DRAGON'S FATE

VALERIE TWOMBLY

INTRODUCTION

One touch will prove fatal.

Caleb is dark, hot, and commanding in human form. As a dragon, he's a force to be reckoned with. When he witnesses the slave Lileta being beaten by his Overlord Odage, he nearly comes unglued. Without understanding why, he asks to take Lileta as his own, but soon realizes his longing is more than an attraction to a beautiful woman. In a sick twist of fate, the gods have given him a demon as his mate—one he can never touch unless he wishes his own death.

His only choice is to grant her freedom.

Abducted as a teen, and later purchased by a dragon Overlord, Lileta's venomous touch remains her only safeguard as a slave. When the demon's rebellious nature brings about a brutal punishment, Caleb steps in and takes her as his own. As if having the sexy dragon save the day isn't bad enough, she soon realizes they are destined to be together.

Mating is out of the question.

The abduction of a goddess intertwines their paths once again, spiraling them to the brink of passion. Unable to resist their fatal desire, the two must trust fate and hope they don't destroy each other.

This book formerly published as Fatal Desire. Revised 2nd edition.

CHAPTER ONE

ODAGE STOOD under the full moon, the desert wind whipped through his hair and grains of sand danced past his boots. Finally, he'd found the other half of the amulet of Tobor.

"I am extremely pleased, Odage. You have done well and will be rewarded. However, you know this journey has only begun," a sinister voice filled the night air.

"Yes, my lord. I'm aware of what is to come next." Odage sneered. He knew the dark demon wanted the amulet. The harmless stone tucked in his curled fingers would somehow open Hell's Gate when combined with the blood of a guardian's mate. His master would then be set free to rain terror on the earth's occupants.

"Good. Then you will start preparations. I am most anxious to leave this realm."

"Of course, my lord." Odage shoved the amulet in his pockct and headed toward Caleb's tent. He wondered how the slave Lileta fared with his second-in-command. He'd been surprised when Caleb had asked for the slave. Odage planned to kill her for her betrayal but decided Caleb deserved a gift, so had agreed. He grinned, knowing the other Draki could be as brutal as he was. She might die yet.

When he reached the tent, he flung open the door and entered. Caleb sat at the table gnawing on a chicken bone. Odage's gaze moved across the room where Lileta was handcuffed to the bed. Her tight, pink T-shirt showed every curve, causing his desire to stir. She pinned him with a death glare. It really was a shame their species were incompatible. She was a beautiful female, with flowing, raven hair, golden eyes, and hips that would fit nicely in his grip. Fortunately for her, the gods saw fit to make her species, the Kothar demon, poisonous to a dragon.

Caleb rose. "My liege, how may I assist you?"

"Sit, finish your meal."

Caleb sat back down. "May I offer you something? Wine?"

"Yes, a glass of wine is in order." Odage waited while Caleb got up and procured another glass, filled it halfway with the red liquid then handed it to him. He raised it. "A toast." Caleb extended his glass. "To finding the amulet." Odage pulled the red stone from his pocket and placed it on the table.

"My liege, this is wonderful news. I know how long you've been searching for it." He leaned in closer. "What happens next? Do you sell it to the highest bidder?"

Odage smirked. "Perhaps." He would keep his master's plans close to his chest, not even Caleb would be entrusted with the information. "But first, we must rid ourselves of the vampires. Prepare to burn down Vandeldor if you must."

Caleb tipped his head. "Wouldn't it be wise to find their queen's murderer? I'd be honored to clear your name."

Odage narrowed his gaze. "Fuck them. They dare accuse me, Queen Daria's closest ally, of killing her? You know as well as I that they will never stop hunting me. Even if they were successful in catching me, they wouldn't stop there. They will massacre our race."

"Perhaps, but we are stronger than they are."

"Yes, but I fear they have the gods on their side."

Caleb furrowed his brows then nodded. "As you wish then. I will devise a plan to take them out."

"Good, I knew I could count on you." He raised his glass again. "To the death of our enemies."

LILETA LISTENED to the conversation between Caleb and Odage until she thought she would vomit. She despised them both and, if given a chance, would rid the world of their stench. When Odage had finally exited their domicile, she relaxed slightly. She recalled Caleb's earlier actions and was dumbfounded by them. Why had he rescued her from the sure death Odage would have meted out?

The Draki leader had tied her to a post and whipped her. It was her punishment for freeing the guardian Marcus, who Odage held prisoner. When she thought he would end her life, Caleb had stepped forward. It wasn't until later she'd learned he had requested her for himself. So here she was, in his tent, cuffed to his bed.

She gazed at the Draki while he finished sucking the meat off a drumstick. If circumstances were different, she would find the man downright sexy. His tousled, dark blond hair and eyes that went from brown to green, depending on his mood, lent a sense of mystery to the dragon. Even his scent made her skin tight. Leather with a tinge of spice tossed in for good measure. When the goddess Qadira created the dragons, she had really outdone herself.

There had been a time when the Draki were allies with the guardians. Something happened in the years that she'd been gone to change that. The animosity between the species sickened her. Bile sat at the back of her throat, but she forced it down. It didn't matter how attractive this man was. *They* could never be. She was a Kothar demon and he a dragon. Everything about her was poisonous to his species.

She lifted her chin. "What do you intend to do with me?"

He looked up from the chunk of meat still left on his plate. He studied her and his gaze filled with lust. She was accustomed to the reaction. Men found her species irresistible. It was why she'd been taken as a teen so many years ago and sold into slavery. She despised all those who'd used her.

"Whatever I fucking wish." He went back to his meal.

"You know Odage lies to you."

His lip curled into a snarl, and he tossed the bone to the floor. "I could kill you for that comment."

Her nostrils flared. "Do it. You don't frighten me, I welcome death," she lied. *Would give anything to see her family one last time and tell them all how much she loved them.* She would die with honor, but if ever the chance presented itself, she would fight. Her body was tired, the only thing that kept her going were the other women. The humans Odage used to birth his spawn. She'd already lost Veronica, the first slave brought to her to care for. The woman had died in childbirth. Lileta needed to find a way to save the others and prayed to the gods every day that Baal and Marcus would come.

"I think I'd rather watch you suffer than take the easy way out."

She curled her lip. "Odage killed Daria. He so much as admitted it and has no intention of selling that amulet. He bargains with the spawn of Hell, and only the gods know what they're planning."

Before she could exhale, he was in front of her, his fingers wrapped around her throat.

"Why did you save me, dragon?" she whispered, watching his eyes swirl. The green flecks came together and made the most beautiful emerald. He released his grip and grabbed a lock of her hair. Letting it slide through his fingers, he brought it to his nose. She held her breath and tried to steady her heartbeat.

Why does he affect me like this? I despise him.

She wanted to touch him in the most intimate way.

"I must protect you," he whispered.

"What?" *He must be deranged. Why in the hell would he want to protect me?* There had to be an ulterior motive.

He released her hair, his eyes transformed back to brown, he reached for the handcuff and unlocked it. "We will be leaving here at dawn. Get some rest. Take the bed and don't even think of trying to escape." He stood and walked toward the exit. "I'll sleep outside," he announced before he disappeared out the door.

She rubbed her wrist, her brow creased in confusion. She had no intention of escaping, knowing as long as she wore the silver bands he'd find her. No, her only way out was to be rescued, or for Caleb to set her free. She laughed. He wasn't likely to let her go. She pulled the covers back and crawled into bed, exhausted from trying to heal the wounds Odage had inflicted.

CALEB STORMED FROM THE TENT.

What the fuck is wrong with me?

Slipping his fingers through his hair, he began to pace a trench in the sand. He should have killed her for the lies she spoke about his leader. A Draki would never tolerate such insolence. So, why had he? After all, there was no way Odage had taken the vampire queen's life. They'd been allies before the guardian king had accused Odage of murder. No, someone else performed the task and tried to pin it on Odage. One who wanted to start a war between the Draki and the guardians. The only problem was...he had no clue who.

Caleb stopped and lowered himself to the ground, his ass sinking into the cool sand. He stared at the tent then closed his eyes. He could hear her breathing, the quiet, steady breath of sleep. His body wanted to go to her, comfort her, and make love to her. His mind said he was a fucking lunatic. He scanned across the landscape and took in the surroundings. He focused on the tall, wooden pole sunk into the ground. The damn image of Lileta's restrained body replayed in his mind. The whack of the *dirise* when Odage beat her rang in his ears. The metal discs had dug into her skin, creating deep wounds across her soft flesh. Caleb had nearly come unglued, wanting to kill his leader. Instead, he'd managed his anger and asked to keep the slave for himself. Odage agreed, had thought Caleb deserved the gift for his loyalty. Caleb didn't feel loyal at the moment. His body betrayed him with desire for one he couldn't have. A woman who despised him.

"I must have been hit on the head and not realized it."

It was the only explanation he could come up with for wanting the demon.

"She is beautiful. No virile male would be able to resist her."

Her golden, cat-like eyes were complemented by the silky, black hair that flowed down to her round ass. Pouty, red lips begged to be kissed, and large, firm breasts to be fondled. His cock stiffened.

"Fuck!"

He jumped to his feet. "And like an idiot, I stand out here talking to myself."

Bones shifted and scales rippled along his skin. Sand swirled upward creating a tunnel around him. He shot through it, his dragon taking flight. He needed to put several miles between them and perhaps find a warm female to lay beneath him. The cool air slid across his skin as he glided high above the desert, but it did nothing to squelch his temper or desire. He fought the urge to return to her but found he was unable to leave her alone. Fear sat like a lead ball in his gut, what if someone tried to harm her? He banked a hard right and headed back toward his temporary accommodations. Landing in the soft sand of the Egyptian desert, he stared at his tent. It was going to be a long, cold night.

LILETA STRETCHED, searing pain shot across her side and caused her to hiss. The door to the barracks flew open with a loud thud and revealed a pink sky. Only a shadow filled the doorway, but she knew by the size that it was Caleb.

"What's wrong?" His voice rough as the sand outside.

"Nothing." She tried to ignore him.

The Draki stepped in, letting the door slam closed behind him. With the blinding light removed from her eyes, she noted he wore only a pair of jeans. His bronze chest covered with flawless skin and corded muscles. With the exception of a long scar across his stomach, he was perfect. She could only guess at the devastating blow that left the pink, raised line from the bottom of his left rib down to his right hip. Someone must have tortured him then kept him from healing. Immortals never scarred.

He caught her gaze and looked down at the old wound. His fingers curled into his palms and nostrils flared. "I asked you a question."

She flung her feet over the edge of the bed and winced. "And I gave you an answer." He was such a snarly beast.

Caleb moved beside her so quickly her breath caught. Grabbing her tee, he lifted it to spy the angry wound that had yet to heal. A deep gash just under her ribs.

"You're still injured."

She reached to push the shirt down. Her fingers grazed across his and sent searing heat over her skin. She lifted her gaze to meet emerald eyes.

He leaned closer.

She swallowed.

Hot breath caressed her cheek.

He appeared torn as if he wanted to kiss her. She should allow him. After all, it would be easy to let their saliva mix, transferring her poison into the dragon's system. True, it would take hours to kill one of his size, but then she'd be free to escape. Instead, she looked away and pulled her shirt down and wondered what the hell was wrong with her.

"It's nothing. It will heal." Her voice cracked, and she fought to control her breathing.

He jumped from the bed and stormed to a chest in the corner. Kneeling, he flung open the lid, tossed its contents into the air like a child looking for a favorite toy until finally he found the prize. He freed a small, wooden box, stood and strode back to her.

"Remove your shirt," he commanded.

She furrowed her brows. "I will not." She might be a slave, but at least she would remain a clothed one.

He set the box on the bed and opened it to reveal some bandages, latex gloves, scissors and a small, crystal jar. He grabbed a glove and pulled it onto his right hand. "Either you remove your shirt, or I'll do it for you. Believe me, you will not like what's left of it should I do it myself."

"Fine." She grabbed the hem and pulled the flimsy, pink tee over her head. Left with only her shorts and a pink, lace bra that formed over her breasts like a second skin, she couldn't help noticing the bulge growing in his jeans.

"Christ," he mumbled as he knelt to the floor.

She hid a grin. *I hope you suffer, Dragon.*

He opened the jar to reveal a thick, black paste. Dipping a gloved finger inside, he scooped out a dime-size glob then proceeded to glide it across her wound. The coolness soothed the cut, numbing it along the way, but searing heat from his touch burned her, causing her to grit her teeth.

"What is that?"

He looked up. "An old family recipe." He reached for a bandage, tore open the package and gently taped it over the wound.

She snorted. "Then why didn't you use it on your own wound?" She motioned to the old scar across his belly.

He stood, lip curling to reveal white teeth. With a flick of his wrist, the glove came off and landed in the corner. He turned and headed for the door, but not before she caught the hurt in his eyes.

"Pack up. We're leaving this shit hole." He exited, letting the barracks door slam behind him. There was more to his scar than a thin, red line. Whatever it was ran deep inside him. For the first time in years, her heart ached and it pained for Caleb.

CHAPTER TWO

MINUTES LATER, several Draki descended on the barracks and began to dismantle it. The sun licked Lileta's skin, and she wanted to bask in it but was interrupted by a shadow looming over her.

"You will fly with me."

She whipped her head around and gazed on the Draki beside her. "I most certainly will not. I will travel with the other women through the portal." She looked around where they stood. "Where are they anyway?"

His jaw flexed. "You belong to me and will obey."

She rolled her fingers into her palms, nails biting flesh. "Where are the other women?"

"Fucking slave, I should cut out your tongue and teach you to mind your manners."

Lileta couldn't stop herself, she let her tongue slip between her lips and point directly at him. Childish she knew, but satisfying nonetheless. Firm hands gripped her arms and pulled her to a muscular chest. She tilted her head to look up at the tall, fierce man.

Caleb laughed. "I should put you over my knee and spank you like a child."

Her skin warmed. "You wouldn't dare."

He squeezed tighter. "Don't tempt me, demon. You will soon learn I dare many things."

She nearly choked on her own breath when she pressed against his erection. All the blood flowed to her core and caused a burning she'd never experienced before. Damn her body for betraying her.

His chest rose and fell in a fast rhythm. He set her away from him. "The women have already left. You are no longer responsible for them." His shoulders dropped. "Have you ever flown with a dragon before?"

She had let them down, all of them. Somehow, she needed to get to the women and help them escape. Glancing into Caleb's eyes, she decided he might prove useful after all and would use him to aid her. She only needed to convince him Odage was wrong.

"No, I've never flown."

He smiled. "Are you afraid?"

Her vision narrowed. "I fear nothing, *Draki.*"

His body shimmered as the transformation took place, and a majestic, blue dragon stood in front of her. She'd seen him in this form before, but never up close. He astounded her.

The sun reflected off the golden scales covering his belly and continued up the front of his long, lean neck. Two long horns crowned his head. His appearance was fierce, a menace with wings. A beast capable of destruction not even she could imagine. However, his eyes told another story. The green orbs stared back at her, and for a moment, she thought she caught a glimpse of pain.

He lowered his massive head to the ground. *Climb on.* His voiced echoed inside her mind.

She scurried up thick muscles and pulled herself into position astride his back, grabbing a smaller horn for balance.

Hold on tight.

His voice sent a shiver up her spine. She was really going to fly, a dream she'd held since childhood. Never would she admit to him how she used to watch the dragons circle high above their mountainous home and wished to join them. That was long ago, nearly a lifetime, and so many things had happened since then. The carefree, little girl was gone forever, replaced by a grown woman with revenge in her heart.

The dragon raised enormous wings, and with a gentle flap, they lifted off the ground. Within seconds, he took them high above the desert. Cool wind blew through her hair and she swallowed a giggle as he increased his speed. The little girl was back, even if only for a moment.

"How do you keep the humans from seeing us?"

He snorted, jolting her. *There is much you don't know about the Draki. I am able to cloak us. No one can see, not even the humans' so-called 'radar' can detect our presence.*

"Really? I wonder why Odage found it necessary to seek a cloaking spell from Sidara then." She'd overheard a conversation Odage had with one of his minions, about going to see the voodoo priestess for a spell.

His muscles tensed beneath her. Good, she'd struck a nerve. Hopefully, he wouldn't try and dislodge her from his back as they flew.

We can only cloak in our dragon form. As humans, we lose that power.

"Ah, I see." Was he going to avoid the subject of his fearless leader?

I'm sure Odage was doing recon and didn't want to be seen. It doesn't make sense to shift to our dragon if we are among the humans. Our bulk is simply too much to get around in their world.

She smiled. "Or perhaps it was because he wanted to steal Marcus's mate."

His wings stopped mid-descent for a brief moment before continuing on. She had his attention, and he couldn't walk away from her.

Where is your proof?

The door was open, now she would glide through. "I spoke with her when he succeeded in taking her. He then sent her to Hell with that bitch Eliza."

This is why you released Marcus?

Good boy, he was finally asking the right questions. "Yes, also I was hoping he could save the others. That is still my hope."

Why should I believe any of this? His voice filled with irritation.

"You were once Marcus's friend. Maybe before you decide to kill him, you should ask him about his human mate." She squeezed the horn in her grip. "Kill first and ask questions later is not a good code to live by." She hoped the seed of doubt had been planted. Perhaps somewhere, deep inside the hulking beast she flew on, there was a conscience that would keep him from killing a longtime friend.

ODAGE STOOD in the location Lowan had instructed for him to wait. Again with the sand, when was he ever going to get away from the shit? He was anxious to be done with this meeting and move on to the next phase. Whatever that might be. When his patience was stretched thin, grains of sand lifted, forming fingers that grasped his ankles. Sharp claws dug into his flesh and pulled. His body sank into an ever-growing hole of gritty darkness. He snapped his eyes shut, unable to bear witness to his sandy grave.

"Open your eyes and look upon me."

Odage did as commanded by the sinister voice, spitting sand from his mouth and wondering why the fuck he couldn't enter Hell in a more dignified manner. The demon in front of him stood seven feet tall, his jet-black hair fell over obsidian eyes. A nasty scar ran from his left temple, across his cheek and stopped just above his lip, which curled into a deadly smile.

Odage dropped to his knees and gazed at the marble floor. "My lord, I am pleased to be in your presence at last."

"Rise, dragon, and let me feast my eyes on the amulet."

Odage shuffled to his feet and removed the piece from his pocket, handing it to Lowan. The Dark Lord turned it over in his palm and then moved to an ornately carved desk a few feet away. Lowan reached for an ivory box sitting under a Tiffany lamp and flipped open the lid. His hand disappeared inside and pulled out the other half of the amulet. The demon placed the two pieces together then cupped them in his palms. Red light shot from between his splayed fingers, and sparks flew into the air with a sharp snap. When Lowan opened his palms, the pieces had fused.

He smiled. "It's a thing of beauty, don't you think?"

"Of course, my lord." Odage swallowed the lump in his throat and stared at the glowing stone. "My lord, what about the girl? You promised—"

"Silence!" Lowan took a step closer to Odage. "You fucked up one too many times, dragon. There will be no visits."

Odage dug his nails into his hands and forced himself not to shift. "But you gave your word."

Cold shadows wrapped around his neck and squeezed. "Do not piss me off. You will not like the consequences." Lowan released his invisible grip. "I have another job for you. If you can manage to not fuck it up then perhaps we can talk about the child."

Odage lowered his gaze back to the floor. "Yes, my lord, how may I serve you?"

"You will kidnap Qadira."

He looked up and dared to gaze directly into the Dark Lord's black orbs. "M-my lord. You want me to kidnap a goddess? May I ask why?"

Lowan laughed. "You may ask, but I will not be divulging that information."

Odage dropped to his knees. "I will do as you bid, my lord." *I have no fucking clue how I'm supposed to take a goddess hostage.*

Lowan patted him on the head. "That's a good puppet. I'm sure you will find a way to succeed."

Odage found himself back in the sand where he'd started. Jumping to his feet, he summoned his dragon, and he shifted. Rage coursed through him as he spat fire across the terrain, turning it to glass. He roared toward the heavens. When he shot into the sky, the wind chilled the wetness on his cheek. He would kill Lowan if only he knew how.

CALEB HAD DECIDED to take Lileta to his home buried in the forests of Romania since it was his favorite and the most secluded. He landed softly in a meadow close by. *We are here.*

She disembarked. "Where is here?"

My home is just beyond that ridge. He indicated by tipping his head. *We will have to walk the rest of the way since the forest is too thick for me to land any closer and I have no desire to advertise our arrival by flashing.* He shimmered back to his human form and shoved his hands into his jeans pockets.

"Who are you worried about knowing we are here?"

"Do not concern yourself with it. Did you enjoy the ride?" The memory of her thighs gripping his back caused his pants to become uncomfortable. He stared at her pink cheeks and wind-blown hair. Fire burned in his groin.

She crossed her arms over an ample chest, obscuring his view. "It was all right, considering."

"Considering what?" He clenched his jaw.

Her golden gaze burned him. "Well, considering I'm your slave. After all, it wasn't like I had a choice."

He let out a low growl. "Move." He gave her a nudge toward the tree line. The woman certainly knew how to push his buttons. *Doesn't she realize it's not wise to piss off a dragon?*

Still, he had to question his own sanity. He could release her, yet he didn't. Caleb had never been one who approved of keeping another being against their will, unless of course they were prisoners of war. There was also the fact she had been Odage's slave, which was confusing on its own and he didn't understand how it had come about, yet he would never question his leader. He was sure Odage didn't care at this point what happened to the demon, but there was always the off chance his leader would still want her dead. Keeping her with him would ensure she remained alive, and for some reason the thought of her death left him cold.

He watched her ass flex in the skin-tight jeans she wore. It didn't help the erection he sported. He shook his head as if the vision might leave him. The response his body had to her frustrated the hell out of him. Yes, the man wanted to throw her to the ground and fuck the hell out of her, even if doing so would kill him. Normal, she was a beautiful woman. His dragon, however, wanted to kill any male who dared hurt her, and that he didn't understand.

After a half mile, they made it to the small clearing where his home overlooked the valley below. He'd chosen the spot for its remote location and built the two-story home with his own hands using local trees and stone. His chest puffed with pride. He hoped she liked it.

You idiot, why do you care? She's only here to maintain the house and nothing more. You can never have her.

He moved across the massive porch and opened the door, allowing her entry.

LILETA BECAME ACUTELY aware he watched her with desire as they trekked through the forest. For a moment, she contemplated tossing him to the ground and rubbing against him. Knew that's all it would take for him to break. He would last long enough to finish the deed then die a slow, painful death. Once he was gone, the silver bands that held her hostage would fall off.

She would be free.

Simple. She'd been trained on how to pleasure a man. Learned to block out her emotions long ago in order to keep her sanity. Sex meant nothing to her, and love was a joke. *So why do I find the act of killing this dragon distasteful?* Every time she tried to plot against him, some strange sensation came over her. The thought of him dead sat like arsenic in her gut.

She crossed the threshold and was greeted with vaulted ceilings and warm, wooden floors. A sitting area with a stone fireplace sat between large picture windows. Four black leather chairs and a couch were strategically placed around the room. It definitely lacked a feminine touch.

"I'll show you to your room. You can have free rein of the house, and I think you'll find everything you need here. If there's something missing, let me know and I'll see to it."

She hid a smile. Did he realize he beamed with pride when he spoke of his home? "You trust me to roam your property?"

He shrugged. "It's not like you can go anywhere." He led her up polished, wooden stairs and down a wide hall, stopping in front of a heavy oak door. "This will be your room." He pushed it open. "Matter of fact, this entire wing is yours."

She entered the most beautiful room ever given to her. Used to cramped, dark spaces for the past several years, she faced him. "Why would you give me—a slave—a room like this?" It had to be some kind of sick joke, and her sense of humor had been buried long ago.

He grimaced. "What were you expecting?"

She turned and walked toward the expanse of windows. "A small hole in the basement." The view overlooked the valley below and snow-capped mountains loomed in the back drop. She sucked in a breath and could almost see herself sitting on the deck each morning sipping tea. *What a stupid idea.* She became angry with herself for being foolish and at Caleb for being the cause of it.

"You mean to tell me that is where Odage kept you?"

"He and all the others."

"How many?" he growled.

She maneuvered away from the window to sit on the bed. "How many what?" Smoothing a hand over the quilt, its softness like silk to her fingertips.

"How many have held you captive?"

She tipped her head back up to catch his gaze, death swirled in their green depths. "Four."

"I will kill them all." He spun on his heel and stormed from the room, slamming the door behind him.

She blinked. *Did he just say he was going to kill them?* Laying back, she reeled in the comfort of an actual mattress. Another luxury she hadn't experienced since being taken as a teen. Caleb was a mystery that needed to be solved, but later. Right now, she wanted to explore. One thing she'd learned during her time as a captive. Adapt to your surroundings and life will be much easier.

CHAPTER THREE

CALEB LAUNCHED into the sky with one mission in mind. Find Lileta's previous captors. For some reason, when he'd heard how she'd been treated like a caged animal, his dragon became enraged. He still didn't understand why but had learned not to ignore that side of himself. Unsure of where he headed, he let the beast in him lead the way.

Hours later, he found himself standing in New Orleans, the flight taking some of the edge off his temper. It also gave him time to think, and he'd come to an impossible realization.

The gods were sadistic.

They were punishing him for some misdeed he'd done, probably something to do with his brother. Payback time and now he was going to get his in a cruel, agonizing way.

Lileta was his fucking mate.

Impossible. He fought with his inner dragon the entire journey. Caleb said no way, they were not compatible, and he could never have her. The dragon in him recognized the scent of his mate. He wanted her in the worst way and now understood his mood swings and why he currently stood thousands of miles away from home in search of those who had hurt her. Neither the man nor beast would be satisfied until her captors were dead.

He wondered if she knew as well. Would the mating instinct affect her as it did him? After all, they weren't the same species. Granted, both mated for life, but he realized he didn't know much about Kothar demons. Something that he also planned to rectify.

Before he searched for his prey, however, there was another he would seek. Sidara, the local voodoo priestess. He had questions only she could answer. He'd stopped along the way to pick up a nice bauble from his collection. The woman was a fiend when it came to gems, so he'd pulled the largest diamond he owned. Hopefully, it would buy him what he needed.

Moving up the sidewalk to her mansion, he crossed the porch and rang the bell. The door opened with a slow squeak, reminding him of the old haunted houses the humans put up at Halloween. If they only knew the real thing existed right under their noses. He slipped inside, letting it close behind him. Sidara stood a few feet away, her raven locks piled on top of her head. She was a ravishing beauty.

The priestess glided toward him. "Caleb, you handsome dragon. To what do I owe the pleasure?" She held out her dainty hand.

He grasped it, bringing his lips to brush across her knuckles. "Lovely as always, Sidara. I need something from you, and I'm prepared to pay handsomely." He pulled the diamond from his pocket and held it up to the light. Her eyes grew in diameter.

"Pray tell, what can I do to earn that?"

He pocketed the gem, and a sigh escaped her ruby lips. Good, she wanted the gem, bad. "Did Odage come here asking you for a cloaking spell?"

"Yes."

He hadn't expected the answer to come so quick. "Did he state why?"

She licked her lips, her gaze focused on his pocket. "Something about the vampires not being able to see him." She held out her hand.

Therefore, Lileta had been right. At least on this anyway. "Not so fast. I have one more thing I require from you."

"What?" This time she met his gaze.

"Well, actually two. I was never here and," he pulled a piece of paper from his pocket, "this must be delivered, discreetly to the person on the front."

She snatched it and read the name. "Done. I will take care of it immediately."

"Good." He removed the gem from his pocket and then hesitated. "Perhaps there is something else you can do for me."

Her eyes swirled with impatience. "What?"

"I need to locate some men..."

She held up her hand. "I know of whom you speak." She grabbed a tablet and pen from the side table and scrawled on the paper then ripped off the sheet and handed it to him.

He smiled and placed the gem in her eager hand. "You've earned this." The woman amazed him with her talent. Perhaps she read his thoughts without his knowing. He folded the paper and slipped it into his pocket on his way to the door then stopped and turned around before he exited. "And remember, I was never here."

He strode down the sidewalk. The sun now completely set, he opened a portal to his destination. Lileta's captors would have to wait while he tended to other business. Within seconds, Caleb slipped into the cave without issue. He was taking a huge risk showing up there. Even though it was a neutral location, it didn't mean there wouldn't be an ambush waiting for him. He had to trust his old friend, but after his actions last time they were together, he wouldn't blame Marcus for showing up with an entire army. He had basically broken relations with the guardians after their king had accused Odage of murder.

Moving along a narrow passage, he headed for the pool, positive that's where he would find the guardian warrior. As he neared, he sensed the power of the other immortal. No one else. Excellent,

Sidara had done her job with her usual efficiency and Marcus had come alone.

Caleb stepped into the vast cavern, the vampire faced him, hands at his side where they could be seen. To demonstrate he was also unarmed, he moved his palms out front. Of course, both men understood this didn't mean a thing and was strictly for show since they were equally matched in strength. They would have to trust each other, and Caleb relied on the fact that his longtime friend wanted peace and not war with the Draki. The two had both fought together in the war with Drayos, and it was then he learned about the curse placed on the guardians' souls. One which was slowly spiraling them into the darkness and would eventually turn them into lethal killers.

Marcus crossed his arms over his chest as his eyes flashed silver. "I came alone as you requested. Only my mate knows where I am."

Caleb nodded. "Good. Thanks for agreeing to meet with me."

"Get on with it," Marcus growled.

"I need to know, what makes you think Odage killed your queen?"

Marcus's lip curled. "She told us it was him. Somehow, he removed her life force."

Shit, Marcus was a guardian, created by the god Zarek to protect the human race. Lying was something a guardian reserved for only life and death situations. This was not the news Caleb hoped to hear.

"Did he abduct your mate?"

"Yes."

He sensed this wouldn't be easy. Marcus wasn't very forthcoming with information. "Is she well?"

Marcus narrowed his gaze. "Why do you want to know?"

He didn't want a standoff with the warrior. Marcus was the only healer among his kind, and Caleb knew his skills would be needed. If it came down to a fight, one of them would not leave here alive. He was going to be the bigger man, this time anyway.

He lowered himself to a nearby rock. "I'm beginning to question Odage and his intentions."

Marcus dropped his arms, his stance relaxed. "What has happened to cause this?"

"Lileta."

The vampire moved with lightning speed and had Caleb around the throat, lifting him off his perch. "Where is she? If you have harmed her, I will forget this is a neutral zone and gut you right here."

"She is unharmed." Though difficult, he resisted the urge to fight back. He needed information from his old friend.

Marcus dropped him to his feet. "Where is she?"

"Safe, that's all you need to know for the moment."

Marcus balled his fists. "Why should I believe you?"

Caleb captured the warrior's gaze. "Because she is my mate."

The guardian's jaw dropped. "Holy fuck."

Caleb sat back down. "Precisely."

Marcus took a seat across from him. "What do you intend to do? Does she know?"

He shook his head. "I can't be sure. She is still bound by the bands but is safe in one of my homes. I dare not release her yet. Odage nearly killed her for freeing you."

"And you rescued her? How did that sit with your leader?"

"Actually, very well. I asked to keep her as my own. At the time, I didn't know she was mine, only that I needed to protect her." The anger he'd experienced when the first lash touched her skin had nearly sent him over the edge. It had taken every ounce of willpower to stand and watch the beating as if he could care less.

Marcus sighed. "Cassie is home safe with me. She is heavy with child and due very soon."

Caleb's eyes widened. "I am happy for you, but how? I mean, she's human."

"She was, now she is one of us."

He dropped his gaze to the floor. "I can't believe my leader was able to do these things right under my nose." He looked Marcus in the eye. "He has ordered me to kill all the guardians. You must get your people into hiding."

"We do not run like a bunch of whiny children. You of all men should understand that. Besides, this is much bigger than you or I. Drayos and Eliza spawned a son named Lowan. He plans to open Hell's Gate. He already has Cassie's blood and now needs the amulet of Tobor. Something about her blood is supposed to be the key to work the damn thing."

"Wait...what?" Caleb rubbed his face. "Son of a bitch! Odage has an amulet. We found it in Egypt only days ago."

Marcus jumped to his feet. "We need to find him. Where is he?"

"I'm not sure. He left with a small army and several human females." He shoved his hair back. "I have to see Aidyn. We need a plan."

"I'm afraid the king might kill you on sight. Let me handle this. In the meantime, we must keep up the front of being enemies. Tell no one."

HAVING FLOWN BACK to the caverns he'd abandoned earlier, Odage paced the limestone floor. The guardians wouldn't think to come and look for him here. They had already searched and concluded he'd left.

"Darling, what troubles you?" Oroumea asked.

He gazed at his ghoul wife who lay in bed. Her cheeks flushed, she seemed sated after their session of sex. "I've been instructed to kidnap Qadira."

His bride sat up, dropping the sheet and exposing ample, pale breasts. His cock stiffened again. "Really? How are you going to do that?"

He continued pacing. "I have no fucking clue."

"Perhaps I can help."

He stopped mid-stride and spun to face her. "How?"

"I know how to contain her, make her weak."

He rushed to the bed and knelt in front of her. "Tell me."

"I gathered the memory from one of my victims. Darazor's tear, it will weaken her."

He pushed himself off the bed before he slapped her senseless. "Damn female, that dragon has been dead for centuries. Hell, before I was even born."

Darazor was the first dragon created by Qadira in the beginning of time. An ancient so powerful it was said his tear held more magic than any dragon after him. Odage wouldn't dispute the claim. All Draki were raised with the tales of Darazor, how he lived and how he died.

A soft hand touched his shoulder. "You know the tale of how he died?"

He turned to look at her. "Of course. He had grown so strong even Qadira feared him. It was she who took his life."

"Ah yes, but there is more. The goddess was so distraught at having to slay her child that she saved his tears, thinking that one day she might resurrect him. They are spread out in secret locations throughout the world. I know where to find at least one."

His jaw dropped. "Where?"

A wicked smile played across her lovely face, and her eyes grew bright like rubies. "It's right beneath our feet."

He snapped his teeth together. "Do not toy with me, it will not bode well."

"I don't toy, my love. It is buried in this very mountain. I know its precise location."

He picked her up and tossed her back to the bed. He knew this ghoul would be a valuable asset when he married her, but he had no idea how much so. Finally, it looked like his plans were going to come together. He and Oroumea would locate the tear and find a way to lure the goddess here.

LILETA SPENT what seemed like hours under the hot spray of the massaging shower head. The luxury was something she hadn't partaken of in a long while. Often, she had been forced to bathe with a sponge and a bowl of tepid water, and when she had been granted a shower, it'd usually been ice cold. When she was finally left shriveled, she turned off the water and exited. Her gaze went to the numerous bottles of lotions lined up on a glass shelf. She selected a thick coconut concoction and slathered it on. Her skin absorbed every drop and was left silky smooth. She grabbed the cotton robe left on a hook and wrapped herself in its downy softness. Padding across the expansive room, she went to the closet and flung open the doors. Large, almost bigger than the master bath, and full of women's clothes. She flicked the garments on their hangers and inspected each tag. All her size. Intentional or did the dragon like all his women petite?

Her temper flared, and she stormed from the closet and grabbed her old jeans and shirt. She wanted nothing to do with some other woman's rags. She pushed one leg into the denim then the other and pulled them up. All the while, her temper grew hotter. Why the hell was she so mad? She shouldn't care about another woman, but for some reason, envisioning the dragon with another female set her blood to a low simmer. She set her jaw, sucked in a deep breath and shook the feeling free.

Now time to explore.

She slinked down the hall like a cat on the prowl. Caleb had said the entire wing was her sanctuary, and she wanted to see exactly what a dragon knew of a demon's comforts. Her first stop was to check out the room she'd spotted earlier at the end of the corridor. What she found took her breath away.

The space was enormous, with vaulted ceilings and walls of glass looking over the forests below. On the other side of the room was a fireplace so big she could practically walk inside. However, what made her squeal with delight was the rack of books. Loads and loads of books. Everything from ancient leather-bound text to current paperbacks. She loved to read and hadn't been allowed to indulge in the pastime since becoming a slave. This would indeed become her sanctuary until she escaped or Caleb released her.

"Lileta."

She spun to meet the handsome Draki, who spoke her name like a caress. "You're back, I see."

His brows scrunched together. "Why are you wearing those rags when you have a closet full of new clothes?"

She snorted and walked to the bookshelf, running her fingers across the leather bindings. "I don't care to wear your whore's clothing."

His power flared, snapping in the air and it sent chills up her spine.

"Those clothes belong to no one but you. I had them purchased before we came here. You will toss out your old things and wear the new ones, or I'll do it for you," he commanded.

"Why, Caleb? Why have you done all these things?" She moved in front of him, the top of her head came to his chin so she was forced to look up. "You rescue me from Odage and tend my wounds. Then you bring me here, and instead of a dark, musty room, you give me this." She waved a hand through the air. "You can't fuck me so what is it you want?"

Strong hands gripped her arms and pulled until her body was pinned against his taut muscles. Warm lips pressed against her ear. "Oh but I want to fuck you. I want to lay you right here, on this floor and lick every inch of your naked body until you scream and beg me to give you release." He nipped her earlobe. Her breathing stopped, caught in her lungs while the fire spread through her core. Christ, she wanted him to do all those things and more. Never had her body betrayed her like this, but it was not to be.

She shoved at his chest. "Let me go!" Free of his embrace, she stumbled backward. Goosebumps developed along her limbs without his touch.

He bared his fangs. "You belong to me. No one else." He stormed from the room.

"What the hell just happened?" She was shaken, the true meaning behind his last words crashed over her like an avalanche. She fell to her knees and planted her face in her palms. "Holy hell! It can't be." Tears that had been denied for years now flowed freely.

She was his mate.

CHAPTER FOUR

CALEB STORMED from the room before he tossed her to the floor and made love to her right there. His desire for her would prove fatal, and he needed to keep it in check. Besides, she deserved better than that. Hell, she deserved better than him. He was a dragon with a shaded past.

Part of him wanted to set her free. It's what she needed and he hated that he kept her bound to him. The other half, the dragon, wanted her by his side. Always. He also feared for her safety. Once free of her magical bands, it would take weeks for her full power to return. She would be vulnerable. Perhaps, he could talk her into staying until she was at her peak. *Idiot, she will never stay here with you.*

Right then, her tears ripped through him like shards of glass. She hated him, he had to let her go. He moved away from the door before he made a complete ass of himself and went back into the room to comfort her. Instead, he headed outside. Maybe a flight around the perimeter would get his mind off the raging hard-on he sported.

"Ah, there you are."

He spun to discover the vampire guardian behind him. "Marcus, how the hell did you find me?"

"He didn't find you, I did." Aidyn stepped beside Marcus.

Teeth bared, his fear for Lileta spiked. "You shouldn't have come here. You have put us all in danger if Odage senses your presence."

"Don't worry, I have cloaked us," Aidyn said.

Caleb let his shoulders drop. "If you could track me then why have you not found Odage?"

"He continues to evade us, always one step ahead," Marcus replied.

"Well, let's at least move out of view of the house." Caleb led them into the forest until he could no longer see the large, wooden structure. He stopped and leaned against a tree, arms folded over his chest. "I'm sure Marcus filled you in on our chat."

Aidyn sat on a nearby log. Caleb raised a brow at the expression of faith. He slid down the tree and sat with his ass in the dirt. Knees bent to his chest, he mimicked the guardian king's submissive posture. Once he had done so, Marcus relaxed and took the spot next to Aidyn.

"Yes," Aidyn nodded. "Marcus has told me everything. So far, we have not sensed any rift. I believe the gate is still closed. But for how long, I've no idea."

"Where to start?" Caleb ran his fingers through his hair. "I have not heard from Odage since we left Egypt. I was instructed to kill all of you."

"Are there any of your people you can trust. Warriors who will side with you should they have to choose?" Marcus asked.

Caleb looked to his old friend. "Yes, there are a few who have questioned Odage's motives. I believe I can gather a small army. What's your plan?"

"Burn Vandeldor," Aidyn declared.

ODAGE AND OROUMEA strode through the tunnels deep beneath his lair.

"How much farther?" he snarled.

"Patience, my love, we are almost upon it." She glided gracefully toward a small opening in the wall no bigger than his pinkie. "It's buried in there." She pointed to the hole.

"Step back." He moved forward and raised his pick, swinging it down in a crushing blow, the rock crumbled. He repeated the process until, half an hour later, they both stared at the glowing crystal. He reached in and liberated it from its prison, holding it eye level.

"There is only one tear inside so be careful."

He glared at his wife. "Of course, I will be careful. Hand me the necklace."

Oroumea produced a large emerald on a gold braided chain and handed it to him. He flicked out a claw and proceeded to bore a small opening in the top of the stone. Once complete, he poured the tear from its crystal container into the emerald. When the transfer was finished, she offered him a golden stopper that he fitted over the opening. Enough heat flowed through his fingers to seal the cover in place, ensuring it couldn't be removed.

He held the gem up to admire his handiwork.

"She will love it," Oroumea cooed.

He grinned. "Yes, she will. Now to set the trap."

The two slid into the darkness, back to the lair. Odage broke out in a cold sweat. He was about to abduct a goddess and not any goddess, but his own creator and the wife of the most powerful god in existence. If it weren't for the girl, he would never have considered this assignment.

A hand touched his shoulder. "We will prevail, my love, and you shall have your goddess."

He feigned a smile. "Of course, I never fail. You will go to the designated spot, and I will bring her there." He kissed the top of her head. If Lowan didn't kill him then Zarek would. Either way, he was a dead man.

Odage arrived at the Cave of the Gods undetected. His return back to Vandeldor proved a bit tricky. He'd opened a portal in their upper atmosphere where the vampires would not sense it and flew through. Once in, he remained cloaked until the last possible second before he had to shift to human form to enter the caves.

He knelt on a large, flat rock in the center of a crystalline room. The veins of blue cast an eerie glow around him when he laid the emerald on the stone. He began to chant in his ancient tongue.

"A son of Qadira summons thee."

Wind whipped through the cavern, and a woman materialized in front of him. Hair like spun copper cascaded down her back. Tight fitting, dark jeans and a pink halter complemented her green eyes. "Odage, my naughty dragon. Why have you summoned me?"

He held out the emerald necklace. "I need your help, but first, my gift to you." He bowed his head. "My lady."

She snatched it from his fingers and rolled the gem in her palm. "It's beautiful."

He waited. She needed to place it around her neck before its powers would take full effect. "It would please me to see you wear it. I crafted it myself."

The goddess gave a weak smile and stared at the gem, as if knowing something was amiss. Finally, she relented. "Thank you, Odage." She placed the gold chain over her head and let the emerald settle between her breasts. "Now, what is it you need?" She touched her hand to her brow, sweat beaded across her skin.

Odage rose to his feet. "My lady, are you all right?"

She swayed. "I'm not feeling..."

He caught her before she hit the floor. The woman was out cold. "I'm sorry, My lady, but you are needed elsewhere." He didn't care about being noticed now and opened a portal back to his home. When he stepped through, Oroumea waited, the door to the cell open and everything was in place just as he had instructed. He hated the fact he had to treat his goddess like this. The least he could do was make the chamber more comfortable. The bunks had been removed, and a queen bed replaced it. White satin sheets and a dark purple quilt covered the bed. He'd also had the bathroom enlarged and decorated in gold and green, her favorite colors. It wasn't anything like her home, but it was the best he could do. He carefully placed her on the bed.

"Is the spell in place?"

"Yes, everything has been attended to, my love," Oroumea said.

"Excellent." He had woven an extra spell on the cell that would help keep her drained of power in case the dragon's tear failed. There was also a cloaking incantation to keep her hidden. If Zarek discovered her location, none of them would survive. He closed the door behind him and stood on the outside. "Now we wait for her to awaken."

The ghoul slipped in beside him. "What about Lowan?"

"We wait for him as well. I have no means of reaching him myself." He turned and walked away, needing a stiff drink.

CALEB LEFT the warriors with a plan of attack in hand. Caleb also had the word of Marcus that he and his mate Cassie would return shortly. He was going to free Lileta. With the impending war, it wasn't safe for her to be near him. She needed her strength and to be home with her family. His only debate now was did he tell her they were mates? Perhaps she already realized it herself.

He stepped through the back door into the kitchen. The room was dark so he climbed the stairs toward her quarters. With each step, his weight seemed heavier, and the dragon fought for control.

They both wanted her to stay.

At her door, he stood and listened. Everything was quiet, but he sensed her awake. He knocked. "Lileta, I must speak with you."

Silence.

He sighed. She was going to be stubborn. "I will break the door down unless you invite me in."

"Idiot, it's unlocked," she yelled back.

He scrubbed his face. Shit, he'd never thought to check. Grasping the knob, he pushed the door open and crossed the threshold. After a quick scan of the room, he spotted her by the window, staring into the darkness. He strode in and took a seat in the chair next to her. Honeysuckle. He leaned in closer, sniffed. How had he missed it before?

"I know," her voice hushed.

He gazed at her, the most beautiful creature he'd ever seen. "You know what?"

She turned to look at him, her golden eyes full of pain. "I'm your mate."

His shoulders sagged. Was it the realization she belonged to him that caused the agonized expression? "Yes."

"What are you planning to do?" She folded her hands in her lap, gold eyes pinned on him.

"I'm going to set you free."

Her jaw dropped. "When?"

He reached for a lock of raven hair and massaged it through his fingers. The silkiness was heaven to touch. He wondered if the rest of her would feel so soft. "Marcus and his mate Cassie will be here soon. They will take you home with them until your strength returns or they find your brother."

Her eyes widened. "You've been in touch with the guardians?"

"Yes. You were right about Odage, and he must pay," he growled.

"He will kill you for becoming a traitor."

He closed his eyes and let her scent wash over him. *I'm already dying inside because I can't have you.* Her emotions filled him. She hated him for what he was, but her body cried out for his. It would be torture for both of them to be near each other much longer.

He detected a disturbance. "They are here."

Marcus and Cassie flashed into the room. Lileta jumped from the chair, ran to Cassie and embraced her.

"I'm so glad to see you're all right." She touched Cassie's swollen belly. "And I see the babe is doing well."

"Yes, she's a very active child." Cassie peered at Marcus. "We're both anxious for her arrival."

Caleb stood but kept his distance. It would be unwise to move too close to the pregnant female. Marcus still didn't trust him completely, not that he blamed the guardian "Lileta, come here, and I will remove your bands."

She walked to him, her wrists held out in front of her. He steadied his dragon who wanted to throw her down and claim her. Instead, he reached for the silver bracelets, placed his hands around them, and chanted the releasing spell. The hoops fell to the floor with a clatter and spun like a top before coming to rest. Lileta pulled from his grip and rubbed her wrists then backed away. Her eyes didn't leave his until she reached Marcus.

She glanced up at the guardian. "I'm ready."

The three flashed away, and she never looked back. His heart fractured, part of him had hoped she might stay. What a fool he was.

He needed to kill someone.

LILETA SQUEALED like a little girl when the three of them flashed to Marcus's home in Vandeldor. "I can't believe I'm actually free."

Cassie giggled. "I'm thrilled we could help you. We both owe you more than we can ever repay. You set Marcus free."

"I would do it again." She smiled. "I'm happy for both of you. I have so many things to catch up on."

Marcus cleared his throat. "Well, while you ladies gossip, I have things to attend to." He leaned into Cassie and kissed her. "You will call if you need me."

She slapped at his chest. "Stop worrying."

He rubbed her belly. "I worry because I love you."

"I love you too, now go!"

He vanished, leaving them alone. Lileta's heart gave a small pang. It was nice to see these two so much in love, and part of her wished she could have the same. Instead, she was tied to a Draki she both despised and could never have. *Do I really despise him?* Positive, if she thought long and hard, she would find no reason for it. He had not harmed her. Matter of fact, he'd saved her then set her free. *No, I'm better off not thinking. Hating him will help me stay away.*

"Lileta, are you all right?"

She jolted back to her surroundings. Cassie sat curled up on the couch giving her a look of concern. "Yeah, sorry." She moved to a chair across from Cassie and plopped down.

"It's all right, you've been through a lot. Marcus is going to find Baal. You must be anxious to see him."

She hadn't seen her brother—what had it been? Ten years? "I am, we were very close, and I've missed him terribly."

"He misses you as well. He spoke of you when we searched for Marcus. He never gave up searching for you."

She could only smile. If she spoke, she feared tears might fall.

Cassie chewed her bottom lip. "Can I ask you something?"

"Yes, ask me anything," Lileta answered.

"What about Caleb? I understand you two are mates."

Lileta let out a long breath. Even his name sent shivers down her spine. "It seems so, but we will never be together."

"Is it because of Odage?"

She nodded. "That would be one reason. However, my kind is poisonous to his. Any intimate contact would be detrimental to him."

Cassie tilted her head. "Then why do you suppose you were chosen as his?"

"Ha! Who knows why the gods do what they do? It seems like a cruel joke, doesn't it?"

"Yes, but it also makes me wonder if perhaps you're wrong...about being compatible, that is." Cassie got up and waddled toward the kitchen. "Would you like some iced tea?"

"Sounds good." She jumped up. "Let me help you." Lileta grabbed two glasses while Cassie pulled the tea out of the refrigerator and set it on the counter.

"Look, I know it's not really the same. I mean, Marcus and I never had to worry about killing each other during sex, but we had our problems. I can't believe the gods would put you two together without some kind of plan. You just need to figure out what it is."

Lileta snorted. "Piece of cake."

"Lileta!"

She spun and stared at the man in front of her. Golden eyes matching her own gazed back. Tears released and streamed down her cheeks. She ran into the open arms of her brother. "Baal, I never thought I would see you again," she whispered in his ear, squeezing him so hard her arms ached. She didn't care.

He kissed the top of her head. "My little pip, I can't believe you're real." He set her back and stroked her cheek. "Let me look at you. You've grown into such a beautiful woman. Pip doesn't seem to fit you anymore."

She smiled at the nickname. He'd always called her pip squeak, later it became 'pip' for short. "I've missed you calling me that, please don't stop. It's the only thing that feels normal right now."

"Why don't we all have a seat, and you two can catch up," Cassie called out, making her way across the room. "Marcus, grab two more glasses of iced tea, would you please?"

"Anything for you, love."

Everyone took a seat, Lileta still clutching her brother's hand, afraid to let go and find this was all a dream. She could scarcely believe she was actually free and staring into her brother's eyes. He looked just as he did the last time she saw him.

"Lileta, have you regained any of your powers yet?" Marcus asked.

She shook her head. "No, I'm not even sure how long it will take. Caleb seemed to think it may be weeks since I've been wearing the bands for so many years."

"I'm going to thank him personally for what he did for you. His leader, however, I plan to slit open and feed his entrails to the seagulls." Baal glanced at Marcus. "Perhaps you can grow him some new ones so I can repeat the process?"

"I'd be delighted."

Cassie placed a hand over her mouth. "Yuck, can we change the subject?"

Baal gave a sympathetic smile. "Sorry, doll."

She waved him off. "No problem. So, Lileta, we would love to have you stay here while you regain your powers." She tipped her chin toward Marcus. "I have a feeling these two are going to be pretty occupied for a while, and I'd really like your company."

"Thank you for the offer, but I don't want to impose."

"You are no imposition." Marcus laid a hand over his mate's belly. "Besides, I would feel better having someone here with Cassie while I'm gone."

"And..." Baal interjected. "Cassie is powerful and can keep you safe while I help the guardians."

She moved her gaze from one to the next then sighed. "All right, I'll stay." It was nice to feel wanted for reasons other than being one's slave.

CHAPTER FIVE

LILETA WAS ENJOYING her visit with Cassie. The new guardian was a strong-willed woman, a good match for Marcus. The two of them, along with Marcus's sister Gwen, had been busy helping Cassie pack up the house in preparation for the move.

"I can't thank you two enough for helping me with all this." Cassie waved her hands in front of her. "I'm afraid I would have never been able to get everything out in time."

"You're actually taking this very well," Gwen replied.

Cassie shrugged. "It is what it is. I'm just glad the men were able to seal off the royal artifacts."

"It would have been a shame to lose all of that history," Lileta commented. She still couldn't believe they were going to destroy Vandeldor. The guardians had moved the entire throne room underground. Creating its likeness buried deep beneath Aidyn's home. Without it, they would be unable to hold any binding ceremonies. All the warriors hoped that they, like Marcus, would be given a mate.

Soon Caleb and his men would burn everything to the ground while the guardians secretly moved to a secure location. She had to admit, the thought of Caleb soaring through the skies sent a chill down her spine. She'd planned to pay him a visit now that her powers had returned. Perhaps she would do that today.

"Cassie, what will you do about birthing your daughter?" Lileta asked. It wouldn't be safe for her to come back here to have the child in the healing waters of the caverns.

The woman rubbed her belly. "Marcus and I are still discussing our options. I'm adamant we sneak back here for her birth. No one is sure what will happen if Ariana isn't born in the healing waters of her home. I'm not willing to find out either."

"You know the guardians can't come back here to watch over you. Too many of us and we would be detected," Gwen said.

"They would think nothing of Baal or I being here." Lileta smiled. "And they would never suspect a thing if Caleb were here."

The other two women looked at her then grinned.

"Do you think he would do that?" Cassie asked.

Lileta folded a blanket and placed it in the box she was packing. "I intend on paying him a visit later today. I'm sure he'd be willing to help." If he wasn't, she was going to make sure he reconsidered.

"That's kind of you, Lileta, but really, you don't need to go out of your way," Cassie said.

"It's no trouble, and I want to help. This baby is a miracle."

Cassie smiled. "Well, all right then. Thank you."

Several hours later, when the final boxes had been packed and transported, Lileta kissed Cassie on the cheek. "I'll check on you later."

"All right, try not to kill Caleb while you're there."

Lileta laughed. "I make no promises." She flashed from the room and back to the human realm. Outside the stone house, she debated on knocking or simply zapping herself inside. She flared her senses out and detected only one Draki. Caleb was alone. Flashing to him, she spotted Caleb wearing only a pair of black sweatpants. His chest shone with sweat as he lifted the weights off the bench. Muscles flexed with every move. She licked her lips.

"Why do you bother with human rituals of working out?"

Dragons certainly didn't need to lift weights to stay in shape. Hell, no immortal needed to worry about diet and exercise, a good thing since she had grown a fondness for chocolate.

"Why are you here?" he asked.

"I think I asked a question first."

"Fair enough. It takes my mind off of other matters." He grunted as he bench-pressed two hundred pounds over his head then set the weights in their rack. "Now, your turn. Why are you here?"

"I came to thank you for releasing me." She leaned against the wall, hands shoved deep into her jeans pockets. It seemed like the safest place to keep them, else she would run her fingers up and down his chest.

One brow rose. "That's it? You could have sent me a card rather than risk coming here."

"Am I at risk?" She let her power flare, sending it across the room with a snap. Let him experience a demon at full strength.

"Ah, I sense your power. You think to scare me off with child's play?" He moved off the bench and grabbed a towel, wiping his chest.

Christ, does he really have to do that in front of me?

He advanced until he stood only inches from her. "You forget"— he leaned in closer— "I'm much older than you." He let his power slide across her skin then pin her in place. "Are you tempting fate, Lileta? Do you want to hear what it is I really wish to do to you?"

She swallowed the lump that crept up her throat. "No."

His eyes flashed green before turning back to brown. "Then I ask again, why are you here?"

She dropped her hands to her side. "I'm here to ask for your help."

He snapped the towel over his right shoulder and released his power, giving her freedom back. "Really?"

She didn't like the smirk on his face and itched to smack it off, but realized his power was far greater than her own. She'd best tread lightly. "Cassie is only weeks away from giving birth and needs to do so back in the caves. I was hoping you might be kind enough to stand guard over them when the time comes. I've offered to help, but no one will question—"

He held his hand up. "No need to explain. I would be honored to assist. It's the least I can do for all the problems my people have caused them."

She smiled. Deep down he had a soft spot. "Thank you."

He turned and walked away from her. His ass flexed in the tight sweats, and she gave a mental sigh. *Damn.*

"So, are you well?" His voice caressed her, and she hated him for it.

"Yes. I'm back to normal and plan on hunting my captors."

He spun and pierced her with blazing green eyes. "I told you, I will kill them for what they did to you. You will stay away from them."

Hers narrowed until she stared through slits. "You don't own me. I will take care of this myself."

In two steps, he stood in front of her, and large hands touched the wall above her shoulders while his body pinned her. She had nowhere to go. His erection pressed into her belly, and her breath caught in her lungs. Hands splayed on his pecs, she shoved. "Get off me."

His upper lip curled. "You will not place yourself in danger."

Her chest heaved as she tried to regain her composure. Having him this close muddled her brain, making it hard to think. "You can't stop me." She spoke through gritted teeth, more from desire heating in her veins than anger at his possessiveness.

His lips brushed the rim of her ear. "Oh but I can. I still hold the magic bands I removed earlier. I will not hesitate to use them again."

"Bastard!"

"Yes, I am. Don't challenge me." He let his power slide along her skin, reminding her what he was capable of.

"Caleb, why do you care? You know it's impossible for us to mate." She could hardly wait to hear his response.

"Irrelevant. You are still mine, and a dragon always takes care of what belongs to him."

Possessive bastard! She wanted to be angry, but wasn't in the mood to fight with him. There would be time for that later. Besides, she hated to admit she could use his help. "Fine, how about a compromise?" She needed him to either stop breathing in her ear or run his tongue along her neck and nip at her flesh. At the moment, she didn't care which.

He leaned back to look at her, still keeping her confined. "Such as?"

"Let me go with you. We can take them down together." She swallowed hard, hoping he'd accept the offer.

His nose ran along the crook of her neck, inhaling. He paused between her breasts and planted a kiss.

Her heart stopped.

The urge to shove him to the floor and have him buried deep inside her made her head spin. She resisted, not wanting to kill him. Yet.

"You know I don't have to accommodate you, but this I will grant." He raised his head from her bosom, eyes swirling back to brown. "I understand the need you have to seek vengeance."

She flicked her tongue out and licked her bottom lip. He stared. If possible, his cock stiffened more against her. "Thank you."

He pushed away and moved back to the bench. While sitting, he wiped the towel across his face. "Why do you suppose they did it?"

She gasped and tried to regulate her breathing after his close proximity. "Who did what?"

He looked up. "The gods. Why do you suppose they did this to us?"

"I wish I knew."

ODAGE STOOD outside the cell where Qadira pinned him with

her emerald gaze. If she had her powers, there was no doubt he would burst into a ball of flames.

"What is the meaning of this?" she hissed.

"I am sorry, my lady, but it was necessary," Odage replied.

Pale fingers wrapped around the bars, and she shook it to no avail. "Zarek!" Qadira looked up at the ceiling as if the gesture would bring her husband, the most powerful god alive.

Odage cringed and hoped like hell the cloaking spell worked. "He can't hear you."

"Odage, I'm giving you ten seconds to release me. If you do not do as I instruct, when I finally free myself from this prison, you will rue the day you were born."

"I already do, my lady." He dropped to the floor and bowed before his creator. So many things needed forgiveness Where to begin? Did he start with the murder of the vampire queen? No. It started way before then. Here, on this very mountain. This fucking piece of rock that had become his prison. The goddess knelt to the floor, legs tucked under her. Her hand reached between the bars and brushed a lock of hair from his eyes.

"What has happened, my son, that would cause you to bring the wrath of the gods down upon you?"

He lifted his head, and their gazes met. Anger boiled beneath the surface, and he forced his dragon to recede. Repose would be his only friend right now. "He has her. I have no choice."

Her eyelashes fluttered. "Who has who? Don't speak to me in riddles."

He let out a mocking laugh. "But the gods speak them all the time. You could have stopped this. All of this could have been avoided if only you would have killed him."

Her lips pursed, and her eyes narrowed. "You try my patience, Odage."

Again, a sinister laugh escaped past his lips. "You know nothing about patience. I've waited a year to see her. Done his bidding." He pulled himself closer until his face touched the bars. "I am the devil's puppet, my lady, and he has my daughter."

Shock registered on her face.

"Well done, Odage. You managed not to fuck this one up." The voice echoed through the room.

Qadira's eyes widened. "Lowan," she whispered.

Odage stood and brushed off his jeans. "I have done as you asked, my lord. You will let me see Leria now?"

"To show you I am a demon of my word, I will allow a brief visit."

Darkness swirled around him and pulled. Distance grew between him and the goddess until she was gone and he stood in a dimly lit room. "Leria?"

"Father?"

A girl ran from the shadows. Her raven hair pulled into a braid. She looked more like her mother than the last time he had seen her. He bent and scooped her into his embrace, squeezing her.

"Child, I have missed you." His voice was unsteady.

Her arms wrapped around his neck. "Daddy, where have you been? Where's Mom?"

Tears threatened to spill, but he forced them away. Instead, he kissed her velvet cheek and inhaled her scent. This would need to last him for a while. He sat in a nearby chair and pulled her into his lap. "I need you to be strong, okay?"

She touched his cheek. "It's okay. I'll be strong, promise."

The child was wise beyond her sixteen years. "Your mother is dead."

He tried to not let the visions of his mate falling from the sky enter his mind, but it was too late. Lowan had managed to force her to shift back to human form in mid-flight. There was nothing he could do. He stood paralyzed on the mountainside and watched in horror. The fall had been too high for her to survive. The love of his life lay in a broken heap at the bottom of the rocks. It wasn't enough to take his mate from him, Lowan had taken his daughter hostage as well, forcing Odage to do his bidding. His mind was shattered. Killing and torture were in his blood now. Stained by the dark seed Lowan had planted, he only had one mission.

See his daughter to safety.

He stroked her hair, cherished every second, for who knew when Lowan would force him to leave her.

"She's with the gods now?"

"Yes, sweetheart. She watches over you every day."

Leria smiled. "I like that. Are we leaving now?"

"No, I have not finished my business yet. Soon, I swear. But first I need you to make me another promise." He placed his palm on top of her head, opened his mind, and flashed mental images to his daughter. "Now promise me should something ever happen, should you ever get free from here, you run and find the man I showed you. He will take care of you."

"Times up, dragon," the menacing voice laughed.

CHAPTER SIX

"MEN, you have your orders. We will rendezvous in the Vutha Mountains in one hour, and then we will burn the guardians from their homes. Capture any females and bring them to me. Otherwise, kill all the men." Caleb watched twenty dragons exit his home and hoped like hell when they arrived, the guardians would be gone. Aidyn had assured him the place would be empty. Caleb hoped they were doing the right thing. He grabbed his dagger from the table and slid it into the sheath at his waist, furious with himself for letting that damn female talk him into allowing her to accompany him while tracking her captors. He must be a sadist, because the only thing the woman did was torture the hell out of him. When he'd pinned her to the wall, he was within seconds of tossing her to the floor and claiming her. He'd wanted to bury himself so deep inside her he would forget his name. One thing was certain, while in Vandeldor, he would be calling on his goddess Qadira to find out exactly what was behind this mate of his. Maybe she could break this bond between them so they both could move on.

He conjured a portal and stepped through. On the other side, he stood on the mountaintop and looked out over his true home. Sadness encompassed him as he remembered the days past when his people lived here in the mountains and the guardians were spread out among the forest and the ocean. Children of both species had played together in mock battles, practicing for the real ones they would encounter as adults. Since the war with Drayos over three hundred years ago, both species had taken a beating. The guardians remained here in Vandeldor, but the Draki had spread out into the human world to live. Perhaps one day they would all come together again and bring joy and laughter back to their home. It would have to wait, though. Today, he was about to destroy it.

"Diego."

"Yes, Commander?" Caleb's baby brother stepped forward to stand in front of Caleb. Donned in a black T-shirt and black jeans, his cropped, brown hair and three-day stubble made him look a menace. He sensed the young dragon's itch for a fight.

"Any activity?"

"Nope." Diego rubbed his chin. "Do you suppose they all left?"

He pretended to scan the area. "Hard to say, either way we need to burn the place down. Leave nothing standing."

Diego stood tall. "Yes, sir."

Caleb shifted to his dragon and took flight. Heading straight for the king's home. There would be no satisfaction gained in completing this task. He circled low and flared out his senses, detecting no life. It seemed they had indeed all gotten out. He let loose the first wave of fire, sending the flames crashing through a window. The front of the house exploded, debris spewed into the air. He circled to the right and came in for another attack, sent another rush of fire until the home was engulfed. He headed back toward the mountains and landed next to Diego.

"Report."

"We found no life, Commander, but not a structure stands." Diego's reply was full of venom.

"Send the others back, we will stand watch."

"Yes, sir."

Diego ran off to relay the command while Caleb stood and watched the fires burn. He half expected the gods to strike him down this very moment for the destruction he created. Perhaps they were waiting until they thought he forgot then would wreak their havoc. Diego moved in beside him, and he turned to gaze at his younger sibling.

"Diego, you trust me with your life, yes?" Caleb asked.

A dark brow lifted. "Of course, what kind of stupid question is that?"

"The guardians knew about the attack and fled." Caleb stared out over the burning terrain.

Diego clenched his jaw. "Who would have told them?"

"I did."

"What the fuck! Why would you do that?"

He pinned his brother with his gaze. "Odage has lied to us. He killed their queen and is in league with a demon High Lord who plans to open Hell's Gate."

Diego's jaw dropped, and he brushed a palm over his face. "I'm fucking stunned."

Caleb laughed. "Not as much as I, dear brother. Not as much as I."

"So, what now?"

"We must play it cool until we figure out where Odage is, and even then, we cannot tip our hand. He must be taken down."

"Son of a bitch. Odage is the strongest among us. It won't be easy. Not to mention those that will follow him no matter what he's done." The young Draki plopped down on a rock.

Caleb sighed. "That is why you must renounce your alliance with me when the time comes."

Diego jumped up, standing inches from Caleb's face. "Like hell I will." He turned and paced, his fists clenched and unclenched. "I wasn't there for you when you were taken and tortured. When you watched our brother die. I'll be damned if I will leave your side now." He moved back in front of Caleb, he jabbed his brother in the chest. "I'm older and stronger now. I can help you."

Caleb remained the epitome of patience. "Your strength is not in question. However, I have another very important task for you."

His brother crossed his arms over his chest. "What?"

"Take care of my mate."

Diego's arms fell to his side. "The hell you say?"

"Yes, seems the gods have seen fit to mate me with a Kothar demon named Lileta."

A fit of laughter erupted from beside him. "What the hell did you do to piss them off?"

Caleb snarled. "Wish I fucking knew. Now if you'll excuse me, I need to go summon a goddess." He flashed away, confident that no matter what happened, Diego would make sure Lileta was safe. Even though they could never mate, she still belonged to him and deserved his protection. It was probably the only thing he could give her.

He entered the Cave of the Gods and walked toward its center, stopping at the water's edge. He knelt and pulled a large ruby from his pocket, placing it on the rock in front of him. He began the chant, calling his goddess to him.

He waited. Nothing.

"Something's wrong." The gods always appeared. It was their own law that dictated they came to this place when summoned. He repeated the chant again. This time the flex of power brushed over his skin, but he knew it wasn't Qadira. He jumped up and spun on his heels to view the god who stood behind him.

"Zarek."

The deity stepped forward. His body clad in jeans and a black Pink Floyd tee. Caleb stifled a laugh. *So, the God is a rocker?*

"Where is she? Did she not come when summoned?" His jaw muscles flexed and his pulse beat at his temple.

"No, I have summoned twice."

"Do it again," Zarek growled.

Caleb flinched. He wasn't afraid of anything, except for Zarek.

The god could smite him down in a heartbeat if Zarek so desired. Caleb wasn't about to give the god any reason to desire his demise.

"Yes, my lord." He dropped to his knees and began the chant.

Silence, not even the water droplets dared make a sound. It was as if every molecule of Vandeldor could feel the god's wrath.

"I don't understand, my lord. Why does she not come?" Caleb dared break the silence.

"Why do you seek her?"

The Draki remained on his knees. It seemed like the smart thing to do. "My lord, I—"

"Tell me!" His voice echoed through the cave. Rocks crumbled, fell to the ground.

"I wanted to know why my chosen mate is a Kothar demon."

The god glared at him, and his eyes swirled like sapphires and coal. "I'm sorry, but it seems my wife, your goddess, is missing."

Caleb jumped to his feet. "What do you mean missing?"

Zarek ran his hand through his raven locks. "Fucking missing. Do you need a damn dictionary?"

"I understand missing, just not how a goddess becomes such." He tried hard to keep his voice even as he watched Zarek pace. The god was about to lose his shit any second. Caleb pondered how he would feel if Lileta came up missing and found the sensation distasteful. He suddenly had a great deal of sympathy for Zarek and the urge to lay his eyes on his own mate.

"I've no clue how, it just is. I can't find her anywhere, and she doesn't answer my calls. When I heard her summoned, I came here to see if she would show up." Zarek grabbed Caleb by the arm. "You're coming with me."

LILETA WAS busy helping Cassie unpack the last box when the air charged with static. Her gaze landed on Caleb, and her heart stopped. His six-foot frame clad in black, leather pants, black T-shirt and combat boots appeared dangerously sexy. A dagger strapped to his thigh and the snarl on his lips indicated he was ready for battle. The sight caused her blood to run hot. Distracted by the delicious picture he made, it took her a moment to realize another handsome man stood next to him, one she didn't recognize. The same height as Caleb, he looked much like him except his hair was brown instead of dark blond and his eyes were lighter in color. He carried himself in the same manner. Possibly a brother? Her gaze continued to the third man and she gasped. *Zarek.*

Cassie stepped forward and threw her arms around the god. "Zarek, what brings you here?"

He kissed the top of her head. "How are you, daughter?"

She looked up at him and beamed. "I'm good." Rubbed her belly. "And Ariana is doing well."

He flashed a smile. "I'm happy to hear that. However, I'm afraid I have some bad news. Call the others please."

Cassie took a step back, her face pale. "Yes, of course."

Within seconds, the room filled with five imposing warriors. Marcus strode toward Cassie and placed a protective arm around her shoulder.

Aidyn stepped forward. "Zarek." He bent on one knee. "How may we serve you, my lord?"

"My wife is missing. Find her."

Aidyn arched a brow. "My lord, how does a goddess go missing?"

Zarek lowered his head so he could stare down at his guardian king. "If I fucking knew, I'd find her myself. All I know is I can't sense her anywhere and she does not heed my call."

Caleb cleared his throat. "I tried to summon her in the caves, but she failed to show."

Lileta wondered if Caleb had summoned the goddess in order to try to break their bond. The thought should please her, but for some reason, she found the idea left her angry. Did he not think her good enough to be his mate? Of course, he didn't. He already thought of her as weak. A Draki such as himself would want a strong female, one who could fight beside him if necessary and one who would bear his children. She clenched her jaw. *Why do I even care?*

The room fell silent. Everyone knew Qadira's body would have been pulled from wherever she was and sent to the caves. The choice was not hers to make. Could a goddess die? Yes, it was possible. This whole scenario left a bitter taste in the back of Lileta's mouth. She couldn't help wondering if Odage was somehow involved. Before she could voice her opinion, the air shifted again and a winged warrior stared at them from across the room. *Gabriel.* She'd heard about Zarek's personal warrior but had never seen him.

If he walked in the human world, he could easily be mistaken for the boy next door. Tousled, blond hair and the bluest eyes she'd ever seen glanced around the room. His bare chest packed with muscle and sinew. Hell, his muscles had muscles. A pair of faded jeans with a hole in the knee sat low on his hips and black, biker boots finished the ensemble. The only thing that told he wasn't your average guy were the large pair of wings protruding from his back. The feathers so black they glistened with a rainbow of colors.

"Gabriel, have you found her?" Zarek demanded.

"No, and I'm afraid I have more disturbing news," Gabriel replied.

Zarek's fangs descended. "What now?" His agitation slid across Lileta's skin like a sheet of sandpaper.

"Hell's Gate remains locked. However, several fissures have erupted along the perimeter. We contain one, and another takes its place."

Zarek fisted his hands and waved them in the air. "Fucking Lowan. I wonder what is stopping him from opening the gate."

"Whispers in Hell say the amulet and Cassandra's blood were not enough," Gabriel stretched out his wings and gave them a shake. "However, he has enough strength to let loose some of his minions. I believe that's the reason why the fissures have formed."

"Someone kill that son of a bitch and find my wife," Zarek growled, glass shattering in the distance.

"Why the fuck don't you kill him yourself?"

"Baal!" Cassie and Lileta cried in unison.

Lileta ran to her brother and gave a pleading look. *Don't anger the god for crying out loud.*

His gaze caught hers. "It's a perfectly legit question."

Zarek narrowed his gaze on the demon, his nostrils flared. "If I could enter his realm, I would. Some things are bigger than even I." He looked around the room. "You all have your orders. I'm leaving before I take entire leave of my senses and destroy this whole fucking planet!"

He vanished.

A woman's cry echoed through the room.

CHAPTER SEVEN

ODAGE FOUND himself sucked from his daughter's grasp. He fought to no avail, unable to hang on to her small frame. Tears stung his eyes as he watched Leria's face disappear. Back in front of Qadira's cell, he clenched his jaw.

"Odage, I hope you enjoyed your little visit. Now, I require the goddess be brought to me," Lowan's voice thundered.

He stared through the hair that fell over his eyes, his lip curled. "Why do you not simply take her? You seem to have no problems shifting me from one location to another."

Acrid smoke closed in around his neck. "I have my reasons. Obey me, or the child dies!"

"As you wish, my lord." Claws dug into his palms as he fought to control his temper. Blood splattered the floor, the pain he inflicted his only solace. "Oroumea?" His ghoul wife was the only one he trusted other than his commanding officer Caleb. He didn't think even the other Draki would understand the kidnapping of his goddess.

"Good, I knew you would see it my way. I'll send you an escort shortly."

Qadira glided to the cage door, still ever the elegant lady. "Odage, release me, and I can help you."

He refused to meet her gaze. "No one can help me now."

"He will never let your daughter go."

"For the time being, she is alive. That is all that matters." He moved from the room when he sensed his wife nearing. In the corridor, he sucked in a deep breath and regained his composure. It was time to try to right a wrong while he still maintained a small amount of sanity.

"Darling, you called."

"Yes, I must take the goddess to Lowan. Take the women to Caleb, he will see to them." Odage wasn't sure if Caleb would know what to do with the pregnant humans, but he would figure it out. Odage had bigger issues now than worrying about creating bastard children for Lowan to lord over.

"Of course. You will find me upon your return?"

He stared into her red eyes. "Yes." He only hoped he did come back. He was about to walk into Hell itself. It didn't take long for his escort to arrive. He took one look and blanched.

Wendigo.

"CASSIE," Marcus yelled.

Everyone turned to witness Cassie clutching her belly, eyes big as saucers. Her breaths came in short gasps. "I think the baby's ready."

Lileta moved toward them. "What can I do?"

"I need to get her back home," Marcus said.

Caleb stepped forward. "Diego and I will go now and make sure the area is secure."

"I'll go with them," Baal called out, and the three men disappeared.

Marcus's pleading gaze met Lileta's. "I'll be right back and let you know if it's okay to leave," she whispered.

"Thank you."

She flashed and found herself at the entrance to the cave. The two dragons soared above her, Baal coming up from behind. "There is no sign of life here. I think it's safe for them to return." Lileta nodded then left, praying everything went without a hitch. This birth could not come at a worse time. Back at the guardian's home, she heard Cassie give out another cry.

"Marcus, the area is protected. Let me take you."

"Are you sure you're strong enough to flash the three of us?" Cassie asked.

Actually, she wasn't sure, but there was only one way to find out. It would be faster than waiting for Marcus to open a portal. The demons were the only species capable of flashing between realms without the need of a gateway.

"We'll give it a try."

The warrior scooped his mate off her feet, and Lileta touched his arm. Before they could vanish, Aidyn stepped up.

"Good luck."

They nodded and flashed from the room.

She took them directly to the bowels of the cavern, where the warming pools were located. Marcus sat Cassie on a nearby boulder and began to unbutton her shirt. Lileta turned her back.

"I'll wait outside." She wanted to give them some privacy. After all, this was their moment and she wasn't even family.

"No, please stay," Marcus begged. "I need someone to help watch over my mate and daughter."

She was taken aback by his request and turned to face him. "Are you sure? I can just as easily guard you from outside."

"Lileta, I have, on many occasions, had to trust your brother with my life. I do not hesitate to trust you with those that are most precious to me. Stay and witness the birth of a miracle." The look in his eyes told her he was sincere.

She nodded. "I'll just step over here where I'm out of the way." She moved into the shadows, touched by the guardian's gesture.

Marcus turned his attention back to his mate. "Concentrate on your breathing. Connect with her, she will be frightened," Marcus said.

Cassie shook her head. "Sorry, I seem to have forgotten everything you told me."

He smiled. "It's all right. Your mind has been occupied." He finished removing her shirt. "Can you stand for me, love?"

She placed her hands on his shoulders as he knelt in front of her. "Normally, you would be stripping me for other reasons," she giggled.

He pulled off her pants. "Oh don't worry, we have a lifetime for pleasures of the flesh." He leaned in and planted a tender kiss on her extended belly. "And many more children."

Lileta felt her cheeks grow hot. It was obvious these two loved each other very much, and she found herself wondering what it would be like to know such joy. Would Caleb love her like that? *Stupid! Why are you even thinking about him?* They were not compatible, so even having children was out of the question. Besides, he had come here earlier to ask the goddess to break their bond.

Marcus rose and began to disrobe. Lileta gasped, but before she could turn away, he scooped up his mate and walked into the water, maneuvering to a spot where the rock gently sloped down to form a seating area. He sat Cassie on the rock so her entire belly was submersed then positioned himself next to her, his hand touching her stomach.

"You're doing a good job, love. Our daughter has calmed."

Cassie flashed him a smile. "I can't believe she is finally coming to us. Oh Marcus, how are we going to shield her from all that's going on?"

"We've discussed this. The two of you will go with Zarek."

Lileta had heard of the decision to send mother and child off to the gods and thought it was a smart move. No one knew what would happen when Lowan or Odage found out there was a guardian baby. In this case, safety was best.

Cassie arched a delicate brow. "I'm not so sure about that now that his wife's missing. What do you suppose happened to her?"

"We are not going to discuss these matters while you're giving birth," Marcus commanded.

Cassie twisted until she faced her mate. "Don't give me that. Ariana isn't ready yet, and you've taken away my pain so we have nothing but time to talk." She crossed her arms over her chest. "And stop staring at my breasts!"

He laughed. "Sorry, you know how much I worship them."

She rolled her eyes. "Ugh, worship them later."

Lileta stifled a giggle.

"As you wish." He smoothed her hair back. "I fear Lowan may be to blame for the goddess's disappearance."

She relaxed until she was leaning against the rock again. "I was thinking the same thing. It frightens me what he's capable of."

Lileta had also come to the same conclusion and wondered what he was doing to the goddess. She hoped for everyone's safety that Qadira would come back alive and safe. If not, who knew what kind of fury Zarek would unleash on the world?

Marcus kissed Cassie's forehead. "I will never allow anything to happen to you or Ariana."

"Yes, I know."

He cupped her chin, leaned in and brushed his lips against hers then pulled back, his forehead touching hers. "Our daughter is ready."

Cassie nodded. "So am I."

Marcus positioned himself between her legs, hands still on her belly. "Prepare for your first push, love."

Cassie pulled in a slow breath then exhaled. Lileta stepped closer, excitement beat in her chest at the prospect of witnessing the birth of a guardian. Every air molecule zinged with magic, and Lileta was certain several pairs of eyes from above were watching this blessed miracle.

"Push, sweetheart," Marcus said.

Cassie leaned forward, blew out a breath and pushed. Marcus rubbed her stomach, and Lileta noticed the white energy he sent to his mate to help keep away the pain and calm the baby.

"Her head is crowning. Take a deep breath and relax."

"How long do you suppose it will take?" Cassie asked as she leaned back.

He smiled at her. "I don't think it will be much longer. She's anxious to meet us."

"I can't wait to hold her."

"Love, give me another push."

Cassie leaned forward and followed his lead. His hands moved from her belly to between her legs. "Her head is out. One more and we'll have her."

Lileta found herself transfixed on the events. Her breath captured in her lungs, and her teeth sank into her bottom lip.

Cassie gave one last grunt, and Ariana floated into her father's waiting hands. Lileta covered a gasp with her palm, not wanting to break the moment. Her eyes glistened with tears, and she swallowed a lump in her throat.

"Oh my gods," Cassie cried out.

Lileta's gaze followed Marcus when he lifted the child from the water and placed her at Cassie's breast. "Look at all that hair," her mother exclaimed.

The baby girl had a head full of dark brown waves. Marcus moved in next to her and planted a kiss on Ariana's head. "She has your green eyes."

Lileta noticed the ancient warrior had a tear running down his cheek. Cassie reached out and brushed it away. "Look at what we've created. She's beautiful."

Lileta found herself brushing away her own tears. The first guardian born in centuries, she was a true miracle indeed. Cassie caught her staring.

"Come here, Lileta. Would you like to hold our daughter?" Cassie asked.

She hesitated, still feeling like an intruder, but the warm smiles that greeted her pushed her feet into moving. Marcus took Ariana from her mother and handed her to Lileta. She clutched the tiny bundle close to her chest. Bright green eyes that matched her mother's looked at Lileta, and a smile crossed little Ariana's lips.

Lileta ran a finger down the soft cheek. "You are the most beautiful girl in the entire world."

Ariana cooed as if she understood who and what she was. Perhaps she did. After all, she was a guardian, a special immortal created by the gods.

The air charged with energy, and a shadow fell upon them.

"I've come to bless the child."

"Ediva." Marcus rose from the water, his nakedness not seeming to bother him in the least and bent to one knee. Cassie followed, and Lileta handed Cassie the baby and dropped to her knees.

The goddess was breathtaking with the black gown that swirled at her feet and her dark hair cascading past her shoulders. Her steely gaze stared back at them. She reached for Ariana and pressed the babe to her bosom.

"Cassandra, you have done us proud. She is beautiful."

"Thank you," Cassie whispered.

Ediva brushed a finger across the child's cheek, and white light surrounded Ariana. The baby smiled at the goddess. "May the gift of light and strength be your guide, little Ariana, for one day you will save the soul of a dark warrior. Let the lightning become a beacon in his darkest hour." She kissed the babe's forehead then handed her back to Marcus. Ediva's form burned bright then vanished.

Cassie stood and looked at her mate. "What just happened here?"

His lips pursed into a thin line. "Our daughter's mate has been chosen." He laced his fingers through Cassie's and led her back to where their clothes were. "Let us hope he lives long enough to claim her."

"I will wait for you outside," Lileta said and made a hasty exit, wondering who would lay claim to little Ariana once she was a grown woman. Would the girl follow her destiny or choose another path?

Lileta stepped into the sunlight of Vandeldor, her thoughts still on little Ariana. She hoped the goddess had at least chosen a compatible mate for the child. Time would tell. Immortals grew up quickly, in about half the time human children did. It seemed unfair, but then when one really pondered it, to be a child in their world was dangerous.

She perched her sword on her shoulder. Baal had moved to the back side of the mountain, covering any other ways into the cavern, and the two dragons circled above. Well, at least until a small dragon landed in front of her. His black scales transformed to the man who had stood next to Caleb back at the guardian's home.

"Hello, I'm Diego. Caleb's brother."

She gave a nod. "Hello, you must be his younger brother?"

"Yes. Our older brother was slain during the war with Drayos." He squatted, picked up a rock, and rolled it around in his hand. "He still blames himself."

She wondered why the young dragon was here divulging this information. "What happened?"

"Diego, what are you doing?" Caleb snarled.

"I was just leaving." He shifted and took flight.

She spun to narrow her gaze on the older Draki. "He was simply introducing himself. What's your problem?" She didn't like the tone his voice carried when he spoke to his brother. There was something about the young Draki she'd liked. In addition, she was sure he could answer some questions about the fierce man who stood before her. Questions her mind demanded answers to, though she was clueless why.

"He has been assigned a job, and it doesn't involve becoming a social butterfly with you."

She pursed her lips, not liking the way his gaze pinned her. She shifted her weight, hand tightening on the grip of the sword. The desire to shove it through his heart and get him to stop staring at her was almost too much to bear. "You might learn something from him, like how to *not* be an ass."

He tossed his head back and laughed. "I doubt there's anything a dragon three hundred years younger than I can teach me."

"Of course, you're right. It was silly of me to even think an old fuck such as yourself could learn compassion. Your brother is more my age, I think I'd like to get to know him better." She turned her lips into the biggest smile she could conjure.

His chest swelled while his hands fisted. "Don't play games with me, Lileta."

Before she could stop herself, the sword moved from her shoulder and the tip touched his chest. "I take orders from no one, especially you. I am no longer your slave."

His eyes swirled green. "That's funny, you didn't take orders as a slave either. Why do you think I released you? I need a woman who can warm my bed, and we both understand you're not it." He leaned into the blade. "As soon as I can, I will be asking the gods to break this bond between us. In the meantime, I'll enjoy another female writhing beneath me."

He stepped off the edge of the cliff and transformed, his dragon taking flight. Her heart sank to her stomach.

CHAPTER EIGHT

CALEB REGRETTED the words as soon as they slipped past his lips. The look Lileta gave him when he'd mentioned the other female nearly undid him. What was he supposed to do? He needed to find a way to break the binding before he lost all control with her. He was a dragon and she a demon, certainly not a match made in heaven. *What the fuck are the gods thinking?* Ending this would be best for both of them, and she could meet someone else. His body tensed at the thought of her giving herself to another man.

"You've always been a moody fuck, but that demon is making you worse. What are you going to do about it?"

Caleb stared at his brother. "The only thing I can. One, stay away from her, and two, find a way to free us both."

Diego snorted. "You are an idiot."

"Explain." Caleb crossed his arms over his chest.

"The gods have given you a gift. Instead of seizing it, you mean to toss it away. Hell, I think any one of the men would be honored to be given a mate." Diego walked to the fridge and fished around before pulling out a beer. He twisted off the top and chugged down half the contents.

"Help your fucking self, why don't you?" He ran his fingers through his hair. He knew the men would love to have a mate. Many of their women fell to the same fate as the guardians. Dead at the hand of Drayos, who centuries ago had laid claim to the females and used them to breed his spawn. Neither the Draki nor the guardians had recovered from that war with the demon. "I mean, Lileta is a beautiful woman. However, you're missing one very important point. I claim her, and I die."

The young Draki waved his hand. "Minor detail."

Caleb arched a brow. "You in a hurry to be rid of me?"

"No, of course not. I just think there's more to this than meets the eye. I mean, why would the gods choose two species that were incompatible to become mates if they didn't have a bigger plan?"

Caleb moved to the fridge and pulled out his own beer. It was times like this he wished he could tie one on and get drunk. It was also when he missed his eldest brother the most. He would have had sound advice for this situation. Guilt wrapped around his gut like a parasite sucking the life force from his body.

"Caleb, stop. His death is not your fault."

He looked across the room at his little brother, twisted the top off his beer, and took a long swig. He enjoyed the bitter taste while he chose to ignore Diego's comment regarding their brother's death.

"I won't argue the gods have bigger plans. Question is what? Maybe they want to start a new race, a hybrid. Demon and dragon. I fuck her, get her with child then die." He wondered if they would even be able to have children. The thought of his children living on without him caused the guilt to squeeze harder.

Diego tipped his bottle in salute. "Good point. I never thought of it that way. Then again..." He took a swig and let out a loud belch. "Why did they mate a human and guardian? Cassie is now one of them."

Caleb turned around a chair and straddled it. "So, either I become a demon or Lileta becomes a dragon? Is that what you're saying?"

"Anything's possible."

"Again, we have a problem. I don't think either of us would agree to the change."

The air shifted. Caleb jumped from his chair, knocking it over, and Diego took a fighter's stance. A woman's figure formed in front of them.

Oroumea.

"How may we serve you, my lady?" Caleb tipped his head. He wasn't fond of the ghoul, but she did belong to his so-called leader and he still needed to keep up appearances.

Three women and a baby came in behind her. "Your leader asked that I deliver them to you. He said you would know what to do. Oh," she reached out for the baby, "and take his screaming brat as well." She practically tossed the child Erebos into his arms before she vanished.

Both he and Diego stared at the three women. "Why does he have pregnant human females in his possession?" his brother asked.

"I believe they are carrying his children."

"Why?"

Caleb looked down at the babe tugging on his shirt. How could he have been so stupid? He never questioned Odage and what he was doing. One didn't question their leader, especially when said leader was a dragon and apparently a very unstable one at that.

"Caleb!"

He cleared his head. "What?"

"What are you going to do? These women will die if they give birth." Diego's voice was laced with panic.

"Ah hell. Go find Lileta. She has a concern for the women, and maybe she'll know what to do." He hoped she could shed some light on the situation. Guilt racked him as he looked down at the baby in his arms. He hoped to the gods that his mother hadn't suffered during his birth, but something told him Odage wouldn't have given a shit.

"OH CASSIE, she is the most beautiful baby I've ever seen," Gwen cooed at the child in her arms.

"She is and now, thanks to all the guardians, the most spoiled as well," Cassie replied.

Lileta watched as the baby was passed around the room. The men were absolutely smitten with the baby, including her own brother Baal. She couldn't blame them. It had been a long time since a miracle of this magnitude had taken place. It was a shame the occasion had to be darkened by the abduction of the goddess Qadira and the Dark Lord's attempts to open the gate. The men would soon be leaving to try to help contain Lowan's demons so it was decided Cassie and little Ariana would stay in the compound with Aidyn. They were secure in a secluded area and as safe as if they were back in Vandeldor. Lileta, on the other hand, would head home for a reunion with her family. She had to admit, she was a little scared at being amongst her own again. Would they look at her with pity? She wanted none of it.

Voices yelling roused her from her thoughts. The men were pushing Cassie and the baby behind them, swords drawn. She followed their gaze.

"I come in peace." Diego knelt on the floor, hands in the air.

"What do you want?" Aidyn asked. "Answer quickly before Marcus loses his head and takes yours."

Lileta glanced at the vampire, his eyes dark and fangs extended. It was evident his instinct to protect was in overdrive and he sensed a possible threat to his mate and child.

"I'm here for Lileta." He looked up at her. "Caleb needs your help."

Marcus's stance relaxed, and he approached the Draki. "Sorry, we are all a bit twitchy right now. I know you were among those who watched over us while my daughter was born. Thank you."

Diego stood. "I understand the need to protect your daughter and mate. After what happened in the past, your instincts will serve you well."

Marcus nodded then walked away.

Lileta crossed the room. The other warriors relaxed, but only slightly. Still mindful of Diego's every move as he greeted her.

"Diego, I'm happy to see you, but what could Caleb possibly need from me?" *This should be good.* He'd made it abundantly clear he needed her for nothing.

The young Draki's gaze shifted from her to the guardians staring him down. "Uh, Odage's women were dumped on Caleb, along with a baby. He said you might know what to do."

"He has the other women? All of them?"

"I'm not sure, were there three?"

"No, eight."

"Then no. We have three that are heavy with child." He shifted his weight.

She wondered where the others were. No time to worry about it now. These women needed help, and she would go to them. "Fine, are they back at his home?"

"Yes."

"Lileta." Aidyn moved to her side. "You don't need to go. I can send one of the men, and we can bring them back here."

"Yes, let one of the warriors go in your place. You need not see him," Baal said, touching her arm.

She waved a hand. "I'm grateful to both of you, but I need to do this. I'm fully recovered. I'll be fine."

Aidyn nodded. "I understand. You will, of course, report back to me their condition? I am after all responsible for them."

"Of course. As soon as I know something, I'll be back."

Aidyn seemed satisfied with her response and walked away. Baal pulled her into a hug. "I would never stop you from doing what you think is right. Just be careful," he whispered in her ear.

"I will." She pulled from his embrace and looked at Diego. "Let's go."

She flashed directly into Caleb's living room. Erebos's screaming laughter rang in her ears, and she stifled a giggle at the sight of the

Draki sitting on the couch bouncing the boy on his knee. Witnessing the hulking dragon playing with the small child pulled at her heart strings. He would make a good father. It also brought home the hard fact that she would never be the one to give him the children he deserved. Tears stung her eyes, but she blinked them back. She would not allow this man to see her weakness.

"I don't understand why you find this a surprise," he called out, never looking at her. "I love children." His soft brown gaze finally caught hers. "What about you? Would you like children someday?"

She could almost forgive him for the comments he'd made earlier. He seemed so sad, holding the child with a longing look in his gaze. "Someday, should I ever find my true mate." She regretted the words as soon as they left her mouth, but it was a means to keep him at arm's length.

His lips pressed together. "I placed the women in your wing. I suggest you go to them and take the child with you. I'll be leaving. Diego will be here should you need anything." He handed her the child and walked away, slamming the door behind him.

Diego whistled. "Boy, you really know how to get under his skin, don't you?"

She snorted. "It's not hard, he's so damn moody." It's what she'd meant to do, keep the distance between them, yet it ripped at her heart. She moved up the stairs toward the rooms he'd given her during her brief stay. This place brought her comfort and for some reason felt like home, but she needed to take care. If she and Caleb were going to continue working together, she would have to harden her heart. The last thing she wanted was the dragon breaking it. Desire for him spread through her like a forest fire. Wild, untamed and burning hot. *I am so screwed.*

"Lileta, what are we going to do about the women and their pregnancies? I don't have to tell you what happens when a dragon procreates with a human."

"I'm well aware." She could still hear Veronica's screams of pain. Dragon babes clawed their way out. These females were not able to bear them like a normal child. She shifted Erebos to the other hip. "Do you think it would be possible to do a cesarean?"

"I don't know. I'm not sure the child could endure the human sedatives." He extended his arms. "Here, let me take him."

She smiled and handed the baby over to him as they approached the women who sat in the library. Their eyes were still glazed over. She moved next to the one named Sarah, but the woman was unresponsive.

"What has he done to them?" Diego asked.

She looked over her shoulder. "He laces wine with his blood and makes them drink it."

"Son of a bitch. I wondered how he made them conceive."

She stroked Sarah's blonde hair. "What do you mean?"

He took a seat in a rocking chair near the window, the child curled up in his lap. "A female can only get pregnant if she ingests our blood after sex. Semen alone won't do it. This allows us to choose when to have children."

"And he continues to give them the blood to keep them sedated and under his control." She looked around the room. "Does Caleb keep any wine on hand?"

Diego rocked. "Actually, he has quite an extensive wine cellar. Why?"

"From what I've seen, the blood wine is like a narcotic. Without it, these women may have withdrawals. I think it might be best if we wean them off it."

"I'm guessing you want me to be the donor?"

"Would you mind?" She chewed her lip. He didn't have any reason to want to assist them.

"I will do whatever needs to be done to help them survive. The babies need the blood as well. We continue feeding our mate our blood to aid the infant's growth."

Lileta realized there were so many things she didn't know about the Draki, but she wanted to learn. "How do your females give birth?"

"It takes the magic of both mother and father to flash the infant from the womb. Should something happen to the female's power..." Diego looked at the sleeping child in his arms. "The baby will claw his way out. A Draki will survive, but it is most painful and she will never bear children again."

Lileta shuddered. Why couldn't they just have kids like everyone else? Sometimes being immortal had its downside. She stood and went in search of the wine cellar.

An hour later, she'd filled three glasses with wine, bled Diego then tucked the women and the baby into bed. Everyone was sleeping while she and the young Draki sat back in relaxation for the first time that day.

"Why did the ghoul bring them here? Did she say?" Lileta asked.

"No, only said Odage told her Caleb would take care of it."

She twisted her hair up into a scrunchie. "I wouldn't doubt Odage has your goddess."

He dropped his head into his palms. "Oh everything is so fucked up." He lifted his head to look at her. "Caleb is going to need you in order to get through this."

She wrinkled her nose. "He needs no one."

"No, you don't understand, he trusted his leader and now feels like he has let us all down. It's Talon all over again."

"Talon?"

He nodded. "Our older brother who was killed."

"Oh yes, tell me what happened." She curled her feet under her on the couch, eager to hear more about Caleb.

"Well, it was during Drayos's reign of terror. Caleb and Talon were doing recon and somehow were captured. We're still not really sure how the bastard did it. His magic was pretty strong. Anyway, they killed Talon while Caleb watched."

Lileta covered her mouth to stifle a gasp.

"The scar that he carries..."

She shook her head. "The one down his chest?"

"Yes. They cut him open then made him drink Drayos's blood,

just enough to make him too sick to heal." His jaw dropped. "Wait a fucking minute. He drank demon blood, you know what that means?"

She held her hand up. "Don't get so freaking excited. Kothars are in no way related to Drayos and his minions, very different demons. Besides, even if that were the case, we hate each other. He has already said he's going to seek a way to reverse this mating with the gods so he can have someone else."

"Oh I'm sorry."

"Why are you sorry? I could give a rat's ass." She voiced her opinion gruffer than intended. "I'm going to check on the women."

She couldn't leave the room fast enough. The information Diego imparted almost undid her. She had to stop halfway and collect her thoughts. Did this really explain how she and Caleb had become connected? Possible, even though her people were not related to Drayos. The idea that she could possibly have the sexy dragon caused heat to settle between her thighs.

"Oh what am I thinking?" She moved down the hall toward the bedroom. "I don't really want him, and he certainly doesn't want me." That, he made abundantly clear earlier. They both were simply following instinct. The gods had messed with their destiny, causing their souls to recognize each other as mates. Hopefully, Caleb would find a way to break the bond and they could go on with their lives. Otherwise, things were going to get difficult. She had no idea how long they would be able to hold out before claiming each other, thus killing the dragon.

CALEB SENT a few trusted men on assignment to look for Odage. Something was up if he was dumping his women and the child off. He hated to believe it, but suspected Odage was somehow behind the goddess's disappearance. In the meantime, he waited in the shadows for his victim to surface. His own recon work had led him back to

Egypt, to the home of one Richard Sanchez. The man responsible for selling Lileta to Odage.

A Mercedes pulled into the driveway of the opulent mansion, and a man with sandy blond hair stepped out. Caleb looked at the photo in his hand, it matched the person crossing the sidewalk. His fingers twitched when Sanchez entered through a side door. It was time. Slipping around the back of the house, he flared out his senses. The home was empty except for his victim who was now moving up the stairs to the second floor.

Perfect.

Caleb flashed to the kitchen. He took in the polished, granite counters covered in a fine, white powder. When he stepped closer, his keen sense of smell caught a whiff of cocaine. Somehow, he wasn't surprised. Slave runners were also known for being drug dealers.

He crept toward the same stairs Sanchez had ascended. Taking two at a time, he reached the top without even a speck of dust being lifted. His enhanced hearing told him the man he sought was in the shower, so he headed into the master suite. Steam rolled out of the open bathroom door. Caleb would wait for his prey and take the opportunity to snoop. Rifling through drawers, he found the usual items any man would keep. His gaze lifted to the mirrored doors across the room. Moving in stealth mode, he made his way across the thick, burgundy carpet to the closet, grabbed the handle and pulled. Nothing except for Armani suits lined the expanse in front of him. Of course, men like Sanchez made a fortune selling sex and drugs.

Caleb's temper flared at the thought of this man forcing Lileta against her will.

He'd gut the bastard.

"Who are you?"

Caleb turned to find Sanchez wrapped in a towel with a pistol pointed in his direction.

"Your worst fucking nightmare," he snarled.

The other man gave a callous laugh. "Really? Seems to me I have the upper hand since I'm pointing the gun at your head."

"Take your best shot, motherfucker." He stormed across the room. Shots fired, bullets ripped into his flesh, a couple lodging into bone. He flinched through the sting, but the one that landed between his eyes pissed him off even more. Sanchez stared, wide-eyed, and backed into the wall.

"W-what the hell are you?"

Caleb grabbed the man by the throat and lifted him off the ground, the gun dropped to the carpet. "I thought we already established what I was. Now, you will answer my questions. Truthfully." He bared his upper and lower fangs and partially shifted, giving the human a glimpse of his dragon. "I will sense if you are lying."

Sanchez whimpered, and a sound Caleb knew oh so well reached him. He looked down to find the man had pissed on his boot. *Son of a bitch.*

"W-what do you want to know?"

"The slave Lileta, did you fuck her?"

The human shook. "I-I don't know who you're talking about."

He pushed his face closer until they were nose-to-nose. "I told you not to lie." His grip tightened.

Sanchez's face reddened. "Are you going to kill me?"

Caleb tilted his head and gazed into the human's eyes. "No, not if you tell me the truth." He released enough pressure so the man's feet touched the floor but still kept a grip around his neck. "Now start talking."

Sanchez swallowed. "Yes. I-I drugged her then had sex with her."

A hot red haze dropped over his vision. He fought to keep the dragon back who wanted to rip the man to shreds for touching his mate. "Does she know? Was she awake enough to understand what you were doing to her?"

"No. She didn't seem to remember. I sold her at auction two days later." The man slumped, his body racked with sobs. "I swear, I've told you everything."

"There is one more thing before I release you. Who did you purchase the slave from?" His lungs burned, and he was covered in blood from the bullet wounds, but he needed this last piece of information before he headed home to heal.

"A man named John Smith. I met him at Roxie's. That's all I know, I swear. I have no way to contact him. The meeting was arranged by a man named Havier. His number is in my phone. I can get it for you."

He was disgusted by the pitiful display of human male in front of him. The man groveled, he drugged innocent women then raped them. He extended a claw and pressed it into Sanchez's abdomen. "Unlike the guardians, I can lie. Never trust a dragon." He thrust his claw upward, letting the man's guts spill out. "And never touch a dragon's mate."

He pushed the limp body to the floor. After moving to the nightstand, he snatched the dead man's cell phone. Pressing the screen, he scrolled through the numbers until he came to Havier. He stuffed the phone in his pocket and ran for the window. As he crashed through glass, he shifted, and his dragon took to the sky and circled. Several fireballs were unleashed until the house was fully engulfed in flames, then he headed for home.

CHAPTER NINE

"HOLY HELL! WHAT HAPPENED TO YOU?" Diego shouted.

Lileta stopped what she was doing and turned to see what all the commotion was. Caleb stood, covered from head to toe in blood and wavered on his feet. Her jaw dropped. His legs gave out, and he fell to the floor.

"Dear gods!" She ran toward him. "Those look like bullet holes."

Diego reached his brother and lifted him, carrying him to the couch. "Christ, I think someone emptied their entire magazine into him." Diego laid him down and began pulling at his clothes.

"Stop fucking poking at me," Caleb snarled and shoved at his brother. "I can take care of myself. I just need a few minutes."

Diego snorted. "Yes, we can both see how adept you are at caring for yourself." He threw his hands into the air. "Fine dickhead, I have other things to do that don't involve getting my ass handed to me for trying to help you." He looked at Lileta. "He's all yours, sweetheart."

She stared at the dragon bleeding all over the couch. "What happened?" She didn't wait for an answer. Instead, she laid a hand on his arm and flashed them to his bedroom.

"Fuck, could you warn me next time you decide to move me like that?"

She narrowed her gaze. He really was a cranky ass, but he did have good reason. Even though he was immortal, bullet wounds hurt like hell and he had several of them. At first glance, she counted at least six holes, one of them between the eyes.

"You are ungrateful. I should leave you here to fend for yourself. Perhaps you can take care of the women and babe while you're mending." She shot him the most menacing stare she could conjure. In reality, when she witnessed him hit the floor, her heart leapt into her throat. For a moment, she feared him dead.

The scowl on his face indicated he didn't find their conversation the least bit entertaining. He ripped off his shirt, or what was left of it, and threw it to the floor. Even though she had seen his naked chest before, she still swallowed a gasp. He reached for the button on his jeans.

Her eyes widened. She turned her back and headed for the bathroom, leaving him standing next to the bed. "I'll grab some supplies." Once out of the room, she clutched her chest. *Holy hell, that was close.* Hopefully, by the time she got back, he would be in bed and covered. She reached for a couple of washcloths and ran them under some warm water, grabbed an armful of towels and made her way back into the bedroom.

She stopped mid-stride. He'd managed to get into bed all right. The covers had been tossed to the floor, and his naked body lay on only a sheet. She skimmed her tongue along her bottom lip. Even covered in blood, he was one delicious morsel.

"Are you here to help or stare?" he growled.

She clutched the towels tight to her chest and tried to steady her pulse. "Well, maybe if you'd show a little modesty, I wouldn't feel the need to look." *Oh I did not just say that.* The urge to drop the fluffy material and run out the door almost overwhelmed her. Instead, she lifted her chin and walked with purpose toward the bed. Upon setting the towels at one end, she took a wet cloth, sat next to him and swiped it across his chest. His muscles were like hardened steel beneath her fingers. She bit her lip to keep her moan from escaping. He didn't look at her but kept his gaze locked on the ceiling. Thank gods, because she dared not meet his stare. It was all she could do to keep her hands from shaking.

When the cloth was covered with blood, she set it aside and grabbed another. This time, she reached for his face, and he grabbed her wrist. His gaze pinned her, reminding her of warm pools of chocolate before they swirled to green. Her heart raced, sending the fire burning in her blood straight to her core. She dared not look past his waist, knowing she would be greeted with his thickening shaft.

"Thank you for helping me." He held her gaze before his eyes changed back to normal. He released his grip, looking back at the ceiling.

She nodded. "You're welcome. You still haven't said what happened. Did you find Qadira?"

"No, but Sanchez is dead."

She stopped wiping his cheek. "W-what?"

He turned his head back toward her. "I told you I would kill the men responsible for taking you hostage. One down."

She proceeded to wipe the other cheek. "Thank you." They were the only words she could choke out. He had promised her she could go on the hunt, she should be pissed. Normally, she would be, but no man had ever done anything like this for her. With the exception of her family, men were usually her abusers, not her savior. Yet this fierce dragon had rescued her from Odage, given her all the comforts and luxuries of a real home, set her free and then killed the one man she hated more than anyone. Heat warmed her cheeks. Did Caleb know what had happened to her? Sanchez had thought her incoherent when he raped her, but she remembered every detail and wanted to kill him with her bare hands, watch him squirm.

"Did he know it was coming?"

His lips curled into a wicked smile. "He pissed himself and begged for his life, right before I gutted him."

Knowing he suffered should've given her solace. Instead, shame blanketed her. Would Caleb still want her as his mate knowing she was damaged? *Why do I even care? We can never be mated.*

A warm hand cupped her cheek. "Lileta, I'm sorry I was not there to protect you from harm, but I swear on my life I will make them all pay."

An ache caught deep in her chest. She fought back a tear. One minute, he talked about taking other women to his bed. The next, he acted as her protector. Part of her wished this relationship could work, the other half knew it was foolish. The mating bond was the only reason he sought to defend her. He wanted to claim her as he felt was his right, but he would never love her. She shook free of her silly fantasy and came back to reality more determined than ever that this relationship could never happen. Hopefully, he would stick to his word and find a way to break their ties.

"I suppose my mouthy brother told you how I received it?"

She jerked her fingers away, not realizing she'd been tracing the scar Drayos had given him. "He did."

His lip curled. "He shouldn't have told you. I may carry Drayos's blood, but I am not like him."

Is that what worried him? "Of course, you're not. Besides, drinking a little of his blood does not make you a demon or his relation. Diego seems to think perhaps that's why we were chosen to be mates."

Caleb snorted. "My brother thinks too much."

She finished cleaning him up, proud of the fact she'd managed to keep from looking below his waist. "I like your brother. I think he's charming," she said, picking up the discarded towels.

"Yeah, well, I like him too, just don't tell him that. It will make his head swell."

"Lileta?"

Caleb tried to get up. "Who is that?"

"It's Cassie, lie still." She kept her hand on his chest. "In here," she yelled out.

Cassie flashed into the room, and her eyes went wide. "It's worse than I imagined."

Caleb quickly grabbed a towel and threw it over his privates. "What are you doing here?"

She waved a hand. "Please, I was a nurse in my human life. Yours is not the first package I've seen." She approached the bed. "Oh for Christ sake, would you shut up!"

Caleb and Lileta gave each other an uneasy look.

"Sorry, really, I'm not going crazy. Marcus is in my head nagging at me to 'be careful, don't touch the dragon, don't look at the dragon's package.' My gods, he is driving me insane. How am I supposed to heal you if I can't touch?" She sat on the edge of the bed. "Diego came and said you were shot up pretty bad. I left Marcus at home with Ariana and came as quick as I could."

Caleb's brows shot up. "He let you come in his place?"

Cassie reached up and twisted her hair into a knot and flashed a smile. "I didn't give him much choice." She looked at Lileta and winked. "I threatened to withhold. Not that I would, but he doesn't need to know that."

Lileta stifled a giggle. She could picture the big, brooding Marcus at home pacing the floor. "It was nice of you to come."

"I can heal myself. You don't have to do this," Caleb said.

"I'm sure you can, but I will have you on your feet much faster. I understand it could take you days to expel the bullets. I can do it tonight." She placed a hand on his chest. "Now is not the time to be out of commission."

He closed his eyes. "You're right, of course. Please proceed."

"Is there anything I can do?" Lileta stepped closer.

"Yes, he will go into a deep sleep once I finish. You must stay and make sure he is protected," Cassie replied.

CALEB'S LIDS FLUTTERED OPEN, and he sucked in a deep,

cleansing breath, his mind clear. He pushed himself into a sitting position. Scattered all around the bed were the bullets his body had expelled. He brushed his fingers over the spot between his eyes, nothing but smooth skin. He glanced at his chest, he bore no wounds to indicate he was ever shot. Cassie was indeed an exceptional healer. He'd have to remember to thank her again for coming to his home. He would also thank her mate, Marcus. He wondered if the guardian knew how lucky he was to have been blessed with such a treasure.

He swung his legs over the edge of the bed. It was then he spotted her. Lileta curled up in a chair in the corner, asleep. With everything she had been through, she came when he needed her to care for the women. Cleaned his wounds when she could have left him to fend for himself. Moreover, she had stayed by his side all night. Why, he wondered. He stared at the rise and fall of her chest. His gaze moved upward to her lips. Pink, pouty flesh he wanted desperately to taste. He realized in that moment he was not letting her go. He would find a way to have her. With the stealth of an immortal, he crossed the room, knelt on the floor, and braced his hands on the back of the chair blocking her escape. Her lids flew open.

"You're awake." Her whisper caressed his cheek.

"Yes." He inched closer, surrounding her in his power to keep her from flashing away.

"What are you doing?"

He smelled her fear. Was she afraid of him? Surely, she had to know by now he would never hurt her. "You stayed here all night?"

"Yes. Cassie said you would be in a healing sleep and vulnerable. I didn't want the women and babe left alone."

She lied. Had that been the case, he would not have found her in his room. He inhaled. Something else mingled with her fear. Her desire. It flooded him and caused his cock to thicken. Without clothes, his shaft jutted forward. *Fuck it. Let her see what she does to me.* "You belong to me."

Her tongue flicked out and ran along her bottom lip. He wanted to claim her mouth until her body trembled. "I belong to no one."

A smile played across his lips. He bent closer and sucked her earlobe into his mouth. She tasted as exotic as he imagined, like spiced lemons.

She moaned.

He gave a nip. "Oh but you do. You are mine, and I will have you one day."

"I thought you were going to find a way to break the bond so you could find another?" Her question came in a throaty growl.

"I lied. I may have set you free, but I will never break our bond. I will find a way to have you and when I do..." He ran his tongue along her neck. Her pulse raced. "You will scream my name in pleasure."

Her chest heaved, pushing her breasts farther into his skin. Her nipples pebbled through her thin shirt. He swallowed hard and forced himself back before he stripped her, tossed her on the bed and fucked the hell out of her. He reined in his power.

"Run Lileta, before I lose control."

She vanished, but he sensed her still in the house. Still, she refused to leave, which could only mean one thing.

Lileta wanted him too.

He jerked on a pair of jeans, finding it difficult to pull the zipper over his erection. He needed to find the guardian king Aidyn, and see about locating Qadira. She was the only hope he had if he wanted to claim his mate and not die in the process.

ODAGE PUSHED the goddess along a narrow passage, frustrated that Lowan didn't simply snatch her and suck her into Hell like Lowan was always doing to him. Something about doing things the old-fashioned way and not stirring up too much magic was the response he'd received.

With a Wendigo in front and one behind, his comfort level was off the scale. These spawns of Hell towered over him, flashing a mouthful of razor-sharp teeth. One wrong move and he'd be dead. He shuddered to think what Lowan could possibly want with Qadira. Did he plan to use her to get to Zarek somehow? He was surprised hell hadn't rained down from the heavens already. Zarek had to know his wife was missing by now.

They'd been walking for several hours when the passage ended at a door. The Wendigo pushed it open and motioned them through. Lowan stood on the other side and greeted them with a smile.

"Ah Qadira, welcome to my home." He grasped the goddess's hand and brushed a kiss across her knuckles.

"What do you want, Lowan, you snake?" Venom dripped from her voice, and she jerked her hand from his grasp.

He placed his palm over his heart. "I'm crushed. I invite you into my home, and you call me names?"

She gazed through slits. "Somehow, I missed the invitation. If you know what's good for you, you'll free me."

Lowan laughed. "Your husband does not frighten me. Perhaps if you play nice, I will consider letting you leave. In the meantime, my minions will do my bidding for me." He produced a silver dagger, grabbed her wrist and sliced. Blood splatted the floor and sent white, acrid smoke swirling into the air. A small hole now marred the perfect marble. Odage's eyes widened, he had no idea her blood was capable of such destruction.

"See what your blood does here?" He motioned to the Wendigos. "Fill several vials and take them to the fractures." He smiled and brushed a finger down her cheek. "You, my lovely goddess, are going to open the fractures and let the evil spill out."

She fought her captors to no avail. A demon made another slice and began filling several vials with her blood. Odage grimaced. No turning back. Had it not been for his daughter, he would have never subjected Qadira to this. Even with his mind now deeply seated in the darkness, he didn't wish for the hell that was about to erupt on the human race.

"What happens to her now?" Odage asked.

"She will be kept in a secured cell until I have finished with her."

"Then what will you do with me?" Qadira pinned Lowan with her emerald eyes.

"That depends on you, my dear goddess." He waved his hand. "Remove her from my sight and get that blood out into the field. I grow impatient."

"Yes, my liege," one of the Wendigos replied as they dragged the goddess from the room.

Odage dropped to his knees. "How else may I serve you?"

"You're dismissed, for the time being."

CHAPTER TEN

LILETA STOOD outside the room where the women were resting. Her knees weak, she leaned against the wall to steady herself. Her body wanted Caleb. Had he pushed her further, she would have succumbed. Somehow, she had to stay away from him before they both broke down. She couldn't risk infecting him. A couple of weeks ago, she considered doing exactly that and allowing him to die, but not now. Time had taught her he really was a good man, and he had already done so much for her. Did he really believe he could find a way for them to be together? The bigger question was if they could, did she want to?

Perhaps they were both fools.

She pushed from the wall and entered the room. It was time to help the women who neared the end of their pregnancies. Cassie had come up with the only idea that sounded feasible, and she would be returning shortly to help relocate the humans.

Caleb strode into the room, his presence commanding attention. Thank gods, at least this time, he had pants on. She felt her face flush at the thought of his naked body kneeling in front of her.

"How are they?" he asked.

"Good, actually. The weaning process has worked well. Cassie is coming soon, and we're going to take them back so she and Marcus can deliver the children. There's only one problem." She picked up a crying Erebos.

He arched a brow. "That is?"

She shoved the child into his arms. "You're going to have to feed the babe. We're also going to need someone to feed the others when they're born since these women are still human."

He scrubbed his face. "Christ, woman, that's four problems, not one." He bit his wrist and placed it to the screaming child's mouth who suckled. "I'll talk with Aidyn and see if we can come up with a plan."

Cassie shimmered into the room. "Caleb, how are you feeling this morning?"

"Fit as ever. Thank you again for coming."

"Anytime. Are we ready to move the ladies?"

"Let's get this done. I need to go hunt for Odage. I suspect he is behind the disappearance of Qadira," Caleb replied.

Cassie nodded. "I'll open a portal directly to the location where we will be taking the women. Oh and you two will be attending the births along with Diego."

"Anything we can do to help, we will." Lileta gave Caleb the I-dare-you-to-argue-with-me stare.

"Why are you looking at me like I have two heads? I said I would help." He growled as he took one woman by the hand and led her through the gateway. When they exited on the other side, Lileta found herself in a large room, outfitted with three beds. It was light and airy with white walls and large windows where the sun filtered in.

"Where are we?"

"Temple of the Gods. Zarek and the others have outfitted a room for the women. Caleb, you and Diego will have to feed the babes unless you have any others you can trust," Cassie said.

Caleb moved toward a crib beneath the window and placed a now sleeping Erebos in it. "Yes, I will get in touch with them."

"Good idea," Marcus voiced behind them. He approached Lileta. "Do you know who is farthest along? We'll take her first."

"Yes." She grabbed the hand of a beautiful blonde, wishing she knew her name. Unfortunately, these women had never been referred to by any given name and they had always been too drugged to tell her. Even now, the ladies were being kept under the influence of the guardians. Enthralled, so they could be controlled and their fear kept to a minimum.

Diego stepped through a portal and tipped his head at Caleb. "Glad to see you in one piece, brother."

"Good, we're all here. Let's go," Marcus ordered.

Everyone followed the guardian down a marble corridor. Lileta couldn't help but notice how stark the place was and wondered if the rest of their surroundings were the same. She had somehow imagined the gods in a more opulent setting.

Marcus turned into a room on the right. It was much like the one they had just left, except smaller and had only one bed. A small table stood to one side and was covered with surgical equipment. Cassie helped situate the young female in bed.

"Here's what's going to happen. Marcus and I will sedate her and keep the babe safe. Then we will cut her open." Cassie fixed her gaze on Caleb. "Caleb, you will remove the child. It's better if his own kind touches him first."

Caleb nodded and positioned himself next to the woman. Lileta handed him a pair of gloves. Marcus placed his hands on her stomach, and Cassie touched her head. They both inhaled and closed their eyes; the female became encased in a soft, white light.

Marcus opened his eyes. "Lileta, the scalpel please."

She grabbed the instrument from the tray next to them and deposited it in his palm. He placed the tip above the pelvic bone and made a six-inch incision, horizontal across her abdomen. Next, he incised connective tissue until he was able to reach the uterus.

He handed the scalpel back to Lileta. Then spread the incision apart.

He looked at Caleb. "Reach for him."

Caleb inserted his hands into the womb and pulled the baby free. Lileta came around and began to wipe him off with a towel. Her heart fluttered. Caleb brushed his hand over the boy's black hair and smiled when the baby let out a cry. He bit his wrist and offered it to the hungry child.

"Everything will be all right, little one," Caleb cooed.

In that instant, Lileta ached for her own children. Anger toward the gods boiled like a cauldron in her stomach. She wiped away a stray tear before anyone noticed. *It's just not fair.* She looked from the baby up to the dragon that held him. *I could love you, Caleb, if given a chance. However, I would never see you look upon our own children like that.* They couldn't mate.

She stepped away and went back to help Marcus and Cassie, unable to look at Caleb for another second. Marcus was already healing the incision, and soon they could take the patient back to her room and repeat the procedure twice more. Lileta left to ready the recovery room for their patient, when she returned she found Diego and Caleb in the makeshift nursery feeding the three newborns. Two boys and one girl.

"So what happens now?" Lileta asked, still fighting to contain the emotions that warred inside her.

Caleb looked up from the pink bundle in his arms. "We have families who will be taking the children into their homes. As far as the women, I haven't heard anything yet."

"I have an answer to that."

The three looked up to see Argathos had entered. He stopped in front of Diego and touched the baby's cheek. "It has been decided the women will have their memories altered and be returned to their families."

Lileta stiffened. "Is that fair? I mean to have birthed a child and then have it erased from your memory? Seems cruel."

"Lileta, isn't it crueler to have them remember the awful things Odage did to them? Not to mention they're not equipped to care for a Draki child," Diego replied.

She exhaled. "You're right, of course." It still didn't sit well with her.

"Look." Caleb touched her arm. "This entire thing is fucked up, but these women have families who are looking for them. I'm sure you understand that."

There were times this man had more compassion than anyone else she knew, and damn if he wasn't right. "I do, thank you. I guess I've been out of touch with reality far too long." She turned and fled the room before her emotions overcame her. Looking for any escape, she ran down the sterile corridor until she found a large atrium. She hardly noticed the lush foliage, her only focus was the door across the room that led to the outside. She flung it open and stepped out. The sound of running water filled the air. Lileta gravitated toward the water and found herself walking along a lazy river. Wild flowers of every vibrant color under the rainbow grew along its banks. Their perfume wafted through the air. She'd never seen anything more beautiful or peaceful. Kicking off her shoes, she rolled up her jeans then stepped into the shallows. The water running across her toes was like a calming massage.

"There you are."

She flinched. Caleb had found her. She really didn't want to talk to him right then. Her emotions were on the surface ready to boil over.

"Why are you following me?" She let her irritation sound through.

"Because you're upset."

She refused to look at him. Instead, she stared into the swirling water and wished he would simply go away. "I prefer you left me alone."

He stepped beside her, grabbed her arm, and swung her around to face his piercing green eyes. "You don't have that choice. There's more to this than you're sharing."

She balled her hands, and her power flared, turning her skin into an inferno. "You have no right," she spoke through clenched teeth.

His lip curled. "Don't think your magic is going to work on me, darlin'. I'm a dragon and playing with fire is in my blood. Your scorching skin does nothing more than make me hard." He looked down at his crotch to indicate his growing erection.

She threw off his grip and stormed from the water, reached down and picked up her shoes then turned to face him. She swallowed. His hair was mussed from where he'd been running his fingers through it. She'd noticed he did that when irritated. The urge to run back and play with the blond spikes nearly undid her.

"You just don't get it, you stupid dragon. I'm stuck with a man who can never give me the family I want." She didn't stick around to watch the expression on his face. She was going home.

CALEB REALIZED AS SOON as the words passed his lips he'd fucked up and big. He never should have tried to dominate her, but his dragon had reared its ugly head and scared her off.

He scrubbed a palm over his face. "Damn it!" His mate was in a fragile state, but the emotions she emitted when she saw those babies and again when finding out the women would be going home without their children had cut through him. There was definitely more that ate at her, and he intended to find out what it was. In the meantime, he would help acclimate the babies and their new families. When that was done, he would be having a very heated conversation with some gods.

He flashed back to the nursery where Diego and Argathos watched the babes sleep. "When will the couples be arriving?" he asked.

Diego faced him. "In the next hour or so."

He nodded. "What about the women, when will they be going home?"

"We will watch over them for a few more days before sending them back," Argathos answered.

"I see, so you erase their memories and drop them in the front lawn?"

"In a sense, yes."

Caleb arched a brow. "How the hell do they explain their absence?"

The god shrugged. "Alien abduction?"

Caleb and Diego looked at each other, both shaking their heads. His brother seemed to sense the need for him to be alone with the god.

Diego cleared his throat. "I think I'll go for a walk." He flashed from the room.

Caleb pinned Argathos with his gaze. "Don't even think of disappearing. We have some very important business to discuss."

"I know." The god crossed his arms over his T-shirt-clad chest.

He snorted. "Of course, you do, no doubt being the god of vision, you saw this one coming."

Argathos didn't respond, simply stared back, making him uncomfortable. He had to remind himself where he was and whom he was with. While most of the gods and goddesses were gentle and easygoing, it still wasn't wise to press one's luck.

"Well, since you know what I want, why don't you save us both some time and simply give me the information I seek?" Caleb stood tall on a wide stance and cupped his hands at his lower back.

The god flashed his white teeth, a hint of fang peeked out. "You will go to Hell and search for Qadira, take Lileta with you."

"The goddess is in Hell?"

He shrugged. "Perhaps."

Caleb pursed his lips then let out a deep breath. "Can we be together without my dying?"

Argathos rolled his eyes. "Of course, you only need to give her what she desires."

His jaw flexed. *Breathe. You can't smite a god.* "And if I don't?"

Argathos laughed. "Then you die, should you try and mate with her."

He scrubbed both palms over his face. "Fuck. What does she desire?" Children? He wasn't so blind not to notice how she'd looked at the babies.

The god began to shimmer, his form fading. "I can't do everything for you, dragon, you must figure out some things for yourself." He vanished.

"Son of a bitch," he whispered under his breath. "Why does everything have to be a fucking riddle?"

"Welcome to the club." Marcus slapped Caleb on the back.

"You heard all of that?"

"Enough to know you're screwed." Marcus laughed. "Sorry, man."

"What? Why is Caleb screwed?" Cassie asked, gliding into the room.

The Draki shook his head. "Great, who doesn't know?"

Marcus pulled his mate to his side and kissed the top of her head. "The gods left him a riddle. It's you and me all over again."

She mouthed an 'oh'. "What did he say?"

Caleb replayed the previous conversation with Argathos, and both guardians listened intently. "Well?"

"Yep, screwed."

Cassie smacked her mate on the arm. "Stop being so mean."

"Ow!" Marcus rubbed his arm. "Jewels, women love big jewels."

Caleb's eyes lit up. "I have lots of those."

"Well then, you should be in business."

Cassie rolled her eyes. "Oh for the love of Pete, you two are idiots. Caleb, are you going to take advice from him or me?"

"I'm not stupid. You, of course. What do I do?" He hoped the female guardian had something he could really use to win his mate.

"Listen to her, don't push and most of all earn her trust. If you can do those things, she will tell you her heart's desire."

The corners of his mouth turned up. "Well, that sounds easy enough."

Cassie jabbed her hands on her hips. "There's only one problem."

"What?" The two men sounded in unison.

She narrowed her eyes. "You immortal men are overbearing, demanding, obstinate, strong willed and sometimes downright cranky." Her gaze shifted between the two then landed on her mate. "And then you can be kind, caring, loving, and the most gentle of men in the world. Caleb, try to keep your dragon at bay and become the latter."

He could only shake his head. *Yep, I'm screwed.*

CHAPTER ELEVEN

LILETA SAT at the kitchen table in her parents' home. She stared out the window, gazing at the turquoise waters rolling into shore. Her village of Vorel sat tucked along the coast of Greece. Hidden away from the human world behind an invisible shield she could see out, but they couldn't see in.

Her mother sat a bowl of ice cream in front of her. "Your favorite. Chocolate."

She looked up and smiled. She had missed her mother terribly these past years. It was nice to be home. "Thanks, Mom. Maybe later."

Her mother took a seat next to her and reached for her hand, squeezing it. "It wasn't your fault."

"I should have listened to you and Papa. You told me not to wander far from home. I knew of the others who had come up missing, but I never thought it would happen to me." She recalled that day so long ago. She'd been sitting in her favorite spot, high up on the rocky ledge overlooking her village. He'd walked up to her and sat down, the handsome stranger. Her instinct told her to run, but before she could, he had cuffed her and drained her powers. That was when her hell began. She looked into her mother's golden eyes and patted her hand. "I'll be fine, Mama."

"Of course, you will, dear. You are a Kothar, and we are a strong people." Her mother sighed. "I worry about the hole you are carrying around in your heart."

Lileta pulled her hand free. She should have known her mother was reading her emotions. Yes, her heart still held a huge void. She tried to play it off, tell herself it was simply because the bonding had yet to be fulfilled. Like the other immortals, when a couple was chosen to be together, their souls yearned for each other.

"I don't understand. Do you think I'm being punished?" Lileta chewed her lip. Her mother was a very old and wise demon. Perhaps she had some answers.

"No. You are not being punished. Just the opposite. Your mate will make you whole again."

Lileta rolled her eyes. She doubted she'd ever be whole again. Part of her had been ripped away in the years of captivity. Her loss so great she feared she would never fully recover, and now she was stuck with a man who could only think of his carnal desires. Desires her body felt as well, but her heart was what really mattered. If any man could ever pick up the shattered pieces and mend it, he would have her undying love for eternity. Caleb would never love her. "I don't see how mating with a dragon will help me."

Her mother stood, came up behind her and grasped her shoulders, kneading away the tension. "You must trust the gods, Lileta. Sometimes, they do things we don't understand, but always there is a reason." She kissed the top of her head. "The second thing you must trust is your heart. Follow it, and it will never fail you."

Lileta moved from her chair and pulled her mother into a hug. "Thank you, Mama. I'm going for a walk." She headed out the door and proceeded to make her way up the cliff to the rocky ledge above. Once there, she took up a spot on the outcrop and pulled her knees to her chest. The sunshine soothed her. She closed her eyes and buried her head on her knees.

"Lileta."

She winced, the voice whispered across her skin like a warm summer breeze. *Damn him.* "How did you find me, and why are you here?" Her dragon was proving to be a real pain in the ass. Like a damn rash, he kept coming back to irritate her.

"Your brother told me where to find you, and I'm once again in need of your help."

She turned to face him. "Remind me to kick my traitorous brother's behind later. What could you possibly need from me now?"

He moved next to her and sat. She tried to ignore him, but his closeness made her squirm. Part of her wanted to shove him over the cliff, and the other half wanted to unwrap him like a birthday present.

"Argathos told me Qadira is in Hell. I need you to help guide me there." He didn't flinch, his attitude matter-of-fact.

She rolled her eyes. "Get my brother to take you. Or for that matter, any of my people would go. You don't need me." She looked back out over the ocean. It was much safer than staring at him. She knew going to Hell's realm would be brutal and secretly welcomed the challenge, but it meant spending way too much time with him.

"I want you to take me."

"No."

"Lileta, look at me."

I can't. I want you too badly. Her body cried for his touch, the gods really were cruel.

"Please," he begged.

Damn it. She was unable to refuse and turned to meet his warm, brown gaze.

"I make you a promise here and now. Go with me, and if at the end of our journey, you still wish to be rid of me then I will beg the gods to break our bond."

Her breath caught. "What if they refuse?"

He tipped his head. "You're so sure you will still want them to?"

She gave a chuckle. "You so sure I won't? You and I are not the same."

"Then if they refuse, I will go to slumber. I only ask you give me a chance." His gaze pleaded, and her heart stopped for a brief moment. Going to slumber for a dragon meant hibernation. Tucked away deep in a dark, cold cave.

"For how long?"

"As long as it takes to break our bond." Yearning gleamed in his expression. "Even if it's forever."

"You are a fool, Caleb, for making such an offer." She could scarcely believe he would agree to such a fate. The thought of him, cold and alone caused her heart to ache. Deep down she knew she'd never let him make such a sacrifice.

The corners of his mouth turned up, and his eyes shifted to light green. "Perhaps."

"Then I will take you." *Who's the fool now?*

GABRIEL STOOD over a map spread out on a large oak table. "The rifts have opened here, here and here."

"Do you have an estimate of how many have gotten out?" Aidyn asked, leaning forward to study the layout.

The angel shook his head. "No, but we need the guardians to station themselves and prepare for an onslaught of demons to come through. There is simply no way we can stop them all from escaping."

"What a fucking mess. Of course, you can count on our help." Aidyn moved across the room to a side table and poured some whiskey into a glass. He swirled and then downed the liquid.

"The world is going to Hell in a hurry," Seth remarked as he stared at the map of Chicago. Something about it pulled at him, but he couldn't pinpoint what it was.

Aidyn nodded. "I think that might be an understatement. Gabriel, I'll begin stationing the others tonight."

Gabriel nodded and left the room. Aidyn sat behind his desk, his forehead planted in his palms as he stared at the grain pattern of the wood. "Seth, I have a bad feeling about this. My gut tells me Lowan is using this as a diversion for something bigger." He lifted his head. "And where the hell is the goddess?"

Seth took a seat across the desk from his king. The man looked almost defeated. He couldn't recall ever seeing his king like this. "My lord, I'm sure we will prevail."

Aidyn brought his gaze to meet Seth's. "I've no doubt we will. Question remains, how many of you will I lose in the process?"

He arched a brow. "I think you and I both know what you really fear. I'm teetering on the edge. My sanity is ready to pull out from under me and send me toppling."

Aidyn scrubbed his face. "Fuck! You will stay here with Cassie and the baby, and she can continue to see if there is any way to keep the darkness at bay."

Seth shook his head. "I beg you to reconsider. If I must die then let it be as a warrior and not a coward. Assign someone to go with me if you must, but do not order me to stay behind." His gaze never left Aidyn's. He needed to do this. If he failed, he already knew the consequences. Losing his head, literally. Drayos's curse had affected him the worst. His gift was slowly making him insane. The memories he took with each feeding stayed with him and melted into his own. Centuries ago, he was able to purge them. Now they refused to leave and fed off the darkness in his soul. Soon, he would succumb to the black hole and force his brethren to kill him.

"Very well, I will allow you to go. Lucan will escort you since he will not hesitate to kill you should the need arise."

"The dark warrior and the lunatic." Seth curled his lip. "We make a fitting pair." He really hated the fact he would one day force his brethren to kill him. Granted, they would do it. Duty required it of them, but it wouldn't be easy. He couldn't ignore the way they looked at him or miss their emotions when they forgot to block them. They would grieve, and that gnawed at him.

"Don't remind me, but I need Marcus elsewhere." Aidyn sighed. "I'm calling in the others."

One by one, the warriors appeared, summoned by their leader's mental tie to each of them. Seth stood and greeted his brethren. They all slapped him on the back, happy that he was still with them. Everyone knew it was a matter of time. Yet they all hoped and prayed he would be next to find his mate. Seth wasn't so sure that was his cure-all.

The group took a seat around the conference table in the center of the room. Aidyn stood at the head and tossed the map to the center of the table.

"Demons have escaped and will soon be creating havoc around the globe."

"Finally, I get to scorch some demon ass. I was getting bored," Garin replied, cracking his knuckles. Seth grinned. Garin looked the part of a bad-ass. Tall and built like a linebacker, he kept his dark hair shaved short, but the man had a heart of gold. He hoped the warrior would one day find his mate. If anyone deserved happiness, it was Garin. The man was lonely, though he would never admit it. Hell, they all were, but with Garin, it was different. It was beginning to consume his soul.

The rest of the men grumbled under their breath. They were all ready for a fight. After all, a warrior couldn't sit idle for long. Other than the occasional immortal who went astray and needed reining in, they had been without a battle for hundreds of years. Now it looked as if they might be attacked on several fronts. Odage was in hiding somewhere. War with the dragons was still a threat even though Caleb was on their side. Moreover, there was Lowan. A combination of demon and vampire and none of them knew what kind of power he wielded. The guardian's numbers had been reduced centuries ago, and he wondered if they would survive an onslaught of this magnitude.

"Are we going to have the support of the gods this time?" Seth asked.

Marcus gave a wicked laugh from the other side of the table. "Highly fucking doubtful."

Aidyn pulled out his chair and took a seat, his eyes sunken as if he hadn't slept in weeks. "I have to believe they will. I think they're trying best they can."

"Not hard enough for my liking. It's no longer about us. I have a mate and daughter to worry about now." Marcus leaned forward. "It brings things to a whole new level for me."

"I understand." Aidyn let out a long breath. "Marcus, I would much rather have you stay with your family, but I need you on the front."

"Of course, my lord, I understand."

"Good, now that is settled, it's time for your assignments." He pointed at the map. "Europe is already covered by the warriors stationed there so we will concentrate on the States." He glanced up then looked back at the map. "They are coming into the cities because they can blend in better and there are more victims. I'm sending Garin and Gwen to Los Angeles, Seth and Lucan to Chicago and Marcus and I will take New York." He straightened. "Any questions?"

Before anyone could answer, a portal opened and four Draki stepped through. Caleb halted, his men fell in next to him and faced the table of warriors. "I am off to look for Qadira, I have several men on the trail of Odage, but I thought you might be able to use some help. I trust these three men with my life." He waved a hand to the man standing next to him. "You already know Diego. This is Jax and Darius. They are at your disposal and will follow your command."

Seth witnessed Aidyn's body relax. It would be a good thing to have eyes in the sky. They all had a lot of ground to cover, and even with the Chosen ones located in different areas working for them, it was still a big job.

"Thank you, Caleb, we could definitely use the extra help. Diego, you can go with Seth and Lucan. Jax, you'll be with Garin and

Gwen. Darius, you're coming with Marcus and me. We know what needs to be done, let's roll out."

The warriors nodded and flashed from the room.

I'M SUCH AN IDIOT. What was I thinking? She couldn't believe she'd agreed to guide Caleb on his mission to find Qadira. Her stomach clenched at the thought of him going into hibernation. Somehow, she would find a way to prevent that from happening. Even though they couldn't be together, she would not be responsible for the loss to his people. Something in her soul told her they were going to need him when this whole mess with Odage became known. He was a born leader, and maybe if she begged the gods, they would release him from the bond, and then he could be free to have any woman of his choosing. One he could be proud to have at his side. One who could bear his children.

She balled her fists. The idea of him with someone else made the acid in her belly swirl upward. *Get over it. You can't have him.* Her jealousy was only due to the bond forming at this very moment. Once broken, she wouldn't care who he slept with. In the meantime, she'd put up a barrier to protect her vulnerable emotions. Her mother's voice came back to haunt her. *Trust the gods.* She sighed. The woman was wise and always right. Something nagged at her, though. A feeling deep in her gut. Her mother was holding back information, something very important. The fact that she stood in the kitchen smiling to herself confirmed Lileta's suspicions. Her mother had been most pleased to hear her daughter was escorting the dragon into Hell.

"Do you know where we're going?" Caleb interrupted her thoughts.

"No, but I know who to ask. Demons like to talk, especially evil ones. They brag about their latest conquests to any who will listen, so it should only be a matter of time before we learn her exact location." She strapped a dagger to her right thigh and another to the belt on her waist. Caleb picked up the pack from the floor and helped ease it over her shoulders.

"Once we locate her, I go in alone. You will turn back and head for safety," Caleb commanded.

Lileta arched a brow. "As you wish." She held no desire to tangle with Lowan and his minions. Word had already filtered back that the guardians were off to fight the ones escaping. Baal had taken some of his men and gone to help Gabriel's warriors, hoping they could squelch the breach from the inside before too many escaped. So far, it wasn't looking favorable.

"Are you ready?" She refused to meet the handsome Draki's gaze.

"Let's go." He picked up the other pack with the rest of the supplies and headed toward the door.

"Wait," her mother called out.

They both stopped and turned. Her mother approached, took Lileta's hand in her right and Caleb's in her left. "Remember, everything happens for a reason. Don't question why, just embrace it." She dropped their hands and backed away. "Be safe."

Lileta nodded, opened the door and stepped into the morning sun, Caleb one step behind her.

"I like your mother. She's a smart woman."

She gave him an eye roll then led him up the narrow path to the ridge above.

CHAPTER TWELVE

"ARE WE NOT FLASHING INTO HELL?" Caleb asked.

Lileta laughed. "You can't flash into or out of Hell. If it were that simple then all of Hades' demons would be escaping."

He lifted his shoulder. "Sorry, it's not like I visit often and know the fucking rules." *Oops.* There was the attitude Cassie had warned him about. How the hell was he supposed to be someone he wasn't? It was beyond reason. Dragons were moody, and everyone knew it. He scratched his head. "So, is there anything else I should know?"

She continued to lead him along a dirt path that snaked along the ragged edge of a cliff. The sea below looked angry as it crashed onto the sandy shore. He would have offered to fly them but figured it best to keep his mouth shut, at least until he learned more about Hell.

"We will have to hike to the entrance then make our way inside." She finally met his gaze. "I should probably warn you that I change when in Hell."

"What do you mean change?" His gut rolled at this bit of news.

"Well first, my magic becomes much more powerful."

"Makes sense. You're a demon, after all," he replied.

"My appearance will change slightly as well." She sucked in a deep breath as if afraid to tell him. "The horns on the top of my head will appear, and my skin will change to accommodate the heat."

His cock grew hard, and his dragon itched to be released. *Son of a bitch!*

"Okay..." He felt like a complete idiot. Here he was, a nine-hundred-year-old dragon with his tongue twisted in a knot like a damn teenager. Right then, he wanted to kill Argathos for putting him in such an awkward position. If he ever figured out the exquisite female in front of him, it would be a miracle. He was used to having women fall over him, begging to be taken fast and hard. Since rescuing Lileta, he'd become celibate. Not something he or his dragon liked, but other females held no interest for him anymore.

"So, what else should I know? Do you think I'll be able to shift in Hell?"

She gave him a glance. "Hard to say. I guess we'll find out once we're in." She stopped abruptly. "Let me do all the talking. You won't be very welcome among the demons." Her golden eyes glowed, and the corners of her mouth turned up. "Matter of fact, you'd be a tasty morsel for many down there. Best to stick close to me."

Oh hell no! His jaw set. His mate was not going to be his protector. "I'm not sure how to take that." He flashed his best smile while gritting his teeth. For the moment, he allowed her this small victory but readied himself for the fight he knew would come later.

She wrinkled her brow as if confused then started moving again, following the path that led to the beach. Lileta took him across a small stretch of white sand then through a narrow crack in the side of the cliff they had just ascended.

"We're here." She waved her hand. "This is the entrance."

He saw nothing. Only a sheer rock face. "It must be well hidden."

Her hand touched the side of the rock, and a black hole shimmered into view. Damp, musty earth assaulted his sensitive nose. "How is it you can come and go into Hell while the other demons can't?"

She stepped into the darkness, and he followed, noticing a soft, yellow glow emanated in front of her, lighting the way. "Kothar demons fought Hades long ago for their freedom. My ancestors broke free of their confinement and journeyed above. Over the centuries, we acclimated to the human world, only going back home when necessary...or when summoned."

He grabbed her arm and spun her to face him. "And what is stopping Hades from keeping you there?" He sensed there was more to this than she was telling and he wasn't going to like the rest of the story.

Her gaze narrowed. "It doesn't concern you." She tried to pull free, but he refused to let go.

"Like hell. You know damn well what the mating bond entails so stop fucking with me," he growled. All immortals knew the bond was strong, even between two who hadn't consummated it yet. The urge to protect her flowed through his blood, just as it flowed through hers.

Her body tensed. "I must provide a sacrifice to Hades. It's the only way I can enter...or leave."

He ground his teeth together. "What's the sacrifice?" If she said her body, he was going to blow apart the entire mountain above them. When finished, his dragon would rip Hades' entrails from his body. God or no.

"It's only blood." Her gaze dropped to the ground. "I must feed him."

"No!" The only one who would ever drink from her would be him, and right then, not even he could do that without a death sentence. Her gaze snapped back up to meet his, the orbs glowing bright. He'd learned when she was pissed, her eyes turned to liquid gold with flecks of red.

"You do not own me, never forget that." She jerked free of his grip. "Now, do you want to rescue your goddess or not?"

He clenched his jaw. "Yes." Why was it every time she became a spitfire, his desire for her increased tenfold? If he was ever going to win her over, he needed to find a way to tame his beast. *Hell!*

She turned her back to him and continued through the passage.

He followed close behind, his senses flaring out, looking for danger. He didn't give a shit if she wanted protecting or not. She was getting it.

"So why blood?"

She let out an exasperated sigh. "Kothar blood is powerful, that is all you need to know."

His current mood gave new meaning to biting one's tongue. At the moment, his bled.

After several minutes and a tight squeeze through a narrow passage, they came out the other end. Caleb stiffened, waiting for some kind of attack that never came. He soon realized Hell looked nothing as he thought it would. There was green grass, blooming flowers, and giant shade trees. He half expected fairies to come dancing out of the thicket.

"Where's the fire and brimstone?"

Lileta tossed her head back and laughed. God, how he loved to see her happy. "Dragon, we're not in Hell yet. This is only a holding area, Hades' idea of a joke. Bring the souls here and let them think they have moved on to the afterlife in heaven. Once comfortable then the demons come and their misery begins."

He crossed his arms over his chest. "Kind of a sick fuck, I think I like him already." He knew the souls here deserved punishment. He wondered if he'd meet up with Sanchez in the other world. Now that would be fun.

"Why are you smiling?"

"I hadn't realized I was." He knew he was smiling. The thought of torturing Sanchez's soul while he was here made him giddy. "So, when do you pay the god of Hell?"

"Come on." She moved across the soft grass with grace. It was then he noticed her appearance began to change. Two, small, creamy white bumps protruded from the top of her head. Horns, just as she had predicted. Her skin also took on a luminous tone with a soft hue of red. His jeans became too tight, and his cock begged for release.

Even his tongue itched to lick every inch of her glowing skin. If possible, his mate was even more beautiful.

"Are you going to stand there with your mouth gaping, staring at me, or are you coming along?"

He blinked and realized Lileta stood with hands on curvy hips, head tilted slightly and her gaze pinned on him. Yeah, he'd been staring, looking like a damn teenager who'd just seen his first naked female.

"Uh, yes." He decided at that moment he was never going to survive this trip. He needed to sink his cock deep inside her until he touched her soul and didn't give a shit if he survived. He only hoped he lived long enough to hear her scream his name.

He shook his head and came back to his senses. "You never answered me. When do you pay the god?"

"Are you still hung up on that?" she asked in a huff.

"Yes, but maybe if you warn me, I can look the other way." Not.

She snorted. "Right. I have to pay when we reach the inside." She shot him an evil grin. "You know, fire and brimstone."

Their journey continued without conflict, and before he knew it, Lileta led them to a secluded spot next to a waterfall. "We'll spend the night here. Tomorrow morning, we'll reach the gateway so we should rest." She reached for her bag.

"Here, let me help." He grabbed the pack and pulled it free from her back. His fingers brushed her skin, sending a visible shiver across her body. Her head tilted back, and her eyes closed. Her arousal wrapped around him as if it were his own. He wondered if it had something to do with the changes brought on since they'd been here. Never had her desire been this debilitating. She was in pain.

He tossed the sack. "You don't have to suffer. I can help alleviate your arousal."

She turned to face him. "You have a death wish?"

He flashed his best smile. "No, but I have ways to please you that will still keep me breathing."

She chewed her bottom lip and looked as if she was considering his offer. "Look, I know you mean well, but it's better if we refrain. It will pass." She reached for her pack and grabbed a bottle of water.

He knew better. Their urges were growing stronger, and for some reason, hers had grown worse since entering this domain. He could hold out but wasn't so sure about her. If they didn't do something soon, she was going to be in serious trouble.

HER HANDS SHOOK as she reached for the water, surprised by how strong the urges had become since returning home. She was angry that her mother hadn't warned her. Surely, she must have known being on home soil with her mate in tow would stir her desires to an almost unbearable magnitude. Maybe that was what her mother meant by embracing it. She was thankful her back was to Caleb so he couldn't see how much his touch affected her. The offer he made for release only caused more pain, and she had been close to saying yes. Her body was strung so tightly it was ready to snap. Her mind unable to focus, which wasn't a good thing considering where they were. She needed to figure out a way to curb this desire before it killed both of them. She took a swig of water, wishing for something stronger.

Her thoughts now under control, she turned to face him. "I'll start a fire. The sun sets fast here, and when it does, it gets extremely cold." She set down the bottle and took three steps to her left, held out her hands and spoke an ancient incantation. Sparks jumped from her fingertips, and a small fire sputtered to life as darkness spiraled down upon them.

"You weren't kidding. The sun literally fell out of the sky," Caleb remarked as he spread out a blanket next to the fire.

Lileta followed suit, placing her own bedding on the opposite side of the flames. Far enough away from the dragon, she hoped. She lay with her back to him, unable to gaze upon his exquisite body any longer, and closed her eyes, praying sleep would come quickly.

Hours later, sweat rolled off her body and heat licked her,

someone needed to help her. She cried out in despair, her body burning with desire. Something brushed her skin and brought relief. A soothing voice whispered in her ear.

"Lileta, wake up."

She jumped with a start and rolled to her back, finding green eyes staring at her. Eyes that spoke of passion and desire. "Caleb, why are you touching me?" *Why aren't you kissing me and sinking your shaft deep inside my sex?* She knew why, but her body didn't care, it needed him.

"You were thrashing and mumbling in your sleep. I thought you were having a bad dream. I realize that's not the case." His gaze roamed over her like a slow burning fire, it devoured her. "Let me help you, please."

She tried to swallow, but her throat was parched. "We can't do this." Gods, how she wanted to pull him to her and slip her tongue past his lips. She wanted to feel the pressure of his weight pressed against her. She should never have brought him here.

His fingers caressed her cheek and brushed hair from her face. "Stop being foolish. You know it will worsen, and soon, you'll be unable to think. You will be a danger to both of us."

"But what about you? The bonding affects you as well."

"I'm older and stronger. Don't worry about me." His voice carried as a whisper. "I promise I won't hurt you. I can't stand to watch you suffer."

She chewed her bottom lip as his hand slid down her arm, causing bumps to rise on her flesh. The knot in her stomach unraveled, but the heat at her apex burned hotter.

He leaned closer.

Her breath caught in her lungs. Was he going to try to kiss her? She would not allow him to sacrifice himself. She swallowed a moan when he brushed his lips along her neck and sent every nerve firing into overdrive. Her body was like an electrical storm and was about to short circuit. For a brief moment, she thought about the past then reined in those memories. What happened to her wasn't her fault, and Caleb was not those men. He was her chosen. *Follow your heart.* Her mother's voice echoed in her head, but she was confused. Was her heart in control or her body? It was hard to tell.

His fingers slipped under her shirt and pushed the fabric upward until her bra was exposed. He leaned down and ran his tongue across her naked flesh. The heat so intense she was surprised her skin didn't blacken. He pushed the bra aside, exposing sensitive nipples. His tongue swirled across the protrusion and pulled it into his mouth. Her vision darkened, she slid her eyes shut and arched her back.

"For the love of gods, don't stop." Her voice came in a rasp, and she grabbed the back of his head, holding him to her. The sensations that racked her body were foreign. Never before had she experienced pleasure from a man's touch, and never had she desired it so desperately. It frightened her, but she reminded herself who she was with.

He nipped then blazed a wet trail across her chest to the other breast. Giving it the same painstaking attention. Fingers found the button and zipper on her jeans and undid them. His hand slid between the denim and the fabric of her panties then palmed her mound.

She groaned. "Caleb..." Was this what it was like to really desire someone?

"Shhh," he whispered in her ear before nibbling on her lobe. "I won't pass the boundary of your panties. I promise I won't sink my fingers deep into your dripping pussy...at least not tonight." His thumb rubbed across her swollen clit and lightning shot through the sky.

"That was you, wasn't it?" He looked upward. "Your arousal has caused the elements of Hell to awaken."

"Yes." She fought for control. She wanted to rip his clothes off and have her way with him, but knew it was impossible.

"Look at me, Lileta."

She obeyed and caught his gaze. Longing swirled in his green eyes. His thumb continued to rub across her nub, sending waves of desire coursing through her. His other hand cupped her breast and pinched the nipple between his fingers.

"I want to look into your eyes when you come. Come for me, angel."

She needed no more encouragement as the first wave picked her up and carried her on its crest. She heard herself scream his name as if no longer in her own body. She thrashed, and nails dug into his arm until the wave set her gently back on the ground.

"That's my demon mate. You're so beautiful when you come." He leaned over and kissed her cheek. Nimble fingers zipped up her jeans and adjusted her shirt. Warm, strong arms pulled her close to his hard body. Her lids fluttered, and sleep finally overtook her.

CHAPTER THIRTEEN

SETH WALKED ALONG LAKE MICHIGAN, snow crunching under his boots. The city now at rest, its occupants slept in preparation for tomorrow's bustling work day. He and Lucan had separated hours ago. The other warrior moved to the interior of the city and he now patrolled the shoreline. The Draki assigned to them circled high above, searching out the demons they knew lurked in the shadows. His breath blew out an icy fog, and he tucked his hands into the pockets of his coat. Even though he was immune to the cold, he hated winter, and he hated Chicago even more.

He searched for the mental link to Lucan and connected. *Have you found any demons yet?*

None. I don't like the feeling riding up the back of my neck, Lucan responded.

Me either. Have you spoken to the others? He pulled up the collar on his jacket. "Fucking windy city, aptly named," he mumbled under his breath.

Yes, all have made contact and had a few kills. The bastards are here, we simply need to find them.

He felt Lucan cut the connection just as a scream shattered the night. With lightning speed, he ran in the direction of a feminine voice.

"Let go of me, you fucking asshole," she screeched.

The disturbance came from the docks. He flashed and appeared behind a man who was struggling, trying to get a very angry woman onto a boat. "It doesn't look like the lady wishes to board this vessel," Seth announced.

The man spun. "Mind your own fucking business, punk."

Seth assessed the situation. He saw no weapons, but the man had his arm wrapped around the woman's neck. Before he could come up with a plan that wouldn't involve giving himself away as not being human, the female stomped a high heel onto the man's foot.

"Bitch!" The man backhanded her, knocking her across the dock.

"Oh you should not have done that," Seth said through clenched teeth then flashed behind the stranger. Seth grabbed the man by the head and jerked the man to his chest. He then snapped his victim's head to the right, exposing the pulse, and sank his fangs deep into the stranger's muscular neck, hitting the vein. He didn't bother with normal protocol for feeding. He wanted this bastard to feel everything.

He took deep pulls. His victim struggled, but he held fast. He wouldn't kill him, it was against their laws, but he would drink enough to cause the man to black out. He kept one eye on the girl who lay sprawled out on the dock. Her life energy still burned bright so he assumed she was only unconscious. The man weakened, and his body went limp. Seth retracted his fangs and dropped the man to the frozen dock.

"It's more than you deserve." If he had his way, he would have tossed the man into the frigid lake. Stepping over the body, he reached the girl, knelt and turned her head so he could examine her. "Oh hell." Already the entire right side of her face was beginning to bruise. Her lip bled from where it had been split open. Still, it could have been much worse. Seth had taken the bastard's memories and seen what he'd intended for her, she would never have survived the night.

He debated calling in Marcus to heal her then thought better. She would wake and wonder how she'd taken such a punch and been left with no marks. She'd be uncomfortable for a few days, but her injuries were not life threatening.

She stirred, her lids fluttered open, and she gasped.

"It's all right. You are bruised, but safe."

She opened her mouth to speak and groaned, her fingers moving to her lip. "Damn."

"May I help you sit up?" he asked.

She nodded her approval, and he placed his hands behind her back, guiding her to a sitting position. Her gaze darted to the man lying behind him. "Did you kill him?"

"No, he is out cold and will be for some time."

"I hope the fucker freezes to death," she spat.

"What—may I inquire—were you doing out this late at night without an escort?"

She narrowed her gaze. "You're a little young to be my father."

He chuckled—if she only knew. "And you are a little ungrateful."

Her features softened. "You're right, I'm sorry. Thank you for coming to my rescue, even though I could have taken him myself."

He arched a brow. "My apologies. Next time, I'll be sure and not interfere."

She patted the ground around her. "Where is it? I need to find it." Her voice rose in panic.

"What did you lose?" He scanned the area. Something silver glinted in the moonlight several feet away. He moved toward it, bent over and picked up the shiny object. He palmed the dagger, and its magic pulsed through his body.

"Give me that." She was beside him, her hand grabbing for the blade. He held it out of her reach.

"Where did you get this?"

"None of your damn business." Her blue eyes flashed with anger.

He sucked in a breath. It seemed this little redhead was as fiery as the locks that framed her beautiful face. No matter, he intended to find out how it was a human had obtained a magical blade.

Her knee made contact with his balls, and he doubled over. She grabbed the dagger and ran into the night. "Son of a bitch!"

Energy stirred behind him, and gruff laughter echoed. "I leave you to fight demons, and instead, you're getting kneed in the sac?"

He turned to glare at Lucan, his balls still begging for mercy. "Fuck you. And by the way, she happened to be carrying the missing dagger of Embara."

Lucan's eyes widened. "Are you certain? The blade of the Phoenix?"

"I had it in my hand and felt its power."

"Holy hell."

"Precisely. We need to let Aidyn know," Seth replied. It was imperative they find her and confiscate the dagger before she killed someone with it. Namely, one of them.

LILETA WOKE with a start and found her backside pressed into something hard. Caleb was curled into her, his arms wrapped around her waist and his erection pressed into her behind. Guilt, surprise, and embarrassment flooded her. She had been taken aback by the need that caused her so much discomfort, and now her cheeks grew warm at the remembrance of the pleasure Caleb had given her. The unselfish act he'd performed to bring her relief now caused his arousal to press into her. Her mind became a whirl of emotions.

What the hell do I do now? Did she offer to bring him the same pleasure he had her? Her body wanted him, but her mind said doing so would only make matters worse. She wanted to curl inside herself and hope this whole damn mess would simply go away. Instead, they had a job to do, and she would not be responsible for refusing to aid the goddess Qadira. With that settled, she slipped from his embrace.

He stirred. "Are you feeling better?"

Her cheeks flushed. "Um, yes. We should be moving. We still have a lot of terrain to cover."

He sat up and ran his fingers through his tousled locks. He wasn't wearing a shirt, and she found herself longing to trace a finger over his scar.

"If you want to know, you only need ask."

"I...um didn't want—"

He stepped in close, so close his breath brushed across her cheek. "Lileta, there will be no secrets between us. Ask me what you wish to know."

She swallowed. Had she been that obvious? "Diego told me the story, but I'd like to hear it from you." She touched the raised skin. Even though it wasn't her people who had done this to him, it was still demons and she felt a sense of responsibility.

He grabbed her hand and raised it to his lips, planting a light kiss on her knuckles. "When my brother and I were captured, Drayos chained me using magic-laced links so I was unable to break free or shift. He then used a special dagger, one that belonged to the Phoenix."

"How the hell did he get that? I always thought that blade was a legend anyway." She watched him pull a T-shirt over his head and tuck it into his unbuttoned jeans. *Oh Christ.*

"No one knows, and no one up top would ever admit to the existence of such a weapon. I can tell you this much, it will kill an immortal if they are struck in the heart."

The only way to kill any immortal was to sever their head. Not even a blow to the heart would do the trick. They'd simply heal. "So, the dagger is real? Where is it now?"

He shrugged. "No one has seen it since Drayos's death. You are familiar with the legend of the Phoenix god?"

"Of course. All children are taught about the great war of Jumaria, where the god lost his life. It is said his power will rise again one day, but it has never been seen. Many believe he was only a myth as was the dagger he carried."

"I can attest that the dagger is very real," he growled.

"How did you escape? I understand he made you drink his blood to keep you from healing." She reached for her pack, but he grabbed it and held it while she slipped her arms through the straps.

"Yes, he forced his blood down my throat every time I would start to heal then slice me open again. Eventually, after about six months, I was rescued, by Odage." He picked up his own pack and slung it over his shoulder.

"No wonder you had a hard time believing he was responsible for the death of the guardian queen." It didn't take a genius to realize Caleb felt he owed his life to the Draki Overlord.

His eyes darkened. "If it had not been for him and Diego, I would never have survived." He looked away. "I was responsible for my brother's death."

Suddenly, it all seemed clear. She placed a hand on his arm. "Was it the blade that killed your brother?"

"Right through his heart. I watched the life drain from his eyes." His sorrow-filled gaze met hers. "When I finally went home, I had to tell his mate he was dead. She was so grief-stricken, she took her own life." He quickly turned his back to her and stepped away. "We should get moving."

"Yes, of course." Resolve coursed through her. She would beg the gods herself to break the bond. This brave man who stood in front of her deserved much more than a broken demon as a mate. Her heart filled with sorrow. A part of her wanted him but knew she was being stupid and selfish. *Follow your heart.* She wished her mother would shut up. "We will be heading into the next realm, and I suspect we might be able to get some answers there."

"Good, the sooner we can find the goddess, the sooner we can leave," Caleb replied.

HIS SCAR still burned where her fingers had caressed him. It had taken every ounce of dragon strength he had not to throw her down and bury his cock into her warm depths. Then she wanted to know what had happened. Was her resolve breaking? He still needed to find out her deepest desire and hoped by sharing his most painful moment it would move them in the right direction. He feared there wasn't much time left to figure out his mate. Something tore at her heart—this much he could tell—and he planned to press the matter to see if she would share it with him. The more time they spent together, it became apparent she was complicated. Not only did he admire her beauty, but her strength and wit as well. She was a strong, proud demon, one he would be honored to call his mate.

They had been traveling in silence for several hours. The terrain turned from lush green to dead and burnt. It was like a desert, barren with nothing but sand for miles. Not even a breeze blew, making the two suns that blazed down on them even fiercer.

"Holy hell. I like hot, but this is ridiculous." He wiped the sweat from his brow and glanced over at Lileta. Her skin was slick and her cheeks flushed. She looked good enough to eat.

"I'm afraid we're going to have to burrow until night fall. We're only halfway across this terrain and can't continue in this heat." She mopped her forehead.

He raised a brow. "Burrow?"

Her lips curled at the corners. "Watch this." She held her palms out flat in front of her, closed her eyes and her lips moved in silence. The ground shook and sand flew until a small tunnel formed in front of them. She stepped back, hands planted on her hips, and surveyed her work.

"What the hell did you just do?"

"I made us a sand cave." She grabbed his hand and pulled. "Come on, let's get out of the suns."

They stepped through the opening, his eyes quickly adjusting to the darkness. Already his skin liked the coolness. Lileta led him through a tight passage. After several steps, it snaked downward then to the left before widening several feet below. The small room was tall enough for him to stand and wide enough they could both stretch out. The temperature had dropped a good twenty degrees. Still warm, but much more bearable.

He brushed a hand across the walls, the texture smooth as glass. "I had no idea you had such power." He let pride carry in his voice. This little minx was full of surprises, and he found himself wondering what other kinds of tricks she could perform. His dragon stirred along with his cock. Christ, both needed a leash.

"You're in my element now."

He adored the big smile on her face.

She threw her pack to the ground, pulled free a blanket and laid it out then sat and began pulling off her boots. "We should get some rest. Once the suns set, we'll have to move quickly to get across the desert before they rise again. In this realm, night is only a few hours."

He followed suit and took up position near the entrance just in case. She rolled her eyes at him.

"Nothing will bother us while the suns are in the sky. It's after they set you need to worry."

He didn't like the sound of that. "And what exactly should I be worrying about?"

She gave a yawn, laid down and folded her arm under her head. "They know we're here now, and the demons will come. Be prepared to fight."

CHAPTER FOURTEEN

CALEB WATCHED her chest rise and fall for several minutes before he finally let his lids slip shut and take him into sleep. He was enjoying the hell out of his current dream. Delicate fingers pulled on his T-shirt, freeing it from his jeans then glided underneath it across his naked chest. Damn, it felt good.

Soft curves pressed against him then climbed onto his lap. His cock stiffened and strained against his jeans, begging to be set free. Hot moist lips brushed his, and he groaned. He reached for Lileta and cupped her face, if he couldn't have her in real life then he would settle for having her in his dreams.

His tongue plundered into her mouth and slid across hers. Desire kicked up ten notches along with the need to possess her.

Honeysuckle mingled with lust assaulted his senses. His hands dropped to her shoulders then slid to her breasts. He squeezed, the soft mounds more than filled his large hands. She moaned into his mouth while rocking against his shaft.

His body was on fire, and his hands moved to grasp her ass.

"Caleb, I need you," she whispered against his lips.

His body went rigid. Something was off, but he couldn't place a finger on it. She pulled on his shirt, trying to rip it from his body.

"Need this off." Her voice came in breathless pants against his lips.

Holy hell! His lids flew open. This was no dream. Lileta rocked on his lap, and they'd been kissing. He pushed her away and shook her.

"Wake up."

Her lashes fluttered. "Huh? What?" Sudden realization crossed her features. "Oh my god, what's going on?"

"You were trying to fuck me in your sleep."

She scurried off his lap and flew across the small room, her pupils dilated and breathing heavy. "Shit, I was dreaming." She scrubbed a hand down her face then looked at him, her jaw open wide. "I kissed you. Hell, why did you let me kiss you?" Her voice was full of panic.

He adjusted himself best he could. His erection was so hard he could have used it to drill for oil. "Fuck, woman, I thought I was dreaming as well," he snapped, not meaning to.

Her lips pursed in determination. "I should have never agreed to this. It was a mistake." Moisture glistened in her eyes. "My gods, Caleb, you could die."

He slid in next to her. "I'm not going to die." *I hope.* He reached for her hand, but she withdrew.

"Don't touch me." The tears finally made their escape and stained her flushed cheeks. "I'm so sorry. I never meant to hurt you."

This time, he managed to grab her hand and bring it to his chest. "Stop." He brushed a drop with his finger, not giving a shit if he came in contact with her body fluids. Her distress fractured his heart, and the fact that she held concern for his safety meant he was breaking through the barrier. He refused to let this minor setback become a roadblock.

They belonged together.

"Angel, I know you hold no malice. I loved your kiss, and gods, do I crave another. I crave all of you and will have you, one day."

"But you might—"

He placed a finger against her swollen lips. "I'm not going to die. I feel fine—well, except for the raging hard-on I have, but even that I will survive." He looked at the bulge in his pants. "See what you do to me, angel? You set me on fire, and soon, I will part those lovely thighs of yours and bury myself so deep I won't find my way out until next week. But not today." He nodded toward the opening. "I think the suns have set. We should go."

She nodded and moved to rise. He gave a silent prayer to the gods that he would indeed survive.

LILETA TOOK the lead and didn't bother to wait and see if he followed. *I've killed him. How stupid I was to agree to help him.* She prayed he was right and would survive. Perhaps a short kiss wasn't enough to end the Draki's life.

When she reached the outside, she was met with two full moons and cool air blew across her skin. It would be a good night to run. She looked up at the tall man who stood beside her. He was a mystery, one she wished she could unravel. Not only did her body crave his touch, but her heart started to have a mind of its own as well. She would never admit it to him, but she was on the verge of falling for him. Hard.

I need to complete this mission and then get as far away from him as I can.

"Are you ready?" she asked.

He glanced at her, his eyes flashing emerald green. "Tell me what to do."

"We need to cross the rest of the desert and quickly. There is no flashing or shifting in this realm, so we run." She pulled out her dagger. "And keep your weapon handy, the demons will come." She took off in a sprint before he could reply, but he was next to her in a snap. "The demons we'll encounter here require you to stab them in the gut to slow them down, and then you can remove their head."

"Sounds easy enough," he replied.

"Yeah, except they have two stomachs and your aim has to be precise." She noticed he ran with ease as if he were on a Sunday stroll with the exception his muscles flexed with power. *Stop looking at him!*

"Great, can you be more specific? I think we're about to have company."

Several demons came into view on the horizon. "Aim two inches below the nodule you'll see on their chest."

"Right."

The demons were upon them in seconds. From what Lileta could see, she guessed there were at least twenty. *Not a problem.*

The first one who came at her flicked out a claw and raised its black, scaly arm to strike, but before it could, everything stopped. She stood, feet planted in the sand and blade ready to slice into the demon.

"What the fuck is happening?" Caleb asked.

All around them, the demons stood motionless, frozen in the last stance they took. "Shit, there's only one with enough power to do this."

"I'm glad you still remember who I am." A low voice growled from amongst the demons. He moved into view, his height towered over her. Black, leather pants covered his lower part while the top half was left bare, exposing heavy corded muscles. Black hair was tied back, accenting a chiseled face and onyx eyes.

Lileta dropped to her knees. "My lord, I come—"

He held up a large palm. "I know why you're here." His gaze traveled to Caleb. "But why is he in my realm?"

Caleb's posture stiffened, and the grip on his dagger tightened. *Great, just what I need. A pissing match between Hades and Caleb.*

Caleb would lose.

"My lord, I brought him here to retrieve the goddess. He...he is also my mate."

The dark god threw his head back and roared with laughter. "Unbelievable. So, the gods above really do have a mean streak. I'm impressed." He stepped closer to the Draki. "Drop to your knees. Do you not know who I am?" He growled.

Caleb clenched his jaw. "I know full fucking well who you are, Hades. I kneel to no one."

Hades' bottom lip turned up. "Oh you will fucking kneel and address me as your lord."

Caleb's face grimaced in pain as his knees buckled. He fought the hold Hades held over him, but Lileta could see he was quickly losing. "Caleb, please obey him," she begged.

"I do it only for you, not him," he said through pursed lips, and he dropped to the ground. He looked up at the demon god. "Fuck you. My lord."

Hades laughed. "You have spunk, dragon. I like that, and because Lileta seems to like you, I'll let you live. For now."

She let the air escape her lungs. "How can I serve you, my lord?"

"I don't wish to discuss this out here. You will be my guest." He tossed a menacing stare at Caleb. "And I suppose I will allow the dragon if you promise to keep your pet on a leash."

"I promise he'll behave." She narrowed her eyes at the Draki and pinned him with a stare that would burn a hole in his soul. So far, it looked as if he might survive her poisonous kiss. Now, she only needed to get him to behave, or Hades would be hanging a dragon head over his mantel.

"Very well then." The demon god clapped his hands together.

ODAGE STARED at the empty cage where Qadira had been held. He closed his eyes, fatigue spread across his muscles. He hadn't rested in weeks, and there was no light at the end of his black tunnel. As a matter of fact, a vortex closed in around him. He wondered how his son was—both his children now lost to him. Actually, all of his children. There were also the humans who had yet to give birth. A directive from Lowan, which he still didn't understand, but they were his children nonetheless. He hoped Caleb had found a way to save the humans and the babies. Before Lowan, he would never have done these vile deeds. He thought of his dead mate, and a tear slipped from the corner of his eye. She would be mortified at his actions, not caring that he had lost control. There was only one thing left to do while Lowan seemed to allow him a lapse back into reality.

Rescue Leria.

He summoned his ghoul wife Oroumea to meet him in the study. Giving one last look around, he flashed from the empty prisoner's area to the room several feet above. The once bustling cavern was now a ghost town. Its silence eerie even to him. He moved to the bar and poured a whiskey, wishing the amber liquid would numb him, but there was nothing that could take away his pain.

"Darling." His beautiful wife called out as she entered the room wearing a long, black gown that clung to her shapely figure. "You seem so glum." She pecked him on the cheek.

He studied her, she was not going to be happy with the news he was about to unveil. Perhaps he could placate her in some way.

"Love, I've made a decision. I'm going to rescue Leria." He waited for her fury.

Her fists clenched, and her already red eyes turned darker. "What a stupid idea. You will never survive Lowan, and that is surmising you can get yourself into Hell." Her chin raised. "Leave the brat to her fate."

His anger boiled to the surface, and he fisted his palms. "You will never speak of her in that manner again. Do you understand?" He had done many unsavory things in the past several months, but he loved his daughter. She was the only link left to his real love, his dead mate. Lowan had sucked all decency from his soul, but before he went totally mad, he had to at least make an attempt. Already the darkness pulled at him and tried to cloud his mind, but he fought with every ounce of energy he had left. Time was running out.

He understood Oroumea's real reason for anger. She felt jilted out of her role as ruler. She had thought he would be her ticket to power. "You will be taken care of should I meet my demise." He held out a piece of paper, and she snatched it from his hand.

"What is this?"

"It is the location to all my riches. Centuries of precious metals and gems worth untold wealth. Should I fail to return, it is all yours. There is enough there to buy the power you seek."

Her bottom lip curled up. "And I'm not required to share this?"

"No. All I ask is you help me find a way to reach my daughter, and then should it become necessary, get her to my people. They will care for her, and you shall be free." He didn't mention the fact he had another stash hidden, one he would save for his children.

She tucked the paper between her breasts. "Done. Let me check on a few things. I'm sure I can get you in."

He took a swig of liquor. "Excellent. Oh and the treasure is protected by a spell that can only be broken by my death." He refilled the crystal glass. "Just in case you were thinking of simply running off with the spoils."

She sneered at him then fled the room.

"Yeah, I thought so."

CHAPTER FIFTEEN

CALEB AND LILETA stood on black, marble floors where the walls were painted a red lacquer. In front of them was a large throne made of gold and adorned with human skulls. Hades sat, his hands perched on two gilded cobras that looked as if they were crawling up the front of his dais.

A Wendigo stood on either side, their jaws slack, exposing a mouth full of razor-sharp teeth. Caleb flinched. He'd rather tangle with Hades himself than either of these two demons.

"Why the hell are we here?" he asked.

Lileta smacked him in the gut, her eyes narrowed. A wisp of raven hair had fallen free of the pile she had on top of her head. Damn, she was sexy when pissed. He'd have to remember and rile her up more often.

"Several reasons. One, I need your damn goddess out of my realm. She is creating all kinds of havoc."

Caleb crossed his arms over his chest. "Well, no fucking shit. I seem to recall that was the sole purpose of coming to this...pardon the expression, Hellhole."

Lileta planted her face into her palms as if trying to hide then dropped her hands to her side and straightened. "My lord, I don't understand why you've brought us here."

Hades' black gaze drifted over Lileta. "Two, my demon must pay her dues."

Caleb's vision became masked in a haze of red. No fucking way was Hades touching her. God or no, he'd kill the bastard.

Hades leaned forward, his fingers steepled under his chin. "My dear, do you really think to waltz into Lowan's home and snag the goddess? Do you even know where she is?" His gaze traveled from one to the other. "I didn't think so."

"Why in the fuck don't you just go get her yourself? After all, you're the god of this realm." He knew Hades was up to something, it was time to find out what.

The deity tapped his fingers on the arm of his throne. "It is not my destiny." He pointed a finger at Lileta. "But it is hers."

Caleb's head snapped to gaze at his mate. Her eyes as big as golden coins. "What do you mean her destiny?"

"You don't know about your father, do you, Lileta?" Hades asked.

Lines creased in her forehead. "I don't understand what my father has to do with this."

Hades rose and stepped off the dais, his tall frame shadowed over her. Caleb went to lunge for the god but found his feet glued to the marble floor.

"I don't speak of your stepfather, but the man who planted his seed in your mother's womb," Hades replied.

Lileta's lips parted, and Caleb could see her breathing increase. "Did you know my real father? Mother never told me much about him. Only that he died when I was a babe."

Hades touched her cheek. "While I adore your mother, I disagreed with her decision to withhold your father's identity. However, I kept her secret, until now."

"I-I don't understand. Why would she not want me to know?"

Hades flashed a grin only the devil himself could conjure. "Your father is none other than Lowan himself."

Lileta stumbled backward. Disbelief and pain contorted her face, and all Caleb could do was watch. "You bastard! Lileta, angel, he lies. There is no way that fucked-up piece of shit is your father. You're too good to be his daughter." He glared at Hades. "Why are you doing this?"

The god turned and walked back to his throne. "I speak the truth, and if she searches her soul, she will see it for herself. Your power has grown stronger since you were freed of the shackles that bound you. I'm right, aren't I?"

She licked her lips. Her gaze flicked to Caleb, anguish hardened her soft features. *Damn it!*

"Why did mother lie to me?"

"Don't blame her. She had your best interest at heart. She was young and thought she was in love and then discovered Lowan's dark side." Hades sighed. "He didn't know she was with child. I arranged for the mating of her and your stepfather. We are the only ones who know your true identity."

"Why tell her this now? Why at all?" If Caleb could free himself from the god's hold, he'd fucking pummel Hades. The pain on her face ripped him in two, and his dragon twisted and screeched to be released. Unfortunately, he'd been unable to shift since coming to this realm.

"Because as I said, your goddess needs to be removed. Lowan is using her blood to open fractures and allow my demons to escape." He leaned toward Caleb. "Your mate is the only one who can find him and free her."

"What? I don't understand. Why can't you find him?" Lileta asked.

He leaned back, his faced looked haggard, and he let out a long sigh. "Drayos was my son. Lowan, your father, is a demigod."

"Shit," Lileta whispered.

"This gets more fucked up by the minute," Caleb replied.

Hades inclined his head. "Indeed, and you, Lileta, can connect to him and find the goddess. He will never sense you since you are part of him."

"Then what?" Caleb was certain he wasn't going to like the answer.

"Then she goes and rescues Qadira. Nothing more."

He narrowed a brow. "She's not expected to kill him?"

Hades tossed his head back and laughed. "While that is a novel idea, she is not that strong. I'm afraid the blending of Drayos and Eliza created something stronger than any of us imagined." He steepled his fingers. "There is only one who can battle Lowan and possibly win."

"Who?" Lileta and Caleb asked in unison.

"I cannot reveal that yet, but the time will come."

Caleb growled. "You're a fucking god. Why don't you kill him yourself?"

Hades raised a brow. "You ask me to kill my grandson. That I cannot do."

"Why doesn't Zarek kill him then? Or any of the other gods?" Lileta asked.

"If only it were that easy. The battle of Jumaria brought laws that prohibit a god from smiting another." Hades leaned forward. "Can you imagine the havoc if we went around killing each other over every little skirmish?"

Caleb could well imagine. Now they were stuck with a fucked-up love child who was part god and part vampire guardian, and his mate was stuck in the middle of this mess. He didn't like it. Not one fucking bit.

"Fine, I will find the goddess." Lileta looked at Caleb. "The sooner the better then we can leave here."

His heart froze at the thought of her going into Lowan's territory. It had never been part of the deal. If anything happened to her, he would rip Hell apart then work his way to the surface. Destroying everything and anyone in his path. He came to a sudden realization.

Fuck me, I'm in love with her.

"YOU CAN'T STAY in my room," Lileta stated as she tossed her bag to the bed. Hades had insisted they stay there and rest then she would go into a trance and try to find Lowan. The whole idea made her sick, but what choice did she have?

"The fuck I won't." Caleb pinned her with his green gaze. She had come to learn when he was upset or full of desire, his eyes changed from brown to green. Funny, she really adored the emerald fire that burned in their depths. Her memories switched back to the other night when he had brought her to orgasm and then again when she found herself in his lap. His eyes had been the greenest she'd ever seen them, and no doubt he would be one hell of a lover. Her body tingled to find out.

She turned her back to him, lest he see her lust.

"Don't think you can hide from me, woman." He slid in behind her and wrapped his arms around her waist. His nose touched her neck and inhaled. "I scent your desire."

"You don't play fair. Of course, I desire you. I can't deny what nature has intended for us. You know as well as I what the consequences will be if we mate." She also knew her heart would break. As much as she had tried not to, she had fallen in love. Hard.

"I still breathe after that kiss you gave me." He moaned. "I want to kiss you again." He sucked her neck between his lips and nipped. "I want to taste every inch of you."

Gods, did she want it too. She needed to savor him, and the memory of his tongue sliding along hers caused her flesh to pimple. Lileta pushed from his embrace. "Granted, you're alive, but that doesn't mean sex won't kill you." She moved to the other side of the room where it was safer. "I need to talk to you about the rescue." He wasn't going to like this.

"You're right. We should go over the details before we leave."

"You're not going." There, she said it.

His gaze narrowed. "Come again?"

"You heard me. It's too dangerous, so I'm going alone." She wanted to shout *I love you and can't stand the thought of losing you.* However, those words wouldn't come. Her heart would break to utter them and be met with silence. No, it was far better to keep her feelings to herself. Somehow, she had to convince him this relationship was a bad idea then break all ties.

"If you think I'm letting my mate go on this mission alone, you are mistaken." He spoke through gritted teeth.

She balled her hands and planted them on her hips. "Don't think to try and dominate me. I'll have Hades keep you here."

"You wouldn't dare," he growled.

She pursed her lips. "Oh I would." They were now at a standstill. What would his next move be?

He scrubbed his hand over his face. "Fuck, woman, but you are stubborn. How can you even think to ask me to allow my mate to go into danger alone?"

"Because you would leave me behind in a second to go fight a battle." She lifted her chin slightly.

"That is different."

Oh he did not just play that card. "How? How is that different, Caleb?" She asked through clenched teeth. "And if you say it's because I'm a female, so help me gods, I'll..."

"You'll what?"

She wanted so bad to show him in some form. Shoot a fireball at him? No, he loved playing with fire. Send a thousand scorpions crawling over his skin? No, she couldn't really bring herself to do him physical harm so that left only one option.

"Get out of my room."

"I thought I already told you." He crossed his arms over his chest.

"That does it." She held out both palms in front of her and summoned a Wendigo. The creature tipped its ugly head.

"How may I serve you, my lady?"

"Escort the dragon to his room." She pinned Caleb with a stare. "And make sure he stays there."

"As you wish." The demon grabbed Caleb by the arm and dragged him out the door. Finally alone, she sat on the bed and tried to wrap her mind around the fact that her real father...her blood, was Lowan which also meant Hades was her great-grandfather. She wanted to vomit. She wished Caleb were there to pull her into his arms and provide the comfort and love she so desperately wanted. Instead, she had thrown him out.

"Probably for the best anyway. If I rely on only myself then I won't be disappointed." She dropped her head into her hands and wished for the pain in her heart to stop hurting so bad.

"You are such a foolish girl."

She whipped around to face Hades. "I don't remember inviting you in my room."

He laughed. "You forget I need no invitation."

She wrinkled her nose then sighed. "Why am I foolish?"

He folded himself into the chair across the room. "Why have you not mated yet?"

She blinked. "Really? You do want the dragon dead, don't you?"

He leaned forward, his lip curled upward. "If that were truly the case, he'd be dead, stuffed and gracing my study." He leaned back. "It's obvious Qadira chose you for a reason."

SETH LEFT Aidyn with a new assignment in hand—find that female and the dagger. Now that it was his top priority, he once again stood where the incident had taken place. His plan was to try to scent her then find where she'd run to.

He was having trouble concentrating.

Voices ran through his head, demanding he do evil things. The man he'd taken blood from in order to save her had a soul as black as tar. Too many more of those and he would soon find his head detached from his body, courtesy of his king. He shook off the insanity and cursed the dark stain that grew inside him thanks to

Drayos. With his head a little clearer, he found a faint trail. Soon, the sun would come up and the city would awaken, making finding the girl even more difficult.

Seth moved away from the docks and headed west until he found himself in a small service alley between several buildings. Something glistened in the distance. His eyes narrowed, and then he realized what it was.

A demon stepped through the fissure, lifted its nose toward the sky, sniffed then motioned behind him.

Son of a bitch!

Five more walked out behind him, all wearing leather pants and jackets, their bodies strapped with half a dozen blades of various sizes. With the exception of their heads—which looked like a ram's with rows of sharp teeth—they could pass for human.

"We have hit the jackpot," the first one said.

"So many humans, we can feast for months," another added.

Seth had no choice. He produced his sword and slinked toward the group. Maybe if he took out the leader first, the others would weaken and become an easier catch. He would call for backup but knew the others were currently waging their own battles. The fractures coming faster than they could keep up.

He stepped from the shadows.

"Go back to the pit you slithered from or face death," he stated.

All six turned to face him, and the leader curled his lip. "Guardian, how kind of you to join us." His expression turned serious. "This one is mine. I shall enjoy tasting you and sucking the life force from your body."

Seth spread his stance and raised his sword. "Come and get me, goat head."

The demons descended upon him with blades in hand. He slashed and spun, making contact with the first one and sent its head rolling. As he fought off a second attack, the scent of strawberries enveloped him. *What the hell?* He knew instantly it was her, the woman he'd been tracking. From the corner of his eye, he caught a glimpse of her red locks as they glistened in the pink rays of the rising sun.

She stabbed an oncoming demon, using the dagger he'd seen earlier. Instantly, the goat-faced terror turned to ash. He continued his onslaught and fought another, but this time their leader tried attacking from the rear and managed to make a slice across his shoulder before she took him out. He had to admire her abilities with a blade, even if it was a magical one a human should never have in their possession.

He made quick work of dispatching the heads of two more while she killed the last one. When the melee was over, he pinned her with his gaze. "Who the hell are you?"

She wiped the blade across black, leather pants and slipped it into a sheath at her waist. "Well, now who's ungrateful? I save your ass and no thanks?" She pushed a lock of hair off her face.

"I could have taken them myself." He lifted his shoulders. "Sound familiar? No human should be fighting demons, and that blade you have—" He nodded to the dagger at her waist. "Where did you get it?"

Her posture stiffened, and he sensed her discomfort with the turn in the conversation. "Your arm, it's healed already. What are you?" She began to back up and was ready to flee. He needed to tread lightly. He contemplated flashing behind her and making a grab for her, but his balls still ached from the last encounter they'd had together. His mind ran through several scenarios on how to capture her. Pinning her to the ground actually sounded ideal, but before he could make it happen, she spun and ran.

"Son of a..." He took off after her as she disappeared around the side of a building. When he rounded the corner, it was empty. He stood gaping at a wrapper that drifted across the deserted street. *How the hell did she vanish?* He raised his nose to the breeze, all that was left was the smell of vomit and urine.

He fisted his hands.

It seemed the redheaded vixen was going to be harder to find than first anticipated. Determination coursed through his blood. It had been many years since he'd given chase to his prey, and his hunting skills were a bit rusty, but he had one thing she didn't.

The ability to obtain memories. Someone in this city had to know who and where she was.

CHAPTER SIXTEEN

CALEB PACED the room that was now his prison, thanks to Hades and of course his own feisty mate. He'd tried shifting, magic and brute force to break down the door, but to no avail.

"I can't believe she fucking threw me out." He ran his fingers across the top of his scalp as he spun on the ball of his foot and crossed the room again. The thought of her going to rescue Qadira left his nerves raw. He had half a mind to toss the stubborn demon over his knee and give her the spanking she deserved. He stopped mid-stride and sucked in a breath, his heart skipped a beat. Lileta was everything to him. She was the air he breathed, the other half of his soul, and if he lost her, there would be no reason to go on alone.

He tried once more to summon his dragon. It was the only way he would stand a chance against Hades and his demons. The dragon was his stronger side and held magical power.

Scales rippled beneath the surface, and the creature screeched. Fire burned in his belly. *Come on, you must succeed for Lileta.* Bones shifted, and muscles flexed. It was working. His dragon was finally emerging, and it was pissed.

Caleb turned the door into splinters. The black magic that had held him in place could no longer confine his beast. As a matter of fact, the dragon thrived on magic, consumed it as if it were a tasty tidbit. Caleb moved into the expansive corridor where he encountered a Wendigo. He snaked his tail around and hooked the demon, sending him sailing down the hall and through the wall at the far end. For good measure, he sent a burst of flame down the passage to clear out any more unwanted guests.

He raised his nose, searching for his mate. Her honeysuckle scent hung in the air and lured him. He moved to follow it, but before he could reach her, she appeared in his path.

"What the hell is going on?" Lileta asked, hands on her hips.

Hades came up beside her. "It would seem your mate will not be subdued. I have to admit, I'm fucking impressed."

Caleb shimmered and shifted back to his human form. He grabbed Lileta by the arm and dragged her into her room, slamming the door behind him. "Don't ever think to lock me up again." He pushed her to the bed, his body covered her and pinned her to the mattress. He blocked her ability to flash.

"What do you think you're doing?" Her voice was raspy, her breathing heavy.

"I'm claiming my mate. I'm done with the games, Lileta. You. Are. Mine."

Her eyes widened. "N-no, you can't. You'll die."

"Fuck that, I'm not dying. I'm too damn stubborn to die." He nuzzled her neck. The scent of her arousal went right to his groin. Oh yes, she wanted him as much as he desired her. He wedged his knee between her legs, the evidence of her need went right through his jeans.

Her pupils dilated. "I can't let you do this." She placed her palms on his chest and pushed, but he didn't budge. "I will not be responsible for your death."

He moved his lips to her ear. "For once, will you trust me?" he whispered then nipped the lobe and sucked it into his mouth causing her to moan. His dragon liked that, wanted to hear her mewl.

She wrapped her legs around him and ground against his thigh. "No, you must have strength for both of us, because I don't." Her lids slid shut, and her tongue darted out and ran across her upper lip.

He grabbed the hem of her T-shirt, the material giving way with ease as he yanked. Her breasts sprang free. He latched onto a rosy nipple and pulled it into his mouth. His teeth scraped against the protrusion. She arched into him, grabbed his head and dug her nails into his scalp.

"Gods, I need you," she whispered.

He ran his tongue along the underside of her breast. Her skin tasted of spiced lemons, hot yet refreshing. He continued across her firm abdomen and stopped to swirl around her belly button. The urge to taste her center consumed him. There would be no stopping now. If he did die then it would be with a smile on his face, but first, he needed to taste her mouth. Caleb straddled her body, grabbed her wrists, and pinned her arms over her head. He crushed his lips against hers and delved in with his tongue. She groaned and writhed beneath him, causing fire to burn in his groin.

"Mine," he growled between tasting her. "You'll not go to Lowan alone."

"You must stop, Caleb. Please," she begged.

He halted, pulled back slightly and gazed into her golden eyes. Desperation and fear resided there. Concern for his safety? Could she care about him?

"Why do you worry yourself with what happens to me?" He needed to know. Could she love him? Did he dare even hope?

Her lips moved, but no words escaped. She was hiding something. One day, he would find out what it was, but today, he would not press the issue. Whatever tore at her like shards of glass, he would not force her to relive. However, he resolved when this was over, he would continue the hunt for her captors and kill them. Slowly. In the meantime, he would give her the only thing he could.

He released her wrists, palmed her cheeks and placed a gentle kiss on her plump lips. "Angel, I know life hasn't been good to you, but I vow to make it better any way I can."

Her gaze softened. "Caleb, that's sweet, and I know we're mates, but you don't have to bind yourself to me. Maybe there's a way to break this, and then you can be with someone else. Someone you could love."

"I've already met the love of my life. The one woman with whom I want to spend eternity. There is only one who can make me whole."

Her expression went slack. "Oh."

He caressed his thumb over her cheek. "It's you, angel. You hold the other half of my soul. Without you, there is nothing worth living for."

Her gaze fell to her empty hands. "Dragon, I'm no good for you. You need a woman you can love." She opened her eyes and pools of liquid gold stared back at him. "Let me go before it's too late."

He dipped his head, and he pressed his nose to hers. "It's already too late. Can't you hear what I'm saying? I love you, and I don't give a shit who your real father is. I'll kill the bastard myself if it will make you happy."

SHE BLINKED as confusion clouded her mind. "What did you just say?"

"I said I don't care who your father—"

She pressed a finger to his lips. "No, right before that. What did you say to me?"

His brows creased. "I love you?"

"Yes, that. You can't really mean it." *Oh gods, please say you do.*

He brushed back a wisp of hair from her face. "I can, and I do. Look, I know I'm an obstinate ass."

She rolled her eyes. "Demanding also comes to mind, as well as overbearing."

He shook his head. "I know, and I apologize for the way I treated you in the beginning. Hell, I had better apologize for things yet to come. I'm a Draki, and I can't change how I am. I will always be over-protective and demanding, and I'll probably piss you off. Know that I will never hurt you, and I'll kill anyone who does." He ran his fingers through his hair. "Shit, I suck at this. Angel, I'll give you your heart's desire. Jewels, mansions, fast cars, you name it."

Tears welled in her eyes, making it difficult to see. This strong man, a dragon who was feared by many, at this moment gazed at her as if she were the most precious gem in the world. This was a side she had only glimpsed before and she loved it.

She loved him.

The tears spilled and slid down her cheeks. "I don't want mate-rial things. My heart's desire is only for your love."

He nuzzled her cheek, licking the tears away. "You have that and more, until my last breath." His lips brushed hers. "Please tell me these aren't tears of sorrow."

"No." Yes. She was happy with his expression of love, but sad that they couldn't be together without his dying. He pulled back to look at her.

"Angel, I can tell you're not being truthful, and I know what bothers you. Don't worry about my welfare. Just tell me you trust me."

"With my life." That wasn't a lie.

He curled his lips into that sexy grin she loved so much. "That's all I need."

He let his right hand trail down her abdomen and under the waistband of her jeans. The next sound she heard was the ripping of denim as it was torn from her body. Cool air brushed over her skin while lava burned her from the inside. Her need for him rose to a level that scared the hell out of her, but something deep inside told her to trust him.

His warm fingers caressed her thigh then moved up to her panties. Grasping the elastic band, he pulled. "No barriers between us this time." His eyes glowed with desire as they met hers.

"Wait."

He stopped. His gaze met hers. "What troubles you?"

"I can't give you children, Caleb. We are not the same," she whispered.

"You don't know that for sure. Look how far we have come already. You once thought a kiss would bring me death, yet I still live." He placed a kiss between her breasts. "We will work it out, and should it never come to pass...then so be it." Eyes filled with desire and longing stared back at her. "Trust me."

"Okay." She barely got the word out. Her breathing was so erratic. All she wanted was for him to ease the ache that beat between her thighs.

He slid down her body until he had a view of her apex. "I want to taste you." His mouth so close she could feel hot breath across her flesh. "Can I lick you until you come, angel?"

She sucked air into her lungs. Gods, if he didn't do something soon, she would burst into flames. "Yes."

He ran the tip of his tongue along her folds, sending shivers up her entire body. "Damn, you are a tease," she whispered.

"You want more?"

"Please." Only moments ago, she'd pleaded for him to stop. Now she begged him for more. May the gods have mercy on them both, because if he died, she would end her own life.

He wrapped his lips around her clit and sucked. She grabbed his hair and pulled as the first wave crashed over her. If she thought she was burning before, she'd been dead wrong. The orgasm engulfed her entire body and left her shaking. When she floated back to normal, he continued a teasing tongue dance along her folds.

"You taste so fucking good. I swear I will never get enough of you." He found her opening and pressed his tongue deep inside, swirling and lapping at her wetness. Driving her insane.

"Oh my." She moved her hands from his hair to the bed and grabbed fistfuls of sheet as another orgasm ripped into her, sucking the breath from her lungs.

He rose, leaving her cold, but when she realized what he was doing, her body flushed. His shirt landed in the corner, and a view of his ripped abs had her licking her lips. He loosened his belt then unbuttoned his jeans. She swallowed, remembering what lay beneath them. She watched his hands disappear beneath the waistband of his pants and slide them down his thighs. His erection sprung free.

She gasped.

His jeans flew across the room then he leaned into the bed and sucked her nipple between his teeth. She groaned and arched into him. His knees planted between her thighs, pushing them apart while he grabbed her wrists and slid them above her head. He looked up from her breast, raw desire on his face.

"I can't do gentle. I've waited too fucking long to have you." His voice was low and feral.

She nearly came again.

"Who said I wanted gentle? Claim me, Caleb, take me like the animal you are."

HE PRESSED the tip of his cock to her entrance and hovered, watching her eyes darken with need. He had given her his love, and now he would give her his soul. However, if Argathos had been wrong and he did die, at least he would know love. He experienced a need so deep it nearly shattered him, but he wouldn't trade it. Not for anything.

Lileta raised her hips off the bed, and he plunged forward. She enveloped him in her warmth and squeezed.

They were a perfect fit.

He pulled out completely then thrust deep. "Dear gods, woman. If I died today, I could want for nothing more." He had all that he needed right there beneath him, more than he deserved. Only one thing plagued his mind. Dare he complete the mating? If he claimed her completely and bound them together—no, he had to trust the gods.

"Don't speak of death, you promised me—"

He sought her mouth. Gentle went out the window as he thrust in and out. His pace quickened until he thought he might hurt her, but she was a demon. Her body responded, and she bit his bottom lip until a coppery tang danced across his tongue.

His desire heightened more, and his dragon hissed. She knew which button to push. He pulled free of her bite. "Who do you belong to?"

"You."

"Mine."

"Yes," she whispered.

It was all he needed. He pulled free of her warmth and flipped her on her stomach, raising her beautiful, round buttocks in the air. He slipped in between her wet folds and dove deep.

She shuddered.

He leaned over her back. "You will wear my mark," he whispered in her ear. His fangs grew, and he sank them deep into her left shoulder. Her blood trailed down his throat. He kept her pinned as the orgasm racked her body and she screamed. When calm came over her, he released his grip, grabbed her hips and thrust in and out. Ancient words escaped his lips.

"I promise to protect you, provide for you, and love you until my last breath. I beg the gods to bind our souls, making us one."

His cock thickened as burning semen made its way to the tip. He dug his nails into her flesh as he erupted. Pain fired through his chest as part of his soul was ripped out. In that moment, the gods connected them, searing their souls together for eternity.

Sweat dripped from his face to land on her back. "Lileta? Are you all right?" He barely recalled her screams as another orgasm ripped through her. He gazed at the mark left on her shoulder, one that would be visible to only his kind and keep other males away. He bent over and planted a kiss on the bite. Guilt racked him for any pain he caused her.

She moaned. "I've never been better."

Contentment, love, and worry flooded his mind, taking him by surprise. His mate's emotions slammed into him. He untangled them and pulled her into his arms. They snuggled into the mattress.

"Lileta, you have to stop worrying about me."

Her golden eyes blinked. "Damn bond." She laid her palm on his cheek. "I can stop worrying about your life no more than I can stop breathing."

He nuzzled her fingers. "I hate to feel your worry." With the bond came the ability to feel each other's emotions. He wondered if their telepathic link was hooked up yet.

She smiled. *You cannot protect me from my father.*

Like hell I can't. His question answered. This soft, beautiful woman in his arms belonged to him and he to her. His determination to save the goddess Qadira ratcheted up several notches. He owed the gods big time, for they had given him the most precious gift ever bestowed on him.

CHAPTER SEVENTEEN

ODAGE TOOK two steps then stopped and looked at his watch. He'd arrived early in the hopes Oroumea would already be waiting for him. No such luck. She'd told him to meet her in the graveyard where they'd first met in New Orleans. Apparently, she'd found a way to get him into Hell.

"Where the fuck is she?" he growled.

"Patience, dragon." Her voice filled the darkness in front of him before her shape appeared. It wasn't lost on him the fact her voice carried disdain. Apparently, she was past giving a shit about his welfare now that she was so close to procuring his wealth.

"You remember our bargain?"

Her ghostly form solidified to reveal a crimson gown that cut halfway to her navel. Raven hair piled high on her head glistened in the full moon like an intricate spider web. "Of course." She gave a smile that would bring any man to his knees.

"I see you're dressed to kill." It was apparent she would be trolling for her next victim once she was rid of him. He supposed it was what he deserved. After all, he'd used her as well.

She flicked her tongue across ruby lips. "I'm confident you'll not be returning."

He curled his lip. "Vile woman. Perhaps you should consider pursuing Lowan as your next mate. You two would be a match made in heaven." He wondered who would win that battle.

A delicate brow arched. "What a wonderful idea." She held out her hand. "Shall we?"

He grasped her cold, ivory fingers. "How do you intend—" Before he could finish the words, they were sucked into a vortex. Blackness swirled and squeezed him before spitting him out onto a hard surface where he landed on his ass. He reached back to pull the rock out from under him when the ghoul's voice echoed out.

"Take care, Odage. Lowan is expecting you." Laughter rained down. That fucking bitch had double-crossed him. He stood, brushing the black dust from his backside and looked around. Lava bubbled only feet away and screams filled the air, definitely Hell. Now he needed to come up with a plan to locate his daughter and get her out of there. Normally, finding his own flesh and blood would prove easy, but Lowan had the child encased in a spell that blocked her scent.

"No matter," he mumbled under his breath as he shifted, glad to be an ancient. Many younger Draki were unable to call forth their dragon in Hell. It was an asset that would come in handy, for he was certain his dragon could persuade some lowly demon to assist him.

LILETA STRETCHED HER SORE LIMBS. Caleb and she had spent the last several hours having sex. *I can't believe we're actually mated.* So far, he appeared healthy. She hoped he stayed that way. A smile crossed her lips as she lay in the comfort of the bed and watched him pull on his jeans. Every muscle flexed with power, and he was a remarkable sight, her dragon.

"If you keep staring at me like that, I'll be forced to come back to bed and take care of that desire smoldering within you," Caleb said, buttoning his jeans.

She sat up, letting the sheet fall. "I am still in awe of this...of us."

He moved in and sat next to her, pushing a lock of hair behind her ear. "I told you not to worry about me."

"I'm happy you're well, I just wish to know how. Did something change in the years I was gone that allowed our species to be together?"

He grabbed her hand and brought it to his lips. "No. After you left me last, I spoke to Argathos. He told me we were meant to be, I only had to give you your heart's desire and I would live to enjoy you for eternity." His eyes flashed from brown to green.

She pulled her hand back. "How did you know...?"

"I didn't."

"Then what you said, you really meant?"

"Why do you doubt me? Tell me what troubles you, angel." He raised a brow. "You forget I can feel you, and the vibes you're sending out are making me nervous."

She bit her lip then looked down at the sheet, pretending to pick off invisible fuzz. "I'm sorry, Caleb, I'm damaged. You should never have mated me. Do you think the bond can be broken?"

He grabbed her chin and pulled her to look at him. "Damn it, stop. It's time to share your demons with me. Don't leave me out here in the darkness alone. Let me help you."

She swallowed, could feel the tears swelling in her eyes. If he left her now, she would be devastated. "When I was taken, I was a slave, used to satisfy a man's needs."

He brushed her cheek. "I know. It wasn't your fault."

"I'm damaged." The tears broke past her barrier.

He kissed her lips then her cheek. "No, stop. You are anything but damaged. You are a strong, independent woman who is braver than many men I know." He pulled back to look at her, and she saw love in his eyes, so real she could almost touch it. It stole her breath. "You are a demon. One of the most powerful beings in existence, and your mate is a dragon. Nothing can come between us. Ever."

It was in that brief moment she finally realized the gift she'd been given. Her past might never be forgotten, but it was just that, her past. Today began her future, and she was blanketed in love from a man who was bigger than life itself. What a lucky woman she was.

She smiled. "I don't deserve you."

He kissed the tip of her nose. "I think you have that backward. Now, let's go kick some ass."

She gave a nod and they ventured out to meet up with Hades. Minutes later, Caleb sat across from her. Insistent he be present when she tried to locate Lowan. He'd not been pleased with the setup but agreed because it made her happy. He grinned.

"What are you smiling about?" she asked.

"You. I was just thinking about running my tongue across that silky skin of yours."

Her cheeks grew hot. "Now is not the time to be thinking of such things." She split her thick hair into three sections and began to braid it. He shifted with a grunt. "What is the matter with you?"

"It's unnatural for a man to sit cross-legged," Caleb moaned.

She rolled her eyes. "Who knew a beast as large as yourself could be such a whiner."

"Remember that spanking I threatened weeks ago? I have no problem laying you over my knee, bare ass and all." He crossed his arms over his chest, as if it would give credence to his threat.

This time, her entire body heated, remembering what he had done to her earlier. She was a lucky woman. Caleb's love encompassed her, made her whole, but she couldn't stop the feeling of dread sitting in her stomach. Weighing thick and heavy like concrete. Something terrible was going to happen.

"Are you all right?"

She met his brown eyes and tried to put a smile on her lips. "I'm fine."

His gaze pinned her, green flecks appeared in their chocolate depths. "You lie."

Before she could reply, Hades stepped into the room. "Are you ready?"

Not really, but what choice did she have? "Yes."

"Good. It took you two long enough to mate," Hades said, running his hands through the air. A ring of fire formed on one side and then circled around until both she and Caleb were in the middle of the flames.

Lileta and Caleb both looked at the god. "What do you mean?" she asked.

"Your mate is the only one other than another shadow walker who can help your soul leave your body," Hades replied.

"And just when the fuck were you planning on telling us this?" Caleb growled.

Hades shrugged. "Nature had to take its own course. Caleb, you will stay connected to your mate. If Lileta fails to pull back from her link to her father then you will need to bring her back."

Caleb reached for her hand. "I will let nothing harm you," he said while bringing his lips to her knuckles. "Ever."

"Then begin when you are ready, you know what to do," Hades said.

"Yes." Lileta dropped her hands to her thighs, closed her eyes and searched inside herself for the stain that would be her father. Once she found the thread in her mind, she grabbed hold and followed. Moving deeper into the inky darkness and despair. Violent images assaulted her and caused her to wince. Caleb was in the distance, his loving power ready to yank her back.

She pressed forward.

Suddenly, she found herself staring at a mural. Tilting her head, she moved closer to study it. Demons of various species were depicted having sex. Some were in beds while others bent their partner over velvet couches. It struck her there was a common theme. The demons were all male, and the females were human. She reached out to touch the painting then pulled back gazing at her fingertips as if they were alien and wondered how she'd been able to feel the wall.

Something tugged at her, causing her head to snap up. A doorway loomed in the distance, beckoning her, pulling her toward it. Her demon sense said the goddess was behind it.

She glided down a corridor, everything around her blurred except for the door at the end of the path. Emotions bombarded her. Did they belong to her father? She didn't think so, finding it difficult to believe Lowan held any despair. No, this was loneliness like she'd never experienced. So overwhelming, it caused her stomach to lurch. When she reached for the doorknob her hand was shaking. Weird, how could that be when she wasn't really in her body? Clasping the cold metal, she turned it and pushed. More darkness. She stepped through and was slapped with so much hopelessness actual tears stained her cheeks. She was now positive the goddess wasn't in here. Qadira was much too strong for the emotions that stung Lileta.

She pushed forward, determined to find the source when she heard a muffled cry.

"Hello?" She wondered if her actual voice would carry or was it only in her head. The sobbing stopped.

"Hello?" a quiet voice called back.

Lileta followed the sound through the dark until a faint light came into view. Her heartbeat increased at what she might find, and when she rounded a corner, she stopped dead in her tracks.

"Oh my gods." In the center of a cramped room sat a bed with a young girl atop a tattered quilt. The teen clutched a purple blanket to her chest, and her eyes were rimmed red from crying.

"What's your name?" So many thoughts raced through her mind. Was this another daughter of Lowan's? She did have long black hair and fair skin.

"Leria. Are you here to rescue me?" She wiped a fist over her swollen eyes.

Lileta moved closer, ever alert of any danger. "You can see me?" She stood at the foot of the bed.

"Of course, am I not supposed to see you?"

Lileta raised a brow. The girl had attitude that was for sure and reminded her of herself before she had been kidnapped. However, she was surprised the girl could see her. For some reason, she'd thought this was all in her mind, but it appeared she had actually left her body behind and her spirit moved on its own.

Realization hit. "Wait, you asked if I was here to rescue you. Who is holding you captive?"

The girl curled her lip. "The Dark one."

Lileta could only guess who that was. She sat on the bed next to the girl and wrapped a protective arm around her shoulders. She would kill her father. "Where are your parents?"

Leria sniffed. "My father said my mother was dead, and I don't know where he is. The Dark one will not let him visit very much."

She stroked the girl's silky hair, her heart breaking with every word the child spoke. A commotion came from outside, someone was coming. She glanced around the room for some place to hide. It struck her as odd that she should have to do so, but if the child could see her then she better not chance anyone else seeing her.

Leria pushed her. "Get under the bed. They are bringing the pretty lady back."

Lileta hurried and hit the floor, clawing her way across the slick marble until she was secure under the bed. From where she lay, she watched the door open.

"You will rue the day you touched me in such a manner."

Oh yes, only one woman could have so much spunk. How lucky could she get to have also found the goddess? Now to figure out how to get them out of there. She waited, wanting to be sure no one else was coming when a pair of emerald eyes peered at her.

"Are you coming out, or do you intend to hide under there for eternity?"

Lileta gave a shove until she slipped out from under her hiding place, stood, and brushed herself off. "My lady," she tipped her head, "there is one very angry god looking for you."

The goddess smiled. "I hope he rips Lowan a new one. I see you have gained your father's powers. That is most excellent."

Lileta's vision glazed over, she really didn't have time to ask questions.

CHAPTER EIGHTEEN

LILETA BLINKED, her mouth suddenly dry. "You know about my father?" She should have known the gods would be behind this.

"Of course, it's all part of the plan." Qadira moved to a dresser across the room, grabbed a comb and began fussing with the girl's hair. "I am the one who decided you and Caleb should be together."

Her jaw tightened, and she wasn't sure if she wanted to kiss the woman or punch her in the face. Fortunately, self-preservation kicked in and she only smiled. "I should thank you then?"

The goddess laughed. "He is a pain, I know. However, he is destined to lead his people and needs a strong mate. He will also require a woman with a kind heart to help raise his ward."

Her brows furrowed. "His ward?"

"Yes, the girl will become very important to us all when she grows up." She glanced down at Leria then back at Lileta.

The girl rolled her eyes. "I know you're talking about me."

The goddess shrugged.

Holy shit! She referred to the girl. There were a million questions flashing through her mind, but she didn't want to ask them in front of the child. "Uh, I don't know what to say."

"You must go before Lowan feels your presence if he hasn't already. When the time comes, should you have to choose between my life and the child's, you will make sure the girl survives."

Lileta shook her head. "Oh no, you both will survive. I'm not about to bring Zarek's wrath down on myself."

Qadira finished braiding the child's hair. "My husband realizes the importance of the girl."

An eerie screech echoed off the walls. "Seize her!"

"Run, Lileta, your father has discovered you," Qadira begged.

She tried to move toward the door, but something held her firm. "I can't move." She was stuck in limbo.

"Call for your mate, call for Caleb. Hurry."

She closed her eyes and tried to push down the panic, as evil grew thick around her.

TERROR REACHED out its jagged claws and sliced through him. Caleb had never in his life experienced desperation like what coursed through him. Not even when Drayos held him prisoner and killed his brother, had he been this frantic. His love, his entire life was in serious danger.

Lileta, angel, focus on my lifeline.

Caleb, I can't find you, all I see is darkness. I'm so sorry. I've failed.

He sucked in a breath, reached deep within and concentrated on the light. It started in his core as a small flicker. He called for his dragon who held the fire. His skin stretched as he and the beast merged. He was neither man nor dragon, but a combination of the two. Together, they stoked the fire and brought forth the light.

I'm here, love. Can you see me now?

I see the line, but I can't move.

Another presence filled his head.

So, the bitch thought to keep you from me, Lileta? No matter, I have you now. Let go, daughter, or I kill the dragon.

Lowan had hold of her. *No! Hold on, baby. Don't listen to him.* Caleb knew if she let go then her soul would be lost, her body now in a trance would only survive maybe a few days at most. Thousands of burning shards blazed a heated trail through his brain. Warm liquid gushed from his nose and ears. He clenched his jaw.

Caleb, I can't let you die.

A vast emptiness filled his mind, quiet and dark.

She'd let go.

"You fucking let go!" His eyes snapped open, and he tried to focus, he reached up to wipe away the blood from his nose and realized something was off. He looked at his open palms and squinted. Wait, he'd been holding her hands. His mind finally started to clear when he noticed she was gone. He jumped up, spun around, and flared out his senses.

Nothing.

The woman he loved, who'd been sitting across from him in a trance had vanished. He quickly made a mental check and had no knowledge of a soul being able to pull its body back to it. Then where the hell was she?

He stretched his neck, bones popped as he continued the shift into his dragon. He was going to kill Lowan.

ODAGE PLODDED through the steam escaping from the underground vents. He had shifted to his dragon hours ago and still hadn't found a demon who was willing to spill where Lowan was hiding. It might have been they didn't really know, but in his frustration, he'd slaughtered them anyway.

"You seek the High Lord?"

Odage turned his head toward the raspy voice.

Wendigo.

He contemplated shifting back to human form. If this was a trick, he wouldn't stand a chance against the creature. However, he was willing to hedge his bets, something said this one was going to talk. He folded in his massive wings and wrapped his tail around his body, letting the shift overtake him. "Do you know Lowan's location?"

The creature wiped saliva from its jaw. "I do."

He eyed the Wendigo's mouth full of razor-sharp teeth, reminding him to find his patience. "What is it going to cost me?"

"His death."

His brows shot to his hairline, this was not the reply he expected and wondered what the hell Lowan could have done to piss off a Wendigo. "I thought you served him, so why murder your leader?"

The Wendigo flexed his fingers, snapping the four-inch claws together.

Odage shuddered.

"He keeps us under his control, we serve no one."

The Draki wondered how the Dark Lord was able to enslave the beast but didn't care to stand around having idle chit-chat. He needed to get to his daughter. "I would love nothing more than to kill the bastard. Any suggestions on how that's done?"

"Take his head off."

Well, no fucking shit, that much he knew, but there was no way to get that close to Lowan. Especially with a weapon that would take care of the deed. "Yes, of course. Can you tell me where the little girl is?"

The demon raised his chin. "I can do better. I will take you to her."

Dare he hope? He'd promise the creature anything if it would get his daughter out of the Dark Lord's clutches. He'd deal with the consequences later. "Take me to her, and I will kill Lowan once she is to safety."

With a grunt, the beast turned and began to walk away. "She is not far."

A sigh escaped his parted lips. Was it possible he might actually pull this off? It was still highly probable he would die in the process. "Wait!"

The Wendigo turned its dark head and pinned him with a fiery gaze. "You change your mind?"

"No. How do I know this isn't a trick?" It would certainly seem more likely, considering whom he was dealing with.

"You don't." The demon turned and walked into a pocket of steam.

LILETA BLINKED, trying to tamp down the woozy feeling that encompassed her. She sat on the bed and grabbed the edge of the mattress for support. "Wait...what the hell?" She realized her body was complete again.

"He is more powerful than we thought to be able to pull a body and soul back together." Qadira paced the small room.

"You mean it wasn't you?"

The goddess stopped, brow arched. "If I had any power right now, I wouldn't be here."

Lileta rubbed her tingling arms, wondering just how much power a demigod could wield. "Right." Panic overtook her upon realizing she had no clue what happened to Caleb. She'd let go of him when Lowan began threatening his life. Had he survived? There were no remnants of him in her mind. She needed to tamp down the fear and figure out how to get them out of this mess. Maybe she could bargain with her father. *Right, and maybe Hell would freeze over.* Her gaze caught the child sitting on the other side of the bed. She had to try, if not for her or the goddess then for the innocent girl. For some reason, this child was important.

Lileta stood on shaky legs and moved toward the door.

Locked.

"Lowan," she yelled out. "Let's play make-a-deal."

"Daughter, what kind of deal do you think to offer me?"

"In person, Lowan. I want to talk to you in person." Cold, black mist encircled her, pinning her arms to her waist. She refused to flinch. The room dimmed. She was sucked through a dark void. A loud buzz hummed in her ears, and a bright light filtered in. She squinted, trying to adjust when a dark figure appeared in front of her.

"So, it's nice to finally meet you. Daughter." She tilted her head back to look up. The High Lord stood several feet over her, his black hair falling to his collar, and his obsidian orbs stared down. Dressed all in black, his brilliant teeth shown bright when he flashed a smile, but it did nothing to take away from the thick scar across his cheek.

"Well, I see you have your mother's eyes, but the rest of you is all me."

Her nose wrinkled. "There is nothing about me that is remotely similar to you."

He tossed his head back and let out a hardy laugh. "Oh my dear, the darkness rests deep inside you. I can feel it." He leaned closer. "There is more of me in you than you care to admit. I own you."

She swallowed the lump in her throat. It was evident the man who stood in front of her possessed a great deal of power. "What is it you really want?"

He grinned then strode across the red-carpeted floor to a mahogany desk where he poured red wine into a crystal glass. "Care for some?" he asked holding the goblet toward her.

"No."

He shrugged then took a sip of the crimson liquid. "I tire of being in this place and wish to move topside." He leaned on the edge of the desk. "As we speak, my minions are wreaking havoc on the human race. Soon, your mate will arrive in hopes of rescuing you, but I have other plans for him."

She stiffened. There was no way she'd let this bastard near her mate. Power coursed down her arms and to her fingertips, blue sparks exited and snapped mid-air. "Leave him alone."

"Well, well. So, my daughter intends to protect her dragon?"

She moved to stand in front of him. "I intend to protect the child and the goddess as well. Let them go, what need do you have of them anyway?"

He swirled the wine in his glass, coating the edges with dark liquid. "The goddess's blood has served its purpose and so has the child. Her father is now my pawn, willing to do my bidding. Perhaps I shall make your mate my lackey as well." He took a sip then flicked his tongue out and ran it across his upper lip. "I might be persuaded to bargain, but I warn you, dear daughter, you may not be willing to pay the price."

She reached for calm. Emotions would prove fatal when dealing with her father. Wit and power now her best allies. "What kind of bargain?" Could she negotiate Qadira's and the child's release?

"You will stay here with me. Together, we can become most powerful." He reached for her hand and entwined his fingers in hers. "I'm sorry I was not given the chance to raise you myself."

I bet you are. His touch brought darkness and evil that pushed at her, trying to gain entry. He wanted in her head, and she refused, building a brick wall around her mind. She pulled from his grasp and took a step back. His power spun a web around the room and threatened to entangle her. She would have to dig deep to save herself if it was even possible.

"You will let the goddess and child leave if I agree to stay?"

"Yes."

"My mate as well. Send him back home unharmed." Her jaw set. "I know you have the power to do so."

"Agreed, and you will stay with me. I will train you. There is much power inside you yet to be harnessed."

Then I will kill you myself. There was one more thing she needed then her fate would be sealed. "I need you to break the bond between Caleb and me. I cannot concentrate with this attachment to him."

The corners of his mouth curled into a playful grin. He rose from the desk, and in one step, was in front of her, his palm placed across her collarbone. Heat seared her skin then entered deep within, filling her entire body with liquid fire. She tried to expand her lungs but could pull in no air. Sharp pain radiated under her breastbone. He was killing her, pulling her insides apart.

A scream stuck in her throat. Tears rolled down her cheeks, more from her failure than the pain. He pulled away, and her knees buckled. She fell to the floor gasping for air.

"Tis done. The bond is broken, and your mate is free. He will come for you no more." He waved a hand in the air. "Watch," he commanded.

She peered through blurred vision. A window opened to show a foggy picture. Qadira and the child stood in the world above. They had been set free. Her lips moved, but her voice was uncooperative.

"Look again."

She focused on the picture, a fuzzy image came into view. Caleb, he appeared next to the goddess, and from what she could tell, he was unharmed. The image snapped shut. Lowan bent down, his black gaze pinned her.

"Tomorrow, we begin your training." He spun on his heel and left the room.

Lileta lay in a broken heap, the pain finally receding, but it left behind something even worse.

Emptiness.

The bond was severed. No longer could she feel Caleb in her soul. That piece of him had been ripped away and tossed aside like garbage. Instead, she was left with an ache in her chest and a broken heart. Their bond might be gone, but her love wasn't.

"I'm so sorry, Caleb. Maybe now you can move on. Gods know I didn't deserve you anyway."

The tears came fast and heavy. The plush carpet absorbed her heart break. Tonight, she'd mourn her loss, tomorrow, she'd bury it deep and learn to embrace her dark side.

CHAPTER NINETEEN

CALEB'S DRAGON screeched as intense pain shot through him. He fought for control, but his wings folded. His body began to shift mid-air and there was no way to stop it. He was going to hit and hard.

He somersaulted out of Hell's copper sky, the blackened ground coming into his vision fast. He braced for impact with the full knowledge he was going to break several bones. His body slammed onto the rocks. Air pushed from his lungs, bones snapped and muscle ripped when he landed flat on his back. Positive his neck had broken along with several vertebrae, he groaned. The pain racking his body was nothing compared to the vise around his heart.

Lileta was dead.

The piece of her soul he held so dear ripped away. Their bond broken. His body would heal, but his heart never would. He failed in so many ways. His older brother, dead because he couldn't save him. His leader now wanted for murder and torture of humans because he couldn't see what was happening right under his nose. Now, the most precious gift ever bestowed him. A mate. Not just any mate, but Lileta. Warm, soft, and beautiful. All his until he fucking failed to protect her. He wanted nothing more than to lie there and perish, but he wouldn't die. No, he'd continue to live with the worst pain of his life.

He sucked in a breath, bones moved into place and mended. He rolled to his knees and stood, flexing muscle. Without his connection to his mate, it would be difficult to find Lowan. Find him he would, if he had to roam Hell for an eternity.

"I will kill you, you son of a bitch." He tried to summon his dragon, but nothing happened. The beast so heartbroken it refused to surface. He let out a sigh. "I know the feeling, but we must avenge her death." The beast stirred in agreement, but before he could shift, he was pulled off his feet. Sucked backward into a black vortex. He tried to resist, but the force was strong.

He landed on his ass in a cloud of dust. "What the fu—"

"Don't say it," a feminine voice cut him off.

He coughed and spat sand from his mouth. When the dust finally settled, he saw Qadira staring down at him along with a young girl. "Oh." Oops, he'd almost dropped the F-bomb in front of a teen. "What the hell—I mean what happened?" He stood and brushed off his jeans.

"Leria, why don't you go look for some shells while Caleb and I talk?" Qadira smoothed a hand down the girl's raven hair.

"Whatever." She folded her arms and began a trek across the sand toward the foaming waves crashing to shore.

"What is going on?" He suddenly realized where he was. "This is the same beach."

"Yes, the one you and your mate crossed not long ago."

He tipped his head and stared at his boots. His lids slid shut, and visions of golden eyes full of life and love for him filled his mind. Delicate fingers ran through his hair. He jerked away. While he was happy the goddess was safe, he didn't want her touching him. He wanted no one to touch him ever again.

"Caleb, look at me."

He raised his head. "Why? Do you find it amusing to give me love then tear it away? She's dead, and had you never thought to interfere with my life..." He closed his eyes and took in a slow breath. "I wouldn't be in such agony right now. The pain compares to none I've ever felt." He opened his eyes and met Qadira's emerald gaze. "Send me back to Hell so I can kill Lowan." He balled his fists and tried to shove his anger deep inside before he killed his own goddess. Gods knew he walked a fine line at the moment.

"Lowan will kill you," she shot back.

His lip curled into a snarl. "I'm counting on it."

"Your mate lives."

He pinned her with a stare. "Don't even think to fuck with me right now." He glanced around. "And where is your husband?" Zarek had threatened to destroy them all if his wife wasn't found. It was one of the reasons Caleb had been sent to Hell.

"The second I remove this necklace he will be able to find me. I wanted to talk to you first."

He noticed the glistening emerald around her neck and wondered what it had to do with all of this. "Then speak your mind so I can be on my way."

She looked down the beach at the young girl then brought her attention back to him. "I don't lie, Lileta is alive. Somehow, she has broken the bond. I surmise her bargain with her father is what set us free."

"You're sure?" Dare he hope?

"Of course. The two of you are destined to be together. You both have a very important job." Her gaze moved toward the girl collecting shells. "Her name is Leria. She is to become your ward."

"My ward? Where are her parents?" He'd sensed right away the child was a Draki but had been too distraught to worry about it further.

"Her mother is dead at the hand of Lowan, and her father is Odage."

His jaw dropped open. "What the fuck? I thought his daughter died with her mother."

"No, she has been held in the demon's lair. Now you

understand?"

"Shit." Yes, he understood his leader had been trying to save his daughter. Caleb surmised the girl had been a prisoner for several years. The last time he had seen her she was maybe eight and now looked to be a teen. "How old is she now?"

"Sixteen. Odage's mind is half consumed by Lowan. I'm afraid he is lost to us, but his daughter is very important." She grabbed the gold chain around her neck. "Break it. I cannot be free until this thing is off me."

He reached for it and snapped the soft metal.

She sighed. "Fling it into the air."

He did as commanded, and she raised her palm to the sky, a bright flash of blue light incinerated the gem. Color flushed her cheeks and power enveloped him, her emerald eyes flashed silver, and her hair shone like spun copper as the goddess of fire became engulfed in flames.

"The war has begun. Find your mate, dragon, and bring her home." She began to fade, the sand beneath her smoldered. "Remember the child, Leria. She may one day save humanity."

She was gone.

He stood stunned. In one day, he'd lost a mate and gained a daughter. Qadira said Lileta lived, but their mating bond was broken, and now, it would prove more difficult to find her. She had wanted to be rid of him, knowing his softhearted mate, she thought to save him. He chuckled, imagining the look on her face when he came for her. This time there was no connection, only the raw emotions that set every nerve on fire. If this didn't prove his love then gods help them, nothing would.

SETH HAD BEEN COMBING the city for several hours but had lost the strawberry scent of the redhead long ago. The sun shone high over the Chicago skyline. He needed to check in with Lucan.

Lucan, where the hell are you?

Seth, you need to come to me. Now.

He slipped into an alley, closed his eyes and grabbed the link he held with his brethren. Seconds later, he found himself standing in a dark room, the coppery scent of blood assaulted him. *Shit.*

"Lucan!" The blood was not human, but that of his friend.

"Here," a weak voice called out.

His movements swift and darkness his friend, he maneuvered down the corridor of an abandoned apartment building. Rats scurried across his boots. and he nudged them out of the way. He slipped into a tiny room, and his jaw dropped. Dark shadows danced across the walls and ceiling, creating eerie figures of death. Shadowy fingers reached out and tried to grab him.

Lucan had lost his ability to control the shadows. Soon, they would begin to envelope everything in their path.

Seth scanned the area. There, under a pile of old mattresses, his friend hid. In three steps, he was upon the scene and tossing the old bedding as if they were throw pillows. When his gaze finally landed on Lucan, he moaned.

"What the hell happened?" The warrior had a knife wound at least seven inches long in his abdomen. Blood pooled under him and continued to seep from the gash. He knelt on the floor next to his friend.

Lucan coughed. "I thought it might be fun to spill my guts."

He raised a brow. "I see your sense of humor is still dark as ever."

"Yeah, well, you should be grateful I have one. Had you checked in sooner, I wouldn't have had to hide under that pile of stench." He indicated to the mattresses strewn about the room.

"You never called me."

Blood trickled from Lucan's lips. "You sound like a nagging female. I was unable to call. I can't link to anyone." His gaze moved down to the wound his bloody fingers covered. "I was stabbed four hours ago. I can't fucking heal either."

Urgency flooded Seth. Why had he not noticed how pale the

warrior in front of him was? Four hours of blood loss, it was a miracle Lucan was still conscience. "Shit, I need to summon Marcus."

His lids slid shut. *Marcus.*

Seth, everything all right?

Thank the gods. *No, Lucan is in need of immediate assistance.*

On my way.

"He will be here soon. Who stabbed you?"

"Fucking demon." Lucan's lids closed, and his chest stopped rising.

"Oh no, you don't. Marcus!" Seth pushed Lucan flat on his back.

"What the hell?" Marcus came up beside him. "Christ, we've lost him. Shit!"

"Dear gods!" A female voice cried out.

Seth turned to find Cassie running toward them. He knew immediately Marcus had called for his mate. A side benefit the guardians had gained when the human Cassie had mated with Marcus was not only another guardian but also a healer whose power, combined with her mate's, could pull back the soul. At least, that is what they were told. He hoped like hell they could do it.

"Hurry, love," Marcus urged.

"Don't lose him," Aidyn commanded.

Seth glanced at their king. Aidyn was tied to each of them and would have felt the loss of one of the guardians. It struck him as odd that he didn't know the warrior had laid there for several hours. None of them had known, and it gnawed at his gut.

Both healers placed their palms on Lucan's abdomen, the light emitting from his body so bright Seth had to squint. He said a silent prayer. If anyone of them deserved to live, it was the warrior who lay in front of him. He would gladly switch places with his brethren. Lucan might be the darkness, but of all of them, he seemed least affected by the curse. At least, for the moment.

"Damn it, Lucan, where the hell are you?" Cassie whispered, her body tense.

"What do you see, Cassie?" Aidyn asked, kneeling beside her.

"Darkness. I can't find his light."

"Try looking for the darkest point you can find and grab hold of it." Aidyn touched her arm. "He may not appear like the rest of us."

"I have something." Cassie gave a nervous laugh.

"Pull it back to you," Marcus spoke softly.

"Dear gods." Seth wondered what Cassie would come back with. Would it be their Lucan or some evil that lurked, waiting for an unsuspecting victim? No one here really knew what the between-realm held.

Lucan gasped, his back arched as he tried to bring air into his lungs, the wound now healed by Marcus. Cassie bit her wrist and pressed it against the dark vampire's lips.

"Drink."

Lucan obeyed, a little color returning to his cheeks, but he needed a human donor to bring him back to full strength.

"Can you tell us what happened?" Aidyn asked.

"Fucking demon stabbed me. I found myself unable to heal or connect to any of you." He pushed himself into a sitting position, and his brows slashed downward. "As much as I bitch about you guys, it was most unpleasant being disconnected from everyone."

The guardians glanced at Aidyn. Unease spread through the room, leaving them unsettled. In all the commotion, Seth hadn't noticed the shadows leave the room. Everything had brightened, and sunlight filtered through a boarded-up window.

Aidyn reached out and helped Lucan to his feet. "I never knew anything was wrong until your soul left and I felt it disconnect." He slapped Lucan on the back. "Do that to me again and I will kill you myself."

Cassie cleared her throat. "By the way, Qadira has returned home safely."

"This is good news. Do you know what happened?" Seth asked.

"We need to leave here. We can discuss what happened to Lucan and the goddess's reappearance back at the compound. Everyone move out," Aidyn commanded.

CHAPTER TWENTY

"LERIA." Caleb came up beside the girl who stared out to sea as if she was lost in her own thoughts. She turned her head and almond-shaped blue eyes stared back at him. The girl was the spitting image of her mother, and her beauty would one day break the hearts of many men. "We need to leave. Do you know how to shift?" Dragons were taught to change at a very young age, but if the changing wasn't practiced, it would become difficult for them, as they grew older.

"You are the one my father said would take care of me should something happen to him. Is he dead too?"

Caleb saw the pain her eyes. "I don't really know. I have not seen him in some time, but our people are looking for him."

She looked back to the ocean as if contemplating her next words. "It has been a long time since I shifted, but I'll try."

He nodded. "Take your time." He took a few steps backward to give her room.

She closed her eyes and flexed her fingers. Her chest rose and fell in rapid succession. She was on the verge, almost there, yet stuck on the edge. He smiled, flared out his power and enveloped her, giving her the boost she needed.

A small golden dragon stood before him, stretched its wings and gave them a light flip. She lifted off the ground slightly, testing her new form. She would do well once she became accustomed to her new body. Caleb stretched his neck and transformed, letting his dragon take over. He nuzzled the smaller Draki, giving reassurance, urging her to take flight. Once she was safely off the ground, he lifted his large body into the air then connected to her mentally.

Follow me. I will open a portal.

Where are we going? the female voice asked.

Somewhere where you will be safe.

Caleb landed on a rocky outcrop, the smaller dragon next to him. He shifted, and she followed suit. He looked at her smiling face. "How was your first flight?"

"So much fun. When can we do it again?"

He laughed. The girl could almost make him forget the hole in his heart. "Soon, but first I have a very important task to take care of."

She touched his arm. "You're going after Lileta, aren't you?"

"Yes, how did you know?"

"I met her. She tried to rescue the goddess and me, but Lowan took her." She wrinkled her nose. "He's a very bad man. He kept me away from my father."

Caleb touched the top of her head. "I'm sorry we couldn't help you sooner. We had no idea...did he hurt you?"

Leria met his gaze. "No. He used me to get to my father, but I was well taken care of."

"Come on, let me introduce you to some very nice people." He took her hand and flashed them inside the compound. The guardians had reactivated an old bunker deep under an inactive volcano when Vandeldor had been burned. The accommodations were not as luxurious as their individual homes had been, but it was shelter and they had their communications system running so they could stay in touch with others around the world. He really wasn't sure why, since they had the ability to communicate telepathically, but guessed technology proved more effective when dealing with several temperamental warriors.

They walked along a concrete corridor, heading for Aidyn's personal quarters. He needed to speak with the guardian leader, find a caretaker for Leria so he could be on his way to retrieve his mate. Urgency ran through his blood, making him edgy. Gods knew what Lowan was doing to Lileta right now.

Aidyn greeted him at the door. "Come in. What news do you…" His gaze traveled to the young girl next to him. He looked back up and raised a brow at Caleb.

"This is my ward, Leria. I'll explain later."

Aidyn gave a knowing nod. "Do you like chocolate chip cookies?"

Before she could answer, Gwen swept through the door. "I heard we had company." She held out her hand to the girl. "Hi, my name is Gwen. Would you like to come help Cassie and me bake cookies?"

Leria chewed her bottom lip and looked at Caleb. "Can I?"

Caleb couldn't help but smile. "Only if you promise to save one for me."

"Okay." She grabbed Gwen's hand, and the two exited the room, their laughter resonating down the corridor.

"I hope you don't mind my summoning Gwen to assist," Aidyn said, motioning to a seat in the small living area.

"Not at all, it was a wise move." He folded himself onto the leather chair. "The girl is Odage's daughter, kept prisoner by Lowan."

"What the hell? Something tells me I'd better summon the others for this conversation." In seconds, Marcus, Seth, Garin, and Lucan flashed into the now cramped room followed by Diego.

Caleb went on to share the story Qadira had told him of how Lowan killed Odage's mate then kidnapped his daughter. He then replayed the scene of Lileta being mysteriously pulled away from him and her body vanishing. He left out the details of becoming mated then unmated all in twenty-four hours. It was still too painful to speak of it.

"Damn it, the poor child. Having a daughter of my own, I can understand he would do anything to protect her," Marcus said.

Aidyn's face gave nothing away, no hint of emotion. "Regardless, he is now even more dangerous, being under Lowan's spell. He must be dealt with." His fingers drummed the arm of the leather chair he occupied. "We also have another issue. Somehow, a simple knife wound to Lucan caused him to not only lose his ability to heal, but he lost all connection to us. Seeing as how Lowan is a demigod, who knows what magic he has performed." His gaze pierced Marcus. "You will inform everyone that they are to remain in pairs at all times. I realize this will limit our ability to track the demons, but I will not have another man go down alone."

Marcus nodded. "Yes, of course."

"Also, if anyone does meet with the pointed end of a demon's blade, I want them brought back here immediately for testing. Cassie will stay here with me so she can be ready at a moment's notice. I want to know what we're up against." Aidyn rose from his chair. "I want you all to return back to your posts, and if Odage is found, he is to be brought to me. Alive."

The warriors left except for Marcus and Diego. "Caleb, you go and get your mate back. Leria can stay here with Cassie and myself."

"Thanks, Marcus, I was hoping you'd offer and save me the trouble of begging a favor. I already owe you all so much," Caleb replied.

Aidyn stepped in beside him. "You have always been a good man, Caleb, and despite our past differences, I don't doubt you will be a fine leader to your people. This war with the demons is not your fight. While I welcome your help, I fully understand if you want to take your people out of harm's way. I think this is going to get ugly."

Caleb balled his fists. "That fucking piece of shit Lowan has my mate, and that alone makes it my war. The Draki will stand behind you." His eyes narrowed. "Any who do not, will answer to me." He spun on his heel and strode toward the door. One way or another, he would get Lileta back.

LILETA SPENT the better part of the day suffering through her father's mind torture. He meant to break her, pull the darkness residing inside her to the forefront through sheer pain. While dabbing at the blood running from her nose, she decided there was only one option open to her. There was no question, if she tried to hold out much longer, he would win. The shards of electrical current he sent through her mind only served to feed the darkness. The evil that was her father was embedded in her DNA, and no amount of fighting would change that. Besides, she had nothing left, might as well give her soul to the devil.

The door to her room, now her prison, flew open, and Lowan's shadow towered over her. "What will it be, daughter? You know the evil in you cries out to be freed." He cupped his palm to his ear and cocked his head. "Yes, I hear it now, begging for release." He threw his head back in a fit of laughter.

She wanted to grab any sharp object and shove it in his jugular. It wouldn't kill him but would feel damn good. Instead, she calmed her features. "You win. I'm tired of fighting."

His brows narrowed, and he glared. "You have made a wise choice, but it has come rather quickly. I question your motive."

She jumped from the bed and was in front of him. "You won, and now you question me? I thought this was what your fucked-up mind wanted. Father and daughter bonded by evil. I have nothing left to care about—"

Before she could finish, he slapped his palm against her forehead. Dark shadows filled her vision, and her stomach lurched. Acid burned through her veins, causing her body to convulse. She slipped to the ground, conscious of only the screaming that filled her mind. So loud she was sure her brain would soon ooze from any open orifice.

Lileta had no idea how long she lay on the floor, quivering like a lump of holiday Jell-O. Her head pounded, and her breaths came in short gasps. Every muscle and joint felt like a jackhammer had been taken to it. Even her eyes hurt, and all she wanted to do was lie there and whimper like a baby. It was not to be. Father dearest beckoned, calling the evil inside her, and it wanted to get up and party.

Slowly, she maneuvered to her hands and knees and crawled like a toddler to the open doorway. Once there, she managed to wrap her fingers around the jamb and pull herself to her feet. She stood, holding on while the room swayed to some unknown beat and talked herself out of vomiting. After several minutes, she was finally able to open her eyes and actually focus without the room spinning. With one foot in front of the other, and her palms flat against the wall, she made her way down a dimly lit corridor. The evil beat on her chest like a drum, urging her to hurry.

"What's your damn rush anyway?" She spoke to the darkness inside her. "I'm going to have to nickname you nuisance because that's what you are. A fucking nuisance." She wanted to reach inside herself and yank the screaming evil from her soul. It would never happen, though. It was a part of her now, awakened by her father. As much as she missed Caleb, she was glad their bond was broken. She didn't think she could stand the disappointment in his expression.

When she finally reached the end of the corridor, the darkness made her take a hard right and head toward the training area. A large room with concrete floors and walls lined with weapons of torture. Lowan stood on the far side, talking to another demon. When she approached, he turned from his companion.

"Well, you took long enough." He waved his hand in the air. "No matter, soon your dark side will have complete control." He bent closer until his gaze was level with hers. The corners of his mouth turned up. "Let's see how much control you still have left, little girl." He scanned the room until his gaze fell on a blade sitting on a table near the wall. "Go fetch that blade and bring it here."

Her feet carried her against her will until her fingers wrapped around the cold steel of the handle. She lifted it, noting how well balanced the weapon was, and took it back to where her father stood. She held it out to him.

"Oh no, I don't want it. I want you to kill this demon here." He pointed at the man next to him whose eyes were now wide.

"My lord, I beg of you. I've been an obedient servant." The demon's red gaze skimmed from Lowan to Lileta and begged for mercy.

Her mouth went dry, and she tried to fight the urges inside her, but the darkness had other plans. Her arms lifted. "I'm sorry," tumbled from her lips right before she swung, sending his head sailing across the room. She stared at the limp body now sprawled out on the floor, blood pooling around it. Lileta willed her arms to raise again and strike her father; instead, she dropped the blade to the floor with a clatter.

Clapping came from behind her. "Bravo, dear daughter, your will has been broken. I now control you, and you will be an evil to be reckoned with in the human world." He stepped beside her. "I rename you Furia. It means Hell-bound."

Her lip quivered. How had she gone from one hell to another, still a slave to another's whim?

"I have the perfect job for you. Turn and look at me," he commanded.

Her feet shuffled until she was facing him. "You disgust me," she spat.

He gave a mocking laugh. "It was never my aim to win your love. No, hate breeds evil. You think you hate me now? I guarantee when you kidnap your first human female and deliver her to me, you will detest me. And when you help me train her in the ways of sexual pleasure, why then, dear daughter, you will loathe me."

Her lungs burned from the rage that boiled in the pit of her stomach and crept up her chest. Her father needed to die.

CHAPTER TWENTY-ONE

ODAGE WASN'T TAKING any chances with the Wendigo. He shifted into his dragon since the beast had superior senses as well as the ability to fry the demon he followed if it became necessary. Once the shift was complete, he was slammed with emotions, causing him to stumble.

"You ill, dragon?" the Wendigo inquired.

Father?

Leria? Where are you? Are you safe?

Yes, father. Caleb brought me to the guardians.

He pierced the demon with a glare. *What trickery do you play, demon?*

"I told you. We want Lowan dead."

I meant my daughter. She is no longer with the Dark Lord. The fact he was able to communicate with her had him overjoyed and weary. Odage was going to fry the demon and relish watching him turn to ash.

A sharp pain stabbed his rib and then a second, and his dragon let out a screech. He began to shimmer into his human form against his will. A burning started in his gut and moved out to his limbs. He looked down and found two darts sticking out from his chest, then fell to the ground, his legs numb.

"What the fuck?" he snarled.

Four Wendigos surrounded him. The one he'd been following stepped forward. "Lowan wants you back at his domicile."

He'd walked right into their trap, but it didn't matter now. His daughter was safe so they could kill him for all he cared. Caleb would make sure she was taken care of.

Two of the demons approached him, one on either side, and grabbed an arm. They began to drag him across hardened lava, his chest ripped open by the jagged stones. After several minutes, he was pulled through a door and dumped onto a cold, hard surface.

"Well, look what the demons have dragged in." He recognized the sinister voice to be that of Lowan. The Dark Lord gave him a kick in the ribs with a booted foot. "You should know better than to fuck with me." He grabbed Odage by the hair and pulled his head off the floor. "Did you really think you could kill me?"

"To save my daughter, I would have died trying."

Lowan released him and laughed. "You might yet. However, I still have use of you."

"Fuck you. My daughter is safe now so you have no bargaining chip left."

Shards of pain ripped through his skull and blood trickled from his eyes before the sweet comfort of darkness overtook him.

CALEB MARCHED down the corridor of the compound with determined strides.

"Wait the hell up," Diego yelled out behind him.

"You want to talk to me then you'd best run. I wait for no one." He flexed his hands. He was on a mission, and when he got his mate back, he was going to put her over his knee and give her the spanking she deserved. Then he was going to fuck the hell out of her.

His brother moved alongside of him. "I'm going with you, and I'm not taking no for an answer." His hazel eyes flashed green.

"Fine. Just stay out of my way and know that if you get into trouble..." He stopped mid-stride and eyed his little brother. "Know that I cannot choose you. My mate comes first."

Diego's brows dipped. "Don't be a dumb-ass, of course she comes first. So, what's your plan?"

Caleb scrubbed his face. "I wish I had one." He continued down the hall.

"We need to get back into Hell. I assume that's where she still is."

He sighed. "I assume."

"Wait...what? Are you short-circuiting? Your bond should tell you where she is," Diego stated.

His jaw tightened. He wanted to strangle anyone in his sight but managed to restrain himself, remembering that Diego would have assumed Caleb finally mated Lileta on their journey.

"Our bond was broken."

"How the—"

Caleb cut him off. "I don't know for sure, but Qadira thought Lowan had somehow pulled us apart."

Diego pinned him. "Yet you go after her, without a bond? Fuck, you have it worse than I thought."

His brother wasn't kidding. Without the mating bond to attract them to each other, he could easily walk away. There was one problem, his body still craved her touch and his heart craved her love. His chest caught. It never occurred to him she might not want him now. Could she love him back? She never spoke the words, but he thought he'd felt her emotions. Panic started to set in. Those emotions might have been only because of the bond. He replaced the panic with determination. He would win her love if that's what it took. There was no way in hell he was giving up. Not now. Not ever.

They'd reached the end of the long corridor and flashed to the outside. "You say that as if I shouldn't bring her back," Caleb bit out.

"You're dead wrong, big brother. She's the only woman who

could put up with your ass, which is why I'm here to help." He lifted his shoulders. "Besides, I really like her, and gods know you deserve to be happy."

He studied Diego for several minutes. "Seriously, keep your ass out of harm's way. If I have to save you, I'll kill you myself." He shimmered, bringing his dragon forward and shifted. Diego did the same.

Aww, you do care for me. The younger Draki tossed his head back and snorted.

Damn punk. Let's go. Caleb curled his lip to expose his incisors, a warning to the younger dragon to behave before he ripped Diego's flesh open.

Where to bro?

Back to New Orleans. We are in need of a voodoo priestess to find my mate.

FURIA WAS DECKED out in leather pants and a tank top. Several daggers strapped to her thighs and waist, but there was one special blade her father had given her, it was clutched in her right hand. She looked at the dragon to her left out of the corner of her eye. "Defy me, and I will kill you myself."

The man tied back his raven hair with a piece of leather. "I am your servant, my lady."

She turned her head to take in the full view of Odage and pinned him with a glare. "You understand our orders?"

"Perfectly."

"Good." She moved her attention to the ten demons behind her. "Let's go. It's time to raise some hell." The corners of her lips turned up when the troops hooted and hollered. She strode with purpose toward the fissure, placed her palms on the either side of the crack, and forced her power into the rock. The crack widened until it split enough to allow them to pass.

She entered first. Enveloped herself in power, thinking of the place she needed to go and flashed to the surface. Odage and the others followed close behind. Furia sucked in a breath of crisp night air. It felt good to be back on top again. "Everyone move into position and keep yourself cloaked. We may have the element of surprise and numbers, but don't let them fool you. The guardians are very powerful," she whispered.

"Won't all the blades strapped to your body make them suspicious?" Odage asked.

"No. Remember, I helped protect them while the child was born." She sheathed the blade she'd been carrying in her palm. "I'll distract them, and you grab the baby. Lowan says her blood is pure." Her gaze focused with intent on the hidden compound. "That child will free my father from his eternal prison." She watched while Odage led the others away. Once they disappeared, she looked down at her trembling hands and flexed her fingers, taking in a deep breath.

"Stop fighting me, you can't win. I am stronger than you will ever be."

Furia, I beg you to stop. Anything but this. Lileta fought to regain control but was shoved back. Her darker side now dominated. She could only watch as events unfolded in front of her like some horror flick. It was like having two personalities. Her evil twin had surfaced and now refused to play nice.

Furia flashed to the hidden entrance and waited. The sensors would tell the guardians of her presence, which they would verify via the video feed. Within seconds, the stone dematerialized and left a black hole for her to walk through. She moved with the grace of a cat down the steel stairs, her boots echoed on the grating. When she took the last step, she was greeted by the king himself.

"Lileta, you just missed Caleb. He left a few hours ago to search for you. Are you all right?" Aidyn asked.

She stepped into his open embrace and hugged him. "I'm okay, shaken to say the least. What about Caleb? Is he all right?" Aidyn led her down the long corridor and into a spacious library where he indicated for her to take a seat in front of the stone fireplace.

"He was fine, except for his concern for you, obviously. Can I get you something to drink?"

"No, thank you." She watched him grab a bottle of water from a small refrigerator then place it on the table in front of her.

"In case you change your mind." He smiled and sat across from her.

"Thanks. So where is everyone?"

Furia, you fucking bitch, let me out! Lileta had never felt more helpless in her life. She was aware of the plan but unable to stop it. It was like being stuck inside a glass bottle. She could look out, but no one heard her screams. Everything was about to come tumbling down.

"Cassie and the baby are in their room, and the others are busy fighting demons," Aidyn replied.

Furia inwardly smiled, this was going to be easier than she thought. "It's just you and Cassie? Are you sure that's wise?"

He tipped his head to the side and gave her a leveled look. "No one knows where we are." His eyes narrowed. "Is there a reason I should be concerned, *Lileta?*"

Yes! Why can't you sense the darkness? Lileta didn't understand. It had been the hope she'd held out for. Aidyn was a powerful guardian, why didn't he catch on?

"No, I just worry that's all. Lowan is more powerful than we expected." She feigned a yawn and relayed the information telepathically back to the demons.

"You're tired. You are welcome to use your old room and get some rest. I'll send someone to locate Caleb and your brother." He rose. "Tomorrow, you can brief me on your father."

"That sounds good. I guess I hadn't realized how worn out I was." She stood and approached him, holding open her arms to hug the king. When he accepted the offer, she pulled the dagger from her thigh and shoved it deep into his heart.

He gasped, his eyes swirled with anger, but there was nothing he could do except drop to the floor. The poison Lowan had developed worked to not only cut off his communication with his brethren and the ability to heal, but rendered his powers useless. Furia was thankful for that because otherwise Aidyn was capable of bringing the heavens down upon them.

You fucking bitch! Help him. You can't leave him to die!

Furia rolled her eyes and pulled the blade from his chest. "I'm getting really tired of you trying to spoil my fun, Lileta." She wiped the bloody blade across her thigh and spun on her heel, heading for the door. When she entered the corridor, she quickly scanned the area then ran back the same way she'd come in. Opening the entry for the rest of her team, she stopped Odage.

"You will kill Cassie and take the child," she commanded.

Odage tipped his head. His gaze met hers and showed no mercy. "As you wish, Furia." He made a quick exit down the hall, the other demons followed. Commotion and blood curdling screams filled the compound quickly followed by silence. Odage exited the room with a crying baby in his arms. He strode toward her.

"It is done. The female is down."

She smiled. "Good. Hopefully, they will both be dead when the others return and there will be two less guardians to contend with later." She reached for the child and pulled the babe into her arms. "Let's go, Lowan awaits his prize."

The good Lileta screeched and clawed, trying to fight her way back into control. She couldn't believe what was happening, but one thing was certain: she could not allow her father to get his claws into Ariana. Right then, she kicked herself for breaking the bond with Caleb. He would have known what was happening through their connection. *I am such an idiot!* She took a deep breath and blocked her thoughts from Furia. At least, that she could still accomplish. Some way, she had to stop this madness.

She concentrated. *Caleb, can you hear me? Please, if you can hear me at all, know that baby Ariana is in trouble. The guardians need you, Caleb. I have done a terrible thing.* She prayed somehow he could sense her distress and come to their aid.

CHAPTER TWENTY-TWO

CALEB AND DIEGO landed in a remote Bayou of New Orleans and shifted back to their human form. "From here, we'll flash to Sidara's door front and ask for her help."

Diego snorted. "You mean pay her?" He eyed the large ruby Caleb carried. "That should keep her in comfort for several lifetimes. Where the hell did you find that anyway?"

"Never mind. I'll see you there." He flashed and, seconds later, found himself standing on the walkway leading to the old, wooden structure. Diego came in beside him, and together, they strode toward the front porch, crossing over creaking boards. They stopped at the front door. Caleb raised his fist to knock, but the door opened. He looked at his brother and gave a shrug.

"Fuck it, let's go." He crossed the threshold.

"Caleb, how nice to see you again, and do my eyes deceive me? Is this your baby brother Diego?" Sidara sashayed closer until she stood in front of the younger Draki. Her gaze traveled from his eyes, down his chest then came to rest on his crotch. She ran her tongue across her bottom lip. "Do tell me what I can do for you, young dragon."

Diego looked at Caleb, panic written on his face. "Uh, I'm just tagging along. Caleb is the one who needs help."

"Hmm, pity. I would have enjoyed you very much." She arched a dark brow, her azure eyes sparkled with mischief. "Should you reconsider, I do love a good fuck."

Caleb rubbed his brow. His head throbbed, and his entire body felt like a compressed spring ready to uncoil.

"Caleb, you okay?" Diego was at his side. "You look kinda pale."

"Yes, the young dragon is right, you look ill. Come sit." Sidara led them to the kitchen and directed him to sit at the table.

"I don't know what's wrong with me. I feel a sudden sense of doom." He jumped from the chair, flipping it backward and began to pace the wooden floor.

Sidara leaned closer to Diego. "Where is his mate?" she whispered.

Caleb barely heard his brother retell the story of what happened and why they were here. He looked down and found his T-shirt was soaking wet, drenched with sweat. His entire body itched, but not the kind you want to scratch. No, it was more of a crawl-out-of-your-skin kind of itch.

"I need to do something," he shouted, but he didn't know what.

Sidara rose from her seat, went to the cupboard, and began pulling plastic bins out, placing them on the counter. She opened one and tossed it aside. Opened the second and threw it next to the first one. She opened the third box.

"Ah, here it is." She pulled out a dried-up eye and headed back to the table.

Diego cringed. "What the hell is that?"

"This belonged to my great-grandmother." She patted the chair next to her. "Caleb, come sit. I think I can help you."

"Well, that's nice, but *what* is it?" Diego asked again.

She flashed him a smile. "No, it really belonged to my great-grandmother. It's her seeing eye. She was a most powerful sorceress and capable of seeing beyond this plane." She shrugged. "Some use crystal balls, I have an eye."

Caleb grabbed the chair and sat as instructed. "How is this going to help me? Can it show me where Lileta is?"

"That is my hope. Hold the eye in your left hand."

He held his palm open, and she placed the eye looking straight up at him. He tried not to flinch. *This is just fucking creepy.* "Now what?"

"Close your palm...gently."

He carefully wrapped his fingers around the object, noting it was as light as a feather. For some reason, he expected it to weigh more. She covered both hands around his, closed her eyes, and started an easy sway back and forth. She chanted something under her breath, but he couldn't make it out. Suddenly, the room began to spin. He closed his eyes to keep from retching.

"Caleb."

"Lileta?" His eyes snapped opened, and he expected to see his mate, but instead, darkness surrounded him. Faint voices carried in the distance, he struggled to hear what they said. "Lileta!"

"Caleb help them."

"Who?" He was so confused. "Where are you?"

"Save Ariana."

"What?" Marcus's daughter, what did she have to do with this nightmare?

Things shifted, and he realized there was light coming from in front of him. He blinked until he became accustomed then looked closer. "Ariana." He saw the baby as if he were holding her himself. Someone else came into view.

Odage.

"My lady, why do we not flash back to the portal? It would prove much faster," Odage said.

"Because my father is unsure of what will happen to the baby. As you know, the way we transport is different than the guardians, and he needs her alive...for now."

That voice, he recognized it to be Lileta's, but what did she mean? He scratched his head. This was so confusing. He could sense his mate's essence, it blanketed him, but something was different. It was darker and surrounded by sulfur.

"As you wish, my lady." Odage motioned, and several demons surrounded him and Ariana. It was then Caleb realized he was looking through someone else's eyes, but whose?

"Lileta?" He waited, only to be greeted with silence. He looked through the eyes again, the terrain familiar to him. Where the hell were they, and who had the baby? A demon stepped into view.

"My lady, we have communication with your father. Seems all the other guardians are being kept busy with fighting the demons. I think there will be a very good chance that by the time they return home, both the king and the healer's mate will be dead," the demon said.

Caleb's blood ran cold. *Oh Christ...Sidara! How the fuck do I get back?*

Close your eyes, dragon. The priestess's voice echoed in his mind. He did as commanded.

"Open your eyes, Caleb, you're back."

He forced his lids to open. The room where he had started his journey came into view. Both Diego and Sidara gazed at him. "Shit, who the fuck's eyes were I looking through?"

Sidara gave him a sympathetic look. "That was your mate, I'm afraid."

"No." His shoulders slumped.

Diego looked between the two. "What the hell happened?"

The priestess turned away and stood up from her chair. "I'm afraid your brother has a hard choice to make." She removed the eye from Caleb's grasp and placed it back in a velvet bag. "He can either save his mate and let humanity slip into the darkness, or he can let her go." She pierced Caleb with intense blue eyes. "What do you think the healer will do when he finds his mate dead and his daughter gone? What about the others when they discover their king has perished?"

Caleb blinked, and his eyes widened. "Leria is with them." He stood. "Son of a bitch!" He knew exactly what would happen. The curse would take hold on the guardians, and Lowan would win. Between the High Lord's disregard of human life and the vampire's bloodlust, the humans wouldn't stand a chance. He curled his fingers into his palm. *Do I care what happens to any of them? My people will still survive.* When he dug deep, he knew Lileta would care, and if he saved her, she would never forgive him. There was also the part of him that would no way in hell let Lowan have that child.

"Caleb?"

He turned to his brother. "Call in any we can trust. Our first priority is saving Ariana. I'll fill you in on the way." He reached into his pocket, pulled out the ruby, and tossed it on the table. "Thank you." He spun and headed for the door, his heart shattering for the second time. Not only was he choosing to walk away from the woman he loved, he was leaving her trapped. It had finally dawned on him what happened. Lowan had forced her dark side out of its slumber.

LILETA HAD FELT Caleb's essence and hoped he'd understood what was happening. She worried briefly he might try to save her but remembered they no longer had any bond. She wasn't even sure how she'd managed to make a connection with him and, frankly, didn't care. The only thing she could think about was Ariana and, of course, Cassie and Aidyn. She'd tried so hard to regain control of her body and shove the darkness back into submission but grew weaker the longer Furia remained in control. Watching her own hand shove the poisoned blade into the guardian had been like watching a movie in slow motion. She prayed he and Cassie held on until help arrived. Right then, she threw all her concentration into the baby. One way or another, she had to slow down the groups escape and give help time to arrive.

Time for a different tactic.

"Lileta, you are quiet. Have you finally given up?"

Yes, I'm tired of fighting you.

"That is a very wise decision. I really didn't want to destroy you completely."

Really? I would think you'd be happy to be rid of me.

"Not really, you are part of my essence, and destroying you would be like killing a part of myself."

Interesting, maybe she could use this to her advantage. *I'm not feeling well, Furia.*

"What do you mean? What's wrong?"

Lileta sensed a shift in the darkness. Was it concern for her welfare? She wondered if the real reason Furia hadn't destroyed her completely was because if she did then she destroyed herself. It made perfect sense. After all, they were connected. She needed to put her theory to the test. *I don't know. I'm tired and cold.* She envisioned herself submersed in ice water. Being an immortal, she wouldn't die like a human, but her body would react in the same manner. It would slow to accommodate for the cold. Not to mention the fact demons hated being cold. They much preferred it hot.

"What are you doing?" Furia asked.

She still found it odd hearing her own voice talk to her as if she were another person. Her mind functioned the same, but she had no control over her body or her will. Furia had taken over. Lileta held a new understanding and respect for those who suffered with duel personalities. Somehow, like them, she had to fight her way back. *I'm not doing anything.*

"My lady, are you all right?" Odage asked.

"I'm feeling the need to rest. Perhaps we can take a break for a few minutes."

"As you wish, but might I recommend we don't dally too long?"

"No, only a few minutes."

If Lileta could have jumped for joy, she would have. Now she only needed to hang on until help arrived. She hoped it would be soon, already Furia began to fight back.

CALEB WAS the first to spot them. He, Diego, and two others flew high above the deserted beach using their power to remain undetected. He motioned for them to follow his lead. Landing close to the camp where he could see what they were up against. They had to work fast. It wouldn't take long for Odage to sense they were there, and it looked like they were outnumbered. This mission would require pinpoint accuracy.

Diego, are you sure about this?

Yes. I will not fail you.

When Caleb had filled his brother in on what had happened to his mate, Diego insisted he could rescue her. *If you pull this off, I will be forever in your debt. I will go after Odage while Darius grabs Ariana. You know we are going to have to hit fast and hard.* While they had firepower, Wendigos couldn't die from being burned. It would only serve to distract them for a brief period. Their heads had to be removed, which required Caleb's men to shift and fight hand-to-hand. He glanced around. There might only be four of them, but he had the best. Diego, a black dragon, was first rate at cloaking, Darius, a sleek green dragon, was built for speed and Jax, a bronze warrior, was one of the best.

I am well aware. Diego raised his massive black wings in preparation for liftoff.

Good, let's go.

The four took to the sky, ready for battle. Caleb was thankful he'd had the foresight to pop back home and grab Lileta's silver bands, handing them off to Diego. He trusted his brother to capture her, he only hoped he could bring her back from the darkness.

Caleb circled, picking Odage out of the crowd. He landed in

front of him and shimmered into human form. He would be the distraction. "My liege." He gave a half bow. The demons surrounded him, and Lileta jumped to her feet. Before Lileta could reach down and grab Ariana from her resting place in the sand, Darius swooped in like a rocket, talons reached out and gently grabbed the baby, taking her into the night's sky.

Caleb gave a sigh of relief and reminded himself the most important part of the mission had been completed. He tried not to look at his mate for he needed to focus on the task at hand. Diego would not fail him.

"Stop them!" Lileta screeched, running forward with her blade drawn.

Diego flashed behind Lileta and body-slammed her to the ground, slapping the silver cuffs on her wrists. Caleb gritted his teeth at his mate being manhandled, but there was no other way. Seconds later, Diego and Lileta disappeared. There was only himself and Jax left to fight Odage and the demons. Not an evenly matched fight. However, Caleb was about to pull his spade.

"Looks like you have betrayed me, Caleb," Odage snarled.

"I think you have that backward. You betrayed your people. I challenge you to Reelojarit." He had hoped Odage would come peacefully, but dragons had a keen eye for evil and Caleb could see the dark, oily stain now occupying his leader's soul. He had no choice but to fight for Odage's position as overlord. The strongest would lead their people.

Odage laughed. "Do you really think to challenge me for dominance, Caleb? I accept, with pleasure." He looked to the Wendigos. "Do not interfere, this is between the two of us."

The demons withdrew, yet stayed close enough they could jump into the fray if needed. Both shifters produced a dagger. Odage's silver blade glistened in the moonlight, and Caleb tightened his grip on the ancient, gold handle of his own. From the corner of his eye, he saw a flash of fire, it appeared Jax was busy dropping fire balls among the demons, causing the Wendigos to scatter in several directions. Caleb hid a smile.

Odage lunged, and Caleb spun, avoiding a slash to the chest. His dragon was on edge, ready to surface at a moment's notice, but waited for Odage to decide to shift and take the battle to the sky. He need not wait any longer.

"Fuck this." Odage shimmered, red scales danced across his skin before he completed the transformation. Caleb's dragon followed suit and they both leapt into the air. Dragons rarely battled on the ground, preferring the maneuverability flight gave them.

Caleb circled, climbed above Odage then cloaked himself. It would take the other dragon a second before Odage could pinpoint Caleb, and he hoped it bought him enough time. Caleb dove, talons outstretched, and before Odage could react, Caleb hit him square in the back, tearing a gash into the webbing of his left wing. Odage faltered then righted himself, banking a hard right. Caleb knew it was going to take much more than one small hit to gain victory. In a battle for dominance, one of them would have to be knocked from the sky and pinned to the ground. It was then up to the winner if he let the loser survive.

Odage vanished, and Caleb flared out his senses in search of the beast. A dark shadow knocked into him and left a deep gash along his backbone. Blood ran down his side and dripped from the tip of his wing. Lightning arched in the night sky, and thunder shook the ground. Already, the fighting beasts stirred the atmosphere, and soon, the torrential rains would start. If the battle continued too long, it would create tidal waves of biblical proportions below. Caleb had to end this quickly before people got hurt.

He sent healing thoughts to his wound and prepared for his surprise maneuver, one Jax had taught him decades ago. He cloaked, came in directly behind Odage, and then maneuvered slightly above him. His claws sank and shredded the fine membrane of each wing wrapping around thin bones. His jaw flexed, and sharp fangs pierced into the dragon's neck. Odage twisted and tried to throw him like a bucking bronco.

Caleb held firm.

He only needed to hold on for another minute, and his poison would begin to pump through the beast's system, slowing him. Odage started a nosedive for the turbulent ocean below, intending to take them both into the water. *Son of a bitch, relent already!* His leader was stronger than he'd anticipated.

Cold, salty water splashed over them as Odage dove deep. Caleb clung tighter. It was a contest of will and strength, but under several feet of water was not where he wanted to take this fight.

Odage twisted, his body spinning like a porpoise. He flipped upside down and swam over jagged coral, ripping open Caleb's back, turning the water red. Soon, the other predators would come and pick at his flesh. Still, he refused to let go.

His lungs burned. Dragons were capable of many things, but holding their breath for extended periods wasn't one of them. Stars danced through his vision, he shook them free. His muscles rebelled, and his heart slowed. He would not be able to hold on much longer. Odage still fought, but Caleb was determined he would end his own life in a watery grave before he would let go. Something flashed beside him, a dark shadow. Had the sharks already come to get a free meal? His eyes rolled shut, and darkness wrapped a cocoon around him, pulling him into its cold embrace.

CHAPTER TWENTY-THREE

CALEB GASPED. Precious air filled his lungs, and his eyes flew open.

"You try and die on me again, and next time, I will kill you myself." Diego held him from behind in an embrace while they bobbed in the waves. They were both in human form.

"Next time, I promise I'll let you." He broke free and treaded water, facing his brother. "The guardians?"

"Both Aidyn and Cassie are well. Your new charge saved the day. And before you ask, Lileta has been secured and Ariana is back with her parents without a scratch," Diego responded.

Caleb relaxed. They were all safe. "Where is Odage?" He twisted and turned in the churning ocean but couldn't see the other dragon.

"Jax has dragged him ashore and is standing guard over him. Last I saw, he was unconscious. Looks like you were the victor."

"I'm not finished with him yet." Caleb gave a kick and began to swim toward shore. Once he reached the beach, he charged up the sandy terrain to where Odage lay. Caleb stood over him and looked at his lifeless form. How had it come to this? Caleb dug into his jeans pocket, relieved the stone was still there. He pulled out the black crystal the size of a large marble. Diego came up beside him.

"Raelgil?"

"Yes," Caleb replied. The only crystal that could drain a dragon of his powers. He would no longer be able to shift or perform magic. The Draki would be left with immortality and the ability to heal, nothing more. He pressed it to Odage's chest and began the ancient chant that would pull the power into the smooth, black orb. "I summon the magic of Darazor, our ancestral dragon. Our people denounce you as their leader and as a Draki. We proclaim you a simple immortal."

The orb glowed a brilliant white. Odage's back arched, and his eyes flew open.

"No!" Odage screamed.

The stone grew dark except for the pinpoint of amber light that pulsated in its center. The transformation was a success. Grains of sand swirled and danced with a fiery light until they revealed Qadira.

"Congratulations, Caleb. You have completed Reelojarit and won." She stepped forward, her crimson gown dragging across the sand. Placing a palm on either shoulder, she leaned in and kissed his cheek. Her warmth radiated through to his very marrow. "You know what must be done next, my dragon. Love can work miracles." She stepped back. "I command you to kneel before me."

The three Draki bent to one knee.

"I, Qadira, the goddess of fire, declare Caleb, son of Andreas and Jonet, the ruling Draki Overlord. May he lead his people with strength and courage." She looked at the other two men kneeling before her. "Jax and Diego will bear witness to this night's event." Her form began to shimmer. *Remember, Caleb, love conquers all.*

She was gone.

Caleb rose, his mind spinning from the riddles she spewed. "Why the fuck can't the gods speak in plain tongue?"

"What are you referring to?" Diego asked, slapping his brother on the back.

Caleb shook his head. "Never mind. Grab that piece of shit and let's go."

Jax and Diego hauled Odage to his feet, and Caleb moved to stand in front of him. "As much as I would love to kill you myself, I am turning you over to the guardian king. Your destiny resides with him."

They flashed from the beach, heading to the vampires' compound. Caleb's heart clenched at the thought of seeing his mate.

FURIA PACED HER CELL. That damn meddling dragon, Diego, had snatched her then hauled her back to the guardian compound where she soon learned both Cassie and Aidyn were recovering. It seemed Caleb's ward, Leria, had been on site where she remained undetected and had called Marcus for help. He had arrived in time to save both his mate and king and then locked her in this cell upon her arrival.

She grasped the cold steel and tried to pry the bars apart. They refused to even groan under the pressure. "Fucking mystical jail cell." She spat on the floor.

I'm very happy to be here, Furia.

"Of course, you would be. I still can't believe you were able to overcome me. I must admit I am impressed. Pissed, but impressed." She turned back and sat on the bed provided for her. "Don't think this is done. This war is far from over. Father will find a way to free us."

"I can help you."

She spun to see where the voice came from. Her brow arched when she spotted the dark vampire, Lucan. "Well, well." She moved closer to where he stood on the other side of the room then gasped. "You are a master of the darkness. Free me, and you can join our cause." She flicked her tongue out to wet her bottom lip. "Imagine how it would feel to be free of all your restraints. You could finally be your true self."

Furia, you are such a bitch! Lileta knew Lucan was gifted with the ability to control the shadows and call the darkness to do his bidding. With the curse in place, she had no idea how it affected him. Did he plan to set Furia her free? She held her breath.

Lucan tossed back his head and laughed then pinned her with his dark gaze. He smiled, allowing his fangs to show. "I'm sorry to disappoint, but the curse has not taken its hold on me. Yet."

"But it will, and when it does, they will kill you. Come join us," she hissed.

His black hair fell over his face when he leaned forward and touched his forehead to the bars. His lip curled into a snarl. "I will not forget who I am and what my duty is." He leaned back. "Besides, she will save me."

It was Furia's turn to laugh. "Who do you think is going to save you, warrior?"

"My mate." His statement was matter-of-fact.

"Well then, I hope she is close by." Furia crossed her arms over her chest. "You have died once. I know the shadows call your name. How long do you think you can wait?"

"As long as it takes." He turned to leave the room then stopped and looked back. "When you're ready, Lileta, I will be here to help you take back control." He left the room.

Furia snorted, but deep down, Lileta hoped and prayed the king would command her death for the attempt on his life, and then it would finally be over. Her dark side could no longer hurt anyone. She was thankful for the short time she had spent with Caleb and would treasure it always. Her only regret was she had never told him how she really felt. Probably for the best anyway.

"You are so foolish, Lileta. That dragon never loved you, he only used you just like all the other men in your life," Furia commented out loud.

"Do you really believe that?"

Lileta recognized the voice. *Let me see him.*

Furia looked up, and Lileta gasped. Caleb stepped from the shadows. His blond hair tousled and his eyes green, the dragon was close to the surface. Dark jeans sat low on his slim hips, and he wore no shirt, causing even her dark demon to lick her lips. Every step he took closer to the cell caused his chest to ripple. She sucked in a breath.

Furia sat on the bed, legs crossed and examined her fingernails as if she were bored. "What brings you here, dragon? You must realize your mate is lost to you."

His fingers wrapped around the bars, causing his biceps to flex. "I know no such thing." He inserted a key into the lock and turned. He opened the door, tossed the keys to the floor and gave them a kick into the shadows.

Furia rose, ready to be freed. Instead, Caleb stepped in and slammed the door behind him. They were locked in. Together.

Caleb. The real Lileta, buried deep in the darkness, wanted to touch him. She also wanted him to run far away. He didn't belong here. The dark demon chuckled. "Seems your mate wants you to leave."

"Not happening." He stalked closer until he towered over her.

"Tell me, dragon. Why are you really here?" She stepped closer. "You can't have her back. You can only have me now." Furia ran a finger down his chest.

He grabbed her arms and walked forward until his body pinned her against the cold, concrete wall. "You broke our bond, Lileta. That does not please me."

She smiled. "I told you, Lileta is no more. You may call me Furia."

His nose ran along her neck, causing her to gasp. "I do not acknowledge that name, only Lileta." His teeth scraped her earlobe.

"Fine, use whatever name you wish, but it won't bring her back."

CALEB HAD her back in his arms and worried if his plan would work. It had to. He would do anything to bring her back to him. He went back to the words Qadira had whispered. *Love conquers all.*

He pressed his erection against her. His raging hard-on urged him to rip her jeans off, but he showed restraint. Barely. Instead, he claimed her lips, forced his tongue past hers and tasted her essence. Spiced lemon, just as he remembered. She moaned beneath him and ground into his erection. He swore his cock could bore a hole through the concrete wall it was so hard.

He broke the kiss and ran his tongue up her neck until he reached her ear. "Lileta, come back to me. I need you," he whispered. His right hand released its grip and slid along her ribs, following the contour of her waist until he found the hem of her shirt. His fingers slipped underneath and touched her warm flesh.

She shuddered.

He gazed into her golden eyes, knowing his mate was buried in there somewhere. "Lileta, I know you can hear me. I love you. I wanted to die when our bond was broken. I thought you were dead." He cupped her chin, his body kept her in place. "It wasn't until Qadira told me you lived that I saw a glimmer of hope." His forehead touched hers. "I don't care about the past. Our future starts here. Right now. This second."

He palmed the soft mound of her breast.

"You should care about the past, dragon. Your mate stabbed the guardian king and ran off with a warrior's child. He will condemn her to death," Lileta whispered, but he knew it was the other who spoke.

"I know my mate. She will come back and face whatever awaits her." Cassie and Aidyn had forgiven her, but he'd keep that close to his chest for now.

Cassie had also encouraged him into coming to see Lileta. "I saw her light, Caleb. Grab onto it," she had told him. That was precisely what he was here to do. Lucan had also reported that he could help Lileta control the darkness. Caleb only need to push back her dark side.

He needed no more encouragement.

Caleb grabbed the collar of her T-shirt and pulled, the fabric giving way easily under his touch. Next, he sliced through the front of her bra with a claw, exposing firm, round breasts. His mouth fastened around a nipple and sucked, pulling the protrusion farther into his mouth and caused her to arch her back. Her nails scraped his scalp when she ran her fingers through his hair.

"More, dragon," she moaned.

He reached for the waistband of her jeans, shredding them to tatters. All that was left was a black thong. He unbuttoned his own pants and pushed them down his legs until they rested at his ankles. No time to kick off his boots, he needed her. Now.

He broke free of her breast, and grabbed her thighs, wrapping her legs around his waist. The only thing between them was the black, silky fabric. He pushed aside her thong then slid through her hot, moist folds. She was ready for him. He poised the head of his cock at her entrance, hesitating.

"Do it," she hissed.

He thrust. Burying himself deep.

Her walls clenched.

He shuddered.

Time stood still. Her golden eyes filled with desire. His lips pressed hers. "I love you. Please come back to me," he spoke against the soft flesh before pushing his tongue past them. He crushed her, swearing one day he would give her gentle. Today, he would dominate and make every inch of her body his.

Their tongues dueled, and his cock slid out of her until only the tip remained wrapped in the warmth of her cocoon. She pulled his hair, nipped his lip, and pressed her heels into his back. He feared shredding her skin on the concrete wall so he wrapped his arms around her, kicked off his boots and jeans then carried her to the bed. He pulled free long enough to push her to her knees and enter from behind, he grabbed a handful of raven hair and twisted it around his palm while he pounded into her.

"Mine," he growled.

"More," she replied.

His dragon surfaced, it was time to take back his mate. His fangs emerged, he licked her right shoulder then sank them deep, pinning her in place. Hopefully, this time his mark would stay. After several seconds, he released her and began the chant. "I promise to protect you, provide for you, and love you until my last breath. I beg the gods to bind our souls, making us one." A sharp pain shot through his chest.

LILETA SCREAMED at the immense pain shooting through her like an arrow on fire. Luckily, it subsided seconds later. His cock filled her as his thrusting continued. He reached around and touched her clit. That was all it took for her to shatter. She screamed again, this time with pleasure and not pain. She felt his cock swell, and he roared, filling her with his semen.

He'd managed to bond them again, but she was still stuck in the dark. He pulled out and flipped her on her back then re-entered her. His hands cupped her face. She tried to look away, but he held her in place.

"No. Look at me," he demanded. "Come back and tell me you love me. Grab the light and pull. You can do it." He closed his eyes, and she felt the brush of him mentally.

Caleb.

Lileta, grab hold and let me pull you back. We can win this battle.

The light almost hurt her eyes it was so intense. She grabbed the thread and began to pull herself forward. Furia fought, screeching in her ear. "No, you cannot beat me."

Fuck off, bitch. I want to go back to the man I love. The man who loves me. She felt a tear slide down her cheek. He really did love her. After all that had happened, he came back for her.

Lileta grabbed the thread of light, and with one hand over the other, she pulled through the dark shadows until she gazed at him with her own eyes. She threw her arms around him and cried.

"I love you." Her grip was tight, but she feared letting go, afraid it was only a dream.

"No dream, angel. I'm real," Caleb whispered. He pulled back far enough to lock his lips onto hers. She opened and gave him access. Rocked her hips against him, urging him to move. Her dragon took the hint and pumped his cock in and out of her wet sheath.

"So good, Caleb." She clawed his back when the wave washed over her. Sending her into a tail spin of pure bliss. Caleb tossed his head back and growled. His release sent her spiraling upward then crashing back to reality.

They lay entwined for several moments, neither moving nor speaking until Caleb finally pulled free. "We should dress," he said.

She raised a brow. "You left my clothes in tatters."

He looked around. "So, I did. Cassie will bring you fresh clothing." He pulled on his jeans.

She looked away from his stare. Heat crawled up her neck and face, she was ashamed of the awful things she had done. "Cassie and Aidyn...?"

"They are both fine." He planted a kiss on the top of her head. "Everyone is fine."

She wrapped the sheet around her. "I will face whatever awaits me." Her gaze met his. "What about you? You should never have bound us together again. I tried to kill a guardian. Surely, my punishment will be death."

He grasped her chin. "You will not die." His eyes narrowed and flashed green. "And you will never break our bond again. Do you understand me?" His features softened. "They have already forgiven you."

She released a sigh. "What of the darkness then? Lowan pulled it forth once, he will do it again." She let a tear escape. "I'm afraid, Caleb. You saw what I'm capable of." She had never feared anything more in her entire existence. All her life she had faced her fears, even when taken from her family and sold into slavery. This was so much different, though. She had zero control when the darkness had taken over. Even with her captors, she had fought back using any avenue available to her. However, this she had watched through her own eyes as she shoved the knife into a person she cared about. She would relive that moment forever.

Caleb sat beside her and pulled her close. "You are the mate of a dragon, and as long as I live and breathe, the darkness will never control you again." He kissed the top of her head. "Lucan has also offered to assist you. If anyone knows how to control their dark side and use it to their advantage, he does." He sucked in a breath. "In addition, the Draki will be joining the guardians in the war against Lowan. You are one of us, and we need you. I need you."

She tilted her head to better look into his eyes. "What about those of your people who still align with Odage?"

He flashed that sexy smile she loved so much. "None would dare. Odage has been caught and is awaiting his punishment, and I have been named their new leader."

She placed a palm on his cheek. The feel of his skin beneath her fingers sent tingles to her core. It felt right. It felt like home. "I'm so proud of you. You will be a great leader."

"And you will be at my side." He slanted his head and kissed her. Her hand traveled up his thigh.

"Ahem."

Caleb and Lileta turned toward the sound to find Cassie staring back at them with a wicked grin. "I brought you something to wear." She held up a pair of jeans and a shirt. "I figured yours would be useless by the time Caleb was done with them." She unlocked the gate and walked in, setting the clothes on the table in the corner. "Come up when you're dressed. There will be a meeting in the main hall." She turned and left.

CHAPTER TWENTY-FOUR

LILETA ENTERED THE ROOM, Caleb holding her hand for moral support even though he had assured her all was forgiven. A large conference table occupied the center of the room. At one end sat Aidyn, next to him was Marcus then Cassie, Gwen and Baal. On the other side sat Garin, Seth, and Lucan. There were two empty seats at the end closest to where she was standing. Aidyn rose and walked toward them.

"Lileta, I'm happy to see you well." He stopped in front of her and pulled her into an embrace. Caleb let out a low growl, and Aidyn pulled back. "Relax, dragon, you know I mean no ill intent."

"Sorry, I'm a creature of instinct," Caleb replied.

"I understand." Aidyn waved his hand toward the two empty seats. "Why don't the two of you sit and we can get started." He turned and headed back to his chair.

"Wait," Lileta called out.

The king turned.

"I don't like how everyone is acting like nothing happened. I need to apologize."

"Will it make you feel better?" Aidyn asked.

She wrung her hands together. "I'll never feel good about what I did, but ignoring it will not make it go away."

"Go on then," the king urged.

"I'm so very sorry for leading Odage and the demons back here. For stabbing you." Her gaze moved to Cassie and Marcus. "For taking your daughter." Then to Baal. "And for letting you down." Caleb squeezed her hand. "I deserve any punishment you see fit to give me."

Aidyn rubbed his chin as if in thought. "Then your punishment shall be to join us in the fight against your father and his minions."

Her gaze shot back to him. He knew about Lowan being her father. "I don't understand."

"You were not responsible for your actions, nor can you help who your father is. I'm confident, between Lucan and Caleb, they can help you keep the darkness at bay. Besides, some interesting information was gained by this and no one was seriously injured." Aidyn pointed to the chairs. "Now let's get this meeting started."

Lileta took a seat next to Baal who gave her a wink, and Caleb sat across from her. She really wanted to crawl under the table and hide. This was a new emotion for her. Normally, she faced her challenges head-on, but this was different. These people had done so much to help her, and she had let them down. She lifted her chin, deciding she would do whatever she could to help.

"As some of you know, we discovered the blades the demons are now using against us have been coated with black magic. This explains why we are unable to heal and find ourselves cut off from each other," Aidyn stated.

"Fucking great. Lowan is following in his father's footsteps," Lucan shot back.

Everyone nodded in agreement. The guardians were already fighting the curse placed on them centuries ago. This simply added gasoline to the fire. Lileta knew since Marcus had found his mate, it appeared his curse had been pushed back. The stain that had grown and threatened to turn him into a blood-thirsty monster had been settled by Cassie. The others hoped finding their mates might do the same. So far, no one else had been lucky enough. Then again, it wasn't as if they'd had time with all the demon activity going on. It looked like they were going to have to wait for a sign from above to point them toward their mate. Lileta glanced at Lucan. From their earlier conversation, she gathered he knew who his mate was. Or was he living on hope?

Her brother looked at her. "Lileta, do you know anything that can help?"

"No, I was given the dagger but have no idea what he did to them." She wished she could be of more assistance.

"Well, we will just have to continue to be careful. At least, we know at this point our healers can reverse the damage." Aidyn leaned forward. "Let us hope this will not change in the future. I stand by my order that you will remain in teams of at least two."

"Have we gained any information from Odage's interrogation?" Caleb asked.

"He is too far gone to be any use to us. I have learned nothing," Lucan piped up.

"Are you still planning on removing his head?"

Lileta made eye contact with Marcus. She couldn't blame him for wanting the Draki Overlord done in. He had caused so much trouble. She'd wondered as well what his fate would be.

Aidyn pressed his lips into a thin line. "It must be done. There is no other alternative." He reached for the glass of water in front of him and took a long swig as if trying to wash down something distasteful. "Seth, what about that female you were tracking? The one who had the Phoenix god's blade."

"Wait...What? You've found the dagger of Embara?" Caleb asked.

Lileta held back a gasp. The legendary dagger that had been used to give Caleb the scar he now bore. She could scarcely believe it had been discovered.

"Seth, why don't you fill our friend in here. He has a special interest in the blade," Aidyn said.

Seth nodded and began to recount his encounter with a human woman. After saving her life, he actually had brief contact with the knife and was certain it was the one and only dagger of Embara. She later had shown up while he was in a fight, taken out a couple of demons, and vanished.

"She is proving most difficult to find," he concluded.

Lucan shoved his elbow into Seth's ribs. "You left out the part about her using your jewel sack as her personal stomping ground. When I found him, he was doubled over whimpering like a little girl."

"I'd be careful pissing him off. He is half crazy, ya know," Marcus replied with an amused look on his face. It was Cassie's turn to shove her elbow into her mate's ribs. "Ouch!"

"Play nice." She shot him a menacing glare.

Seth raised a brow. "How can you determine that I am only half crazed? I may have crossed all the way over, and you just haven't figured it out yet." He flashed a crooked grin, and Cassie snorted.

"Regardless of Seth's sanity or his jewels, we need to get that blade." Aidyn tapped the table. "I don't need to remind any of you how dangerous that thing is in the wrong hands. We must find it and seal it away."

"I might be able to help," Caleb spoke up. "I'm a pretty good tracker. Do you have anything other than a description?"

"I have her scent, she smells of strawberries," Seth replied.

He tilted his head. "Well, that's not much to go on. I guess we can start at the location you first encountered her and move from there."

"I'm going with you," Lileta stated.

Caleb looked over at her. "I think, considering the events that are about to transpire, you should stay with Leria."

"Oh right." She turned back to Aidyn, having forgotten all about Odage. "When do you plan to execute Odage?"

The guardian leaned back in his chair. "Today. Delaying it will not change anything."

She nodded. "I need to see Leria. Has she been informed?"

"Not yet, we'll go together." Caleb stood. "We should do it now."

"We can finish up our business without you. Go, I certainly don't wish to be in your shoes," Aidyn replied.

Lileta grabbed Caleb's hand once they exited the room and strode down the hall. Leria was with Ariana and the nanny at the other end of the compound. Beth a lovely middle-aged woman, who was the daughter of a Chosen, had been brought in to care for the children only a few days before, or so Lileta was told. She was familiar with the Chosen. Humans who'd been with the guardians since the beginning of time and helped with their affairs. In turn for their loyalty, they were given a home, money, and schooling. Marcus and now Cassie tended to any health issues that cropped up as well.

"I'm concerned about Leria. How was she the last time you saw her?" Lileta asked.

Caleb squeezed her hand. "You will be a wonderful mother to her. Stop worrying." They rounded a corner. He stopped and pulled her into an embrace. "She is a remarkable girl, considering all she's been through. You were my chosen, Lileta, for so many reasons."

He brushed his knuckles across her cheek and sent shivers racing up her spine. She gazed into the depths of his brown eyes where love and desire stared back at her.

"I know, but what if the darkness takes over again?" She fought back a tear. "What if I hurt her? Caleb, I could never live with myself. I—"

He placed a finger on her lips. "Stop it right now. Haven't you learned to trust me yet?" He cupped her face, pressed his fingers around the back of her neck and pulled her toward him. He dipped his head, his mouth consumed hers, and his tongue forced past her parted lips.

She moaned.

He nibbled her bottom lip before pulling back. "Have I failed you yet?"

She became mesmerized by the green flecks that swirled in the depths of his warm cocoa eyes. His dragon was challenging her, daring her to find fault. When she looked back, everything that had gone wrong had been from her own doing, and here he was. This glorious man standing in front of her. He had come back for her even when their bond was broken and he had no reason to. She lowered her gaze to his lips. She was ashamed of herself.

"No. It is I who have failed you. I should have trusted you when Lowan discovered me." She tipped her head back and met his fiery gaze. "I feared for your life and could not stand the thought of your death. Your people need you."

"I need you, damn it." His features softened. "My people can survive without me, but I cannot live without you. Bond or not, I love you, and the fact I came back for you even after our bond was broken should prove that I am no longer in possession of my heart. You are."

Overwhelming love wrapped around her like a warm, snuggly blanket. He'd opened his emotions and merged them with hers. Allowing her to feel what his words could hardly express.

She smiled and palmed his cheek. "Caleb, my dragon mate. I love you. When this is over, I want to take Leria and go home. Back to the Carpathian Mountains where the three of us can begin our life together." She brushed her thumb over his cheekbone. "I swear to the gods, I will never doubt you again." She stood up on her toes and planted a firm kiss on his lips. Sighed then leaned back. "We better go see Leria. This will not be an easy task."

WHEN CALEB and Lileta entered the room, Beth gave them a sympathetic look. Leria glanced up from the paper she had been drawing on, her lips turning up into a big smile.

"Lileta!" She jumped up and ran into Lileta's open arms.

Caleb grinned, watching the two embrace each other. Dread filled him at what they were about to do. The poor girl had already been through so much it seemed unfair taking away her last living parent. However, Caleb didn't have a say in this matter, it came from higher up than him. He was grateful the gods had chosen Lileta as his mate for many reasons. Helping Leria cope with her losses was one of them.

Beth picked up a sleeping Ariana and walked toward them. "I'll leave you alone." The door closed quietly behind her.

"I want to see the king," Leria stated, pulling free from Lileta's embrace.

Caleb took a seat at the table where the girl had been drawing and spotted her picture. A black dragon covered the page along with a smaller, golden one. *Fuck. This is going to be harder than we thought.*

Lileta caught his mental thoughts and glanced at the drawing. Her shoulders sagged. They both knew it was Leria and her father on that page. Lileta steered the girl toward the couch. "I'm sure Aidyn would love to see you as soon as he has a free moment," Lileta said.

"No. I want to see him now." She placed her hands on her hips. "It is my right to make this request."

Caleb cleared his throat. Lileta gave him a pleading stare. "I see. This is official business then and not a social call?" This was exactly what he hoped to avoid, but it seemed the teen was well versed in politics. As the only living relative of her father, she had the right to request an audience with his jailer and ask for a stay of execution. According to the laws of the gods, the audience must be granted.

Leria approached him, her eyes flashing to her dragon green. "We must go now."

Caleb nodded and took her hand. "Then we shall go." He rose, and Lileta followed. The three walked down the same corridor he and Lileta had just passed through. Caleb headed for the study, hoping that's where the king would be.

They were in luck. Aidyn sat at his desk, his head in his hands.

He must have sensed their presence. He looked up. "I've been expecting you."

Caleb inhaled. "Then you know why we're here."

Aidyn rose from his desk and walked around to greet them. "I have my suspicions. Please come in."

Lileta closed the door behind her and had no sooner joined Caleb's side when Leria stepped forward and dropped down to one knee.

"My lord, I request your audience," Leria stated.

Aidyn squatted to her level. "Leria, I am not your king, therefore you are not required to kneel before me."

She brought her gaze to meet his. "I understand, but I am here to beg you for mercy."

Lileta looked at Caleb. *When the hell did she grow up? She seemed such a small fragile child when I saw her last.*

Draki children grow up fast. This one even more so than most. Caleb sighed. *I fear she has had no time to be a child.*

Aidyn let out a long breath. "Very well. I will hear your plea then."

Leria's gaze darted around the room. "Here?"

The guardian raised a brow. "You're going to stand on formality?" He spread out his arms. "As you can see, we are no longer in Vandeldor. The official throne room is buried under ground." He walked behind his desk and rolled out his chair, bringing it to the center of the room. "We will make do with what we have."

He sat and gave Caleb a weary glance. Everyone in the room, except for Leria, knew what the outcome of this meeting would be. However, they had to abide by their ancient laws. Caleb scrubbed a palm down his face. *Lileta, love. Be prepared, we are going to have to pick up the pieces.*

His mate gave him a sidelong glance and wrung her hands together. *Yes, but we will get through this. Together, as a family.*

Leria stood and walked toward the guardian king. Her steps sure and her head held high. When she reached Aidyn, she once again knelt at his feet. Caleb hid a smile. Leria was going to follow protocol to the letter, leaving no room for error.

"My lord. I come to beg you to spare my dad—my father's life. I know he committed a crime and should be punished, but he is all the family I have left." Leria's voice cracked, but she held back the tears.

Lileta grabbed Caleb's hand and squeezed. He sensed it was the only way she could keep from running to Leria and throwing her arms around the girl.

Aidyn gripped the arms of the chair, his face tense. "I understand. I wish I could. However, I am unable to grant your request."

Leria chewed her lip. "My lord. I'm sorry for the death of your mother, but my father was not himself."

Aidyn reached out and touched the child's shoulder. "If she were the only victim, I would grant your request without question." He tipped her chin up to meet her gaze. "However, he committed crimes against humanity. The gods require his punishment. I am so sorry, Leria, I must carry out his execution."

Caleb's heart cracked when the girl's eyes watered. Not only did he have to keep his mate from running to Leria. He had to keep his own feet planted firmly in place. The child who was trying so hard to be an adult would never forgive them for interfering.

"May I see him? Please," she pleaded.

Aidyn sat back and glanced at Caleb who gave the slightest shake of his head. Odage was too far gone, and it would only break her heart further.

"I'm sorry, your father is no longer himself and is a danger to you. I must deny this request." The king sucked in a breath. "His execution will be carried out at midnight. You are dismissed."

The tears rolled down Leria's cheeks as she rose to her feet. She balled her fists at her side. "I will never forgive you for this," she whispered through clenched teeth then turned and ran. Lileta followed her while Caleb stayed behind.

Aidyn picked up the chair and threw it against the wall, leaving splinters on the floor. "I never wanted to hurt her." He leaned over his desk, his eyes closed and his chest expanded in a deep breath. The ground beneath their feet shook, and the walls of the compound bulged. Caleb felt a great power swirl around the room. The king was struggling to keep his power in check.

"Aidyn, she's a child. Give her time. She will one day understand duty," Caleb said. He'd never experienced the full power of the guardian before and was certain if Aidyn didn't calm, the entire mountain would crumble. "Do not make me remind you my mate resides down the hall. If you force me to dig her out, I will be sorely pissed."

Aidyn stood erect and fisted his palms. "I have control. You are wrong, though. Leria will never forgive me. I felt her hatred. It cut me like a white-hot blade." He faced Caleb. "One day, she will seek her revenge, and may the gods have mercy on us all."

Caleb shook his head. "I don't understand. Does this have something to do with her saving humanity?"

His fangs elongated. "Yes."

Caleb rubbed the back of his head. "I don't get how a Draki is going to stop this war and save the human realm. We are not their guardians." He crossed his arms over his chest. "What the hell are the gods up to?"

Aidyn's gaze pinned him. "Her destiny is not to save humanity directly. It is to save my soul."

Caleb dropped his arms to his side, and his jaw went slack for a brief moment before he snapped it shut. "Son of a bitch!" He spun on the ball of his foot and stormed from the room.

CHAPTER TWENTY-FIVE

CALEB FLASHED to where his mate resided. He found her and Leria sitting on the couch, embraced in each other's arms. The girls' eyes were rimmed red, and it ripped his heart open. They needed to leave there.

He knelt in front of the girls. "I think we should leave." He reached for Leria's hand. "How would you like to see your new home?"

"I think that is a wonderful idea. You'll love it, Leria. Caleb has built a beautiful home high in the mountains," Lileta commented while stroking the child's hair.

Leria sniffed. "Can we fly?"

Caleb looked to his mate, Lileta gave a nod of approval.

"Yes, of course we can," he replied and grabbed Lileta's hand, the three flashed outside the compound.

They stood on the rocky surface as the sun was beginning its descent on the horizon. Soon, darkness would fall and help cloak them, making their flight much easier. Leria was still too young to be able to cloak herself, and Caleb would not be able to assist her. When they returned home, he would speak to her about bringing her into his family.

"You go ahead and shift first," Caleb said.

The young girl's image shimmered and was replaced by the golden dragon. Lileta gasped.

"Leria, you are the most beautiful creature I've ever seen." She extended her hand and touched the small dragon's nose. The beast nuzzled into her.

Caleb shifted then placed his head on the ground, giving his mate a platform to climb. When she was settled, he looked to Leria and nudged her, encouraging her to take flight. Once they were airborne, he climbed above the clouds and headed toward the setting sun. Leria flew up beside him then dropped several feet in a spin only to bank left and pull back up again. She zipped in front of Caleb and swished from the left to the right.

"Dear gods, please tell me she's not going to crash," Lileta yelled.

Caleb snickered. *No, she's behaving as a young dragon should. I wish you could hear her laughter.*

"Whew. I'm happy to hear that." Lileta's body relaxed, but Caleb noted her disappointment.

Angel, once Leria is brought into my family by the blood bond, you will be able to share these experiences as well.

"I have so much to learn about you. What does that mean?"

I look forward to your exploration. Caleb chuckled when she gave him a lighthearted swat on the back. He certainly was looking forward to finally getting to savor every inch of her and intended to do just that when they got home. *It is when Diego and I will share our blood with her in a family ritual. This is witnessed before our people thus making her one of us. She will become our daughter, Lileta.*

"I like the sound of that. She deserves stability, I only hope that—"

Stop. Don't even say it!

"I can't help it. I still fear Lowan and his power. He will not give me up so easily." She laid down and wrapped her arms as far around his neck as possible. *I have never feared anything as much as I do this.*

She had switched to her telepathic link and opened up her emotions, allowing him to experience everything she felt. He was humbled she now trusted him enough to make herself so vulnerable. Along with her fear, overwhelming love caressed his skin. He fully understood her concerns. *Angel, I love you. Remember you carry part of my soul and, along with Lucan's training, Lowan will never control you again.*

Of course, you're right. Lucan said he would come by soon. I'm actually looking forward to training with him.

Just don't look too forward to it.

Caleb switched his focus to the smaller dragon who buzzed around him. *Leria, I'm opening a portal directly home. I will lead. You follow close behind me.* The three were greeted on the other side by Diego, Jax, and Darius. Caleb sensed trouble. It wasn't like them to come unannounced.

Lileta jumped down, and he shifted. "What's wrong?" He flared out his senses, looking for trouble.

Diego stepped forward. "There have been rumblings coming from Soreth's clan. He plans to challenge your position." He tipped his head toward Leria. "He also wants the child."

Lileta's eyes widened, and she drew the girl close to her bosom. Caleb's jaw tightened until he thought every facial muscle might snap. He understood this was more than simply leading their people. Soreth wanted the girl so he could use her to gain more wealth. Being how there were so few females, he thought to sell her to the highest bidder once she was of age, with no regard to who her destined mate was. If the poor bastard was outbid, both her mate and Leria would suffer greatly.

"Caleb, no!" Lileta begged.

He glanced at his mate from the corner of his eye. He'd forgotten to close his thoughts. Better for her to know what she was a part of now. Dragons were feral, territorial creatures, and he wasn't surprised by the challenge. He'd not expected it so quickly, however, and he certainly had not entertained the thought of being challenged for the girl.

"Do not worry yourself, angel. I will take care of this matter." He moved closer to his mate, kissing the top of her head. "Take Leria and go to the house. Jax is one of my best warriors, he will go with you and stand guard."

Jax stepped forward, tipped his head. "I'm at your service, my lady." He extended his arm toward the house. "Shall we?"

Lileta gave him a weary look but said nothing as she walked away. Something told him they were going to have a long, ugly discussion when this was done. Once she was out of range, he closed his thoughts.

"Diego, do you have the plan in place?"

"You are not going to die, but yes. Several guards have been placed around your home. Should it even look like you might lose, they will take your mate and Leria to safety." Diego's brows lowered. "No fucking way in hell will I or anyone else allow Soreth to get his hands on them."

Caleb scrubbed his face. "Fuck! As if I don't have enough to deal with. Lowan has not been stopped and is still a threat to my mate. If I die, you will make sure to seek protection with the guardian king, Aidyn. He is powerful enough to protect them."

"It will be done."

"How long do I have before the fight?"

"The battle will begin tonight at midnight," Diego replied.

Caleb nodded. "Then I'm going to enjoy the next four hours with my mate. I will see you later."

LILETA HAD SETTLED the young girl into her room and tucked her into bed. The poor child had fallen asleep as soon as her head hit the pillow. She was worn out. Lileta stood in the kitchen, refrigerator door wide open and peered inside. Empty.

Warm arms slipped around her waist, and she smiled. "Do you not eat?" She closed the door then turned to face the man that held her. A warm brown gaze flecked with green greeted her.

"I've been a little busy chasing my mate." He flashed a wicked smile.

She melted. He had a way of doing that to her. "I see." She planted her palms on his firm chest. "Tell me what's going on."

He spun her so she was now facing the refrigerator and pushed her up against the counter. His erection pressing into her backside. "Later. Right now, I have other things on my mind. He scraped his teeth along her jaw, sending shivers down her spine.

"Mmm...I like where this is going, but not here." She flashed them to his room. She reached for the button on his jeans and pulled. "This time, I'm in charge."

He moaned, and his eyes swirled with lust. "I love a woman who knows what she wants."

"Oh I know exactly what I want. These jeans off you." She lowered the zipper and shoved them to his ankles. He pulled his shirt over his head and tossed it across the room then kicked off his boots and pants. She took a step back, wanting to take in every inch of him. Starting with his glowing eyes that burned with desire for her. To those fleshy lips that caused her to shudder when she recalled how they felt on her skin. Down to a broad chest, and abs you could bounce a quarter off. Her gaze moved past narrow hips and landed on the prize she sought. She gave him a shove, pushing him to the bed. Wrapped both hands around his thick erection, gave a squeeze and settled between his legs.

He groaned.

She flicked out her tongue and ran it along the ridge of his cock before she sucked his length in.

"Damn angel, that feels so damn good," he whispered.

She let his cock pop free from her mouth. "It's my turn to bring you pleasure." She kissed the tip then sucked him in again. Power engulfed her when his body responded with a shudder followed by a moan. She'd ached to do this for so long.

He entwined her hair around his fingers and thrust his hips. She lay still, allowing him to slide between her lips, her gaze focused on his face, his lids at half-mast. She had him exactly where she wanted. She flicked her tongue across his velvet head, and cupped his balls. His body stiffened as the first surge hit him.

"Oh shit!" he cried out.

Claws dug into her skull and spurred her on as she took every drop of salty goodness he had to offer. She pulled back and licked her lips, her body on fire, and she was in desperate need of him.

Caleb leaned forward, grabbed her top and ripped it, sending the tatters flying.

"You really need to stop ruining my clothes."

"Then you need to stop wearing them," his husky voice replied.

She shoved him back to a lying position then slipped out of her jeans. "I can't go around naked all the time." She flicked out her tongue and licked his hardened abs. Gods, he was perfection.

"You're too beautiful for clothes." He rolled a nipple between his fingers, causing her to moan as her tongue continued to explore his chest.

She wanted him. Needed to feel his length slip inside her and rub every nerve until she screamed from the sheer pleasure. This time, though, it would be she who called the shots. "You want me, Caleb?" She sucked his bottom lip between her teeth and gave a gentle nip before releasing it.

His fingers dug into her ass. "I don't just want you, angel. I need you."

She rubbed her slit over his cock, teasing. Locking her lips onto his, she slipped her tongue into the warmth of his mouth, sweeping and tasting every inch. When she could stand no more, she raised her hips, positioned herself over the head of his cock and slid down, taking his entire length. He stretched and filled her and sent every nerve firing into overdrive. She pulled back from the kiss and gazed into emerald pools. He opened his mind and blanketed her with so much love her breath caught. Life had handed her many obstacles, but in turn, it also rewarded her with this man. This fierce dragon who brought her back from the brink of Hell. Like any young girl, she dreamed of a knight in shining armor. A man who would sweep her off her feet, and right then, she was connected to that very man. A connection of the mind, body, and soul. Lileta decided in that very moment she would not lose him. Whatever she had to do to keep him with her, she was going to make it happen.

Caleb cupped her face. "I love you. The only thing that matters is you and now Leria."

Her heart melted. She lifted until only the tip of his cock was left inside her. He latched onto a nipple and pulled it into his mouth. Her inner walls clenched, and she slammed back down, taking him in again. She'd planned to go slow and savor the moment, but plans changed and she needed release. Digging her nails into his chest, she quickened her pace. Her thighs quivered.

"That's it, angel. Take what you need." He threw his arms over his head and grabbed the headboard, giving her complete control.

She arched her back and they moved in unison, creating heated friction in her core. She was close. Pressure built until she thought it would split her in two then sweet release came. She tossed her head back and cried out. Her body racked with wave after wave of pleasure. His cock stretched her farther, and Caleb growled with his own orgasm.

Lileta lay her head on his chest and listened to the beating of his heart. His arms wrapped around her and pressed her tight to him.

"You've closed your mind. What troubles you?" He stroked her hair.

"We've come so far, Caleb." She turned her head, touching her chin to his chest. His eyes still smoldered with a green fire. "I'm coming with you when you fight Soreth." She held her breath, waiting for his refusal.

"It's my battle, not yours." His voice remained calm.

She planted her palms on his chest and pushed up until she stared down at him. "No, that's where you're wrong. It's our battle, Caleb, and we stand together." He opened his mouth to speak, but she placed a finger over his lips. "You saved me, more than once." She ran her finger across his soft, fleshy lips. "You saved us, and now I'm asking you to trust me."

He sighed. "I do trust you, but you're asking me to put my mate in harm's way, and that I cannot do."

She rolled off him and stared at the ceiling. "Yet you ask me to let you go into harm's way. How do you suppose you're going to stop me from showing up?"

He pinned her to the bed with his body. Eyes swirled with determination. "I will place guards on you if I have to, and you will stay here." His face pressed closer until his hot breath caressed her. "And should I fail, you and Leria will be taken to safety."

She licked her lips. Torn on whether to kiss him or hit him. He was stubborn, but then so was she, and at this moment, she would name him the victor. She didn't want to argue, that would come later after she disobeyed him. Instead, she lifted her head, allowing their lips to touch. She was going to savor him until the last possible second.

CHAPTER TWENTY-SIX

"YOU NEED TO FOCUS," Lucan ground out.

"I'm trying!" Lileta stared across the table at the dark guardian who had come to help her. Caleb had left half an hour ago for some last-minute training, and Lucan was now trying to help her tap into and control her she-bitch Furia. Aidyn had only granted him two hours, saying he was needed in the field. Demons were escaping at an alarming rate, and already there had been human casualties. All hell had broken loose, literally. If that wasn't enough, Caleb was challenged to a battle of dominance, and according to Diego, this Soreth was a very powerful dragon.

"You know he is going to be pissed as hell when you show up." Lucan broke her train of thought.

She pursed her lips. "Why do you men feel the need to dominate everything in your sight?"

He smirked. "We are warriors, it's what we do."

She wanted to reach across the table and smack him, but she needed his help. "Women are warriors, yet they do not feel the need to hold a pissing contest to prove their worth."

He placed both palms flat on the table and leaned forward.

Raven hair fell over his equally dark eyes. His lip curled to expose a fang. "Women are weak. You don't belong out there in battle." A full smile was plastered across his face. "We much prefer your naked bodies underneath us, screaming in orgasm." He stood, towering over her. "You are a fucking fool if you think you can help your mate. Do him a favor and strip naked, spread your legs and wait for his return."

Lileta sucked in a deep breath. Anger boiled under the surface, threatening to explode. Furia screeched, wanted to gouge his eyes out. She jumped to her feet, palms on the table and leaned in. "You arrogant, self-centered bastard." Her nails extended into claws and gouged the wooden table. Blue sparks snapped from their tips. Her skin became hot and tight and her vision red.

He threw his head back and laughed. "Well, it's about damn time you let that bitch loose." He straightened. "Look in the mirror, Lileta. You're pure demon."

She didn't need to gaze at herself in a piece of glass to know what was happening. "This only happens when I'm in Hell. It's never happened here in the human world." She lifted her right hand from the table and twisted it to look at her palm. Blue lines crisscrossed in an intricate pattern where the current ran through. She looked up at the vampire. "You did that on purpose. You didn't mean a damn word of it."

There was that cocky grin again. "Nothing like a good dose of anger to bring out your evil side." He stepped around the table until he stood in front of her. "Your mating will anchor the darkness. Now, loosen the leash, and let's have a little fun." He flicked his wrist, and a shadow emerged from the corner of the room. Floating toward her was nothing more than an inky form with blood-red eyes. "Take control from me, or he will kill you."

She gasped and quickly formed a white ball of raw power in her right palm then launched it at the shadow. It penetrated and came out the other side, striking the wall and leaving a hole the size of a dinner plate.

"Really?" Lucan shook his head. "Caleb's gonna be pissed when he sees that." He crossed his arms over his chest. "You are not letting your dark side take complete control."

The shadow reached a claw out to grab her, but she managed to scoot out of its reach in the nick of time. "I'm afraid of my darker side. You saw what Furia did. I can't give her control."

"Fear is your enemy, demon." He outstretched his arms. "You leave me no choice," he growled. Another shadow emerged from the wall, this one complete with a shiny sword. It moved toward her, slashing the blade through the air. It meant to take her head. She screeched and darted across the room, pinning the vampire with a glare. He wasn't going to relent, another of his dark beasts entered from the doorway. The room was becoming a bit cramped, and now she was backed into a corner. She tilted her chin, determined to make this work. She hated to think Lucan had wasted his time here with her when he could have been slaying the enemy.

She centered herself and allowed the darkness to spread. Furia laughed as she came to the forefront, ready to wage war. Lileta held the invisible leash, maintaining control. She raised her hands to waist level, palms facing upward. Closed her eyes and called to the darkness in the room. Beckoned it to come forth. Her eyes snapped open and focused on the image to her left. The shadow with the sword inched forward. She grabbed the thin black line that ran through her mind and yanked, pulling the shadow closer until it was within inches of touching her.

Let me have it. Furia begged like a child asking for candy.

Lileta turned her palms outward and touched the darkness. Furia screeched and lashed out at the shadow walker, pulling the darkness inside. Lileta gasped and jumped back. "What the hell just happened?"

"I'll be damned." Lucan appeared in front of her, his head bent down, eyes staring into hers.

"What?" The way he was looking at her made her feel like a freak on display.

"Your dark side just consumed the shadow walker." He stepped closer, his eyes squinting as if he was trying to see into her soul.

She glanced around the room, nerves on edge. "Where are the other two shadows?"

"I got rid of them the minute your dark bitch ate one." He stepped back, giving her room to breathe, his arms folded over his chest. "Not even I can do that. I can only manipulate the darkness, but if it ever was to turn on me, I could not consume it." His eyes grew darker. "Your father gifted you with some amazing power. Why the hell the gods mated you with a dragon..." He looked away. "I must go." He started to walk away.

"Wait!"

He stopped but didn't turn back to face her. "What is it?"

"What am I supposed to do with this power?" It was like being handed a new gadget without the instruction manual.

"You have more control over your dark side than you realize. Believe in yourself, and you will not fail." He cocked his head and gazed over his shoulder at her. "Aidyn can use someone like you to fight these demons."

"Yes, as soon as this battle with Caleb is over and we get things settled..." She took a step closer. "I want to help. We could team up, and you can continue to be my mentor."

He shook his head. "No. Your darkness is too tempting." He balled his fists. "You should have been mine." He turned and stalked into a black mist, vanishing, taking the darkness with him. It had never occurred to her that she and the dark guardian would have been a well-suited match given the power she'd come into. Fate was fickle, but she loved Caleb and was not about to question the reason for their mating.

"One day, dark warrior, you will find your true mate. Thank you," she whispered.

CALEB WORRIED HIS BROW. Things had been much too quiet in his head. Lileta had kept herself blocked from him, and that could only mean she was up to something. He took a blow to the stomach and doubled over in pain.

"If you don't get your mind off that damn mate of yours, Soreth is going to kill you," Jax spat. "Fuck, you just let me kick you right in the gut."

Caleb stood and stretched out the pain. His friend was right, he'd been otherwise occupied, and that could be the edge that Soreth needed to take him down. If that happened, Diego, Jax and Darius were sworn to take Lileta and Leria to the guardians where Aidyn would protect them. Still, the thought of losing and leaving his mate alone sat like a cold chunk of ice in his gut. He didn't like it. Not one bit.

"You're right, I know." He looked over at his brother, Diego. "She is up to something, I can feel it."

Diego pushed himself off the wall he'd been leaning on. "You want me to go check on her?"

He shook his head. "No. Lucan is helping her control her powers. I'm sure she is simply busy training." He forced himself to swallow down the lump that had formed in his throat. Leaving his mate with another male had taken every ounce of self-control he had, and when it came to her, he didn't have much. He trusted his mate, and he'd known the dark warrior for centuries. Lucan was a good man and loyal to his king and brethren. Still, self-doubt was trying to gain entry and convince him that the gods had made a mistake. Soon, they would realize it and take Lileta from him just as they had taken his brother Talon, while he watched, helpless to save his brother.

Someone shook him. Diego came into view.

"What the fuck is going on with you?" Diego held Caleb's arms in a death grip. He looked to Jax and Darius. "Leave us." The two dragons bowed their heads and vanished. "They're gone, now speak!"

Caleb pulled from his brother's grip. "You presume much, little brother," Caleb growled.

Diego fisted his hands. "Don't pull the Draki Overlord bullshit on me. If you want me to kiss your fucking ass then you better start acting the role of leader."

"I should break your neck for that and teach you proper manners." Even being brothers, Caleb was taken aback by the lack of respect Diego showed him. It was not to be tolerated. As a Draki leader, weakness would get him killed, so even his family must show the respect due his station.

Diego flew at him, shoving him into the concrete wall of the abandoned building they currently occupied. Air escaped his lungs in a whoosh, and then rage blanketed his mind, blinding him. He grabbed the younger Draki by the throat, wound back his right arm and threw a punch square in the nose. Blood splattered his bare chest. The scent caused his dragon to claw to the surface. He drew back again, this time landing the punch to his brother's gut, sending him flying across the room.

Caleb stalked toward the heap on the floor, grabbed Diego's shirt and pulled him to his feet. "Fight back!"

"No!" Diego stood with his hands limp at his side.

"Are you a fucking idiot?" He shook him. "Why would you let me beat the shit out of you?" Caleb was wound so tight every muscle felt as if it would snap.

"If it gives you the release you need to forgive yourself for Talon's death...then I'm willing to take a beating."

Caleb released his brother and stumbled backward. "What the hell am I doing?"

Diego raised a brow. "I believe you were giving me a royal ass kicking." He took slow steps until he stood in front of Caleb. "If you don't put Talon to rest, you're going to lose everything. He would never have wanted that." He placed a hand on Caleb's shoulder. "Mother and Father would not have wanted that."

Caleb dropped his gaze to the floor. "I was helpless to save him. I watched as Drayos shoved the knife into his heart and twisted." He raised his head and looked Diego straight in the eyes. "I watched the fire burn out of his eyes, and it has haunted me ever since. I failed in protecting my own."

Diego squeezed his shoulder. "Then honor his memory by protecting the woman you love. Honor him by keeping the child safe and above all..." Diego dropped to one knee. Jax appeared to his left and Darius on the right, both kneeling. The room filled with hundreds of Draki—men, women and children all kneeling before him. "Above all, brother, honor him by leading your people. He would be proud of you." Diego raised his right arm high over his head and fisted his hand. "Who here among you swears loyalty to Caleb, son of Andreas and Jonet, brother of Talon?" he shouted.

"I do!" Roared a chorus of voices, hands fisted in the air.

"My liege, your people have spoken. We'll take care of Soreth." Diego winked.

Caleb was stunned. Warm arms encircled his waist. "Look at them, Caleb. I knew you were destined for greatness. Your people love you," Lileta whispered in his ear.

He pulled the raven-haired beauty to his side. "I love you." He then pulled Leria to his other side. "Leria, I'd be honored to have you as my daughter." He glanced at his mate. "We'd both be honored."

The girl smiled. "I'd like that."

"SO, you don't have to fight Soreth, ever?" Lileta asked, holding her breath, afraid to believe it might actually be so easy. She didn't want anything to ruin this day.

"No. The people have backed me, and they will strip him of his power then banish him." Caleb reached out and caressed her cheek. His soft touch sent a tingle down her spine. She wished they were alone right then so she could have her way with him. However, they were in the midst of preparations for Leria's ceremony. Soon, Leria would be Caleb's and her official daughter in the eyes of the Draki. Unfortunately, this happy occasion was to be followed by a somber one. Odage's funeral.

Caleb and she had discussed at length if they should wait until after the ceremony to tell her or prepare her now. It was decided they would hide nothing from her so had smoothed the way as best they could. Soon, they would be leaving for Vandeldor, heading to the Draki's homeland in the Vutha mountains. Lileta was anxious to see it, she'd never been deep in the sanctum of the dragon before.

"Are you ladies ready?" Caleb asked.

"Yes, Leria should be down any moment." Lileta smoothed a

hand down the black dress she wore. It had been difficult to decide what to wear on a day such as this, but Caleb had assured her the dress was perfect. She'd chosen a simple, straight gown made of black silk with a modest cut bust and thin straps. Caleb had given her a teardrop emerald that now adorned her neck.

"Before we leave, I have one other thing to give you." Caleb reached into his trouser pocket and produced a black, velvet box. "My father had this ring made for my mother." He opened the box.

Her breath caught in her chest as she brought her hand to cover her mouth.

Caleb pulled the gem from its secure cushion in the box, grabbed her left hand, and slipped the ring on her third finger. "I would be honored if you would wear this as a symbol of my love. Perhaps one day passing it to our daughter."

Tears formed, but she held them at bay. "It will never leave my finger." She glanced down at it. "It's beautiful. Thank you for allowing me to wear something that belonged to her. I will treasure it always." She couldn't help but stare at its blinding beauty. A three-carat square-cut emerald sat between two smaller trillion-cut diamonds, all mounted in white gold. She threw her arms around his neck, pulled him close, and pressed her lips against his. Their tongues slid together, and her core heated. Damn, they needed to get this day over so she could seduce her mate.

"I'm ready."

They broke their kiss and turned to admire the young girl who walked into the room. Leria wore a gold dress that matched her dragon. A single, round, red ruby had been placed in the middle of her forehead to signify her blood heritage belonged to the house of *Dastudr*. Odage's house of Strength. On her right upper arm, she wore a cuff of white gold and emeralds. A gift from Caleb to proclaim her loyalty to the house of *Vers*. Caleb's house of Power.

Lileta swept across the room and pulled the girl into a hug, careful not to mess up her coiffed locks. "You are beautiful."

"We should leave now," Caleb stated, pointing to the open portal.

Lileta took the girl's hand in her right and Caleb's in her left, and together they stepped through the millions of diminutive white lights.

SETH BLENDED into the mass of people walking the Chicago streets. His senses overloaded from all the fumes, he wanted to choke. *How humans choose to live like this, I'll never understand.* He'd grown tired of waiting for assistance from the dragons in locating the female. They had their own issues to deal with and would come when they were able. His brethren were spread thin. The demons had gotten smart in their assault on the human realm. They'd abandoned their tirade on the cities and started overtaking the smaller communities. Realizing that while there were fewer souls to consume, it was easier and faster to start small and work their way up. The guardians feared that soon they'd begin to procreate just as Odage had tried to do. If Lowan couldn't escape his hell then he'd simply create one above him and let his minions run amok. Eventually, the Dark Lord would find a way out.

Seth shivered, not against the cold but rather at the thought of what was yet to come. He worried that even with the help of their allies, they were fighting a losing battle. Already, Aidyn had hinted that his guardians should be on the lookout for superior humans. Perhaps military special ops who knew how to fight and survive. The only thing his king had left unsaid was when the time arrived, would they reveal themselves to these humans or would Aidyn convert them? The guardian king was the only among them who could perform this task on a mortal that wasn't a mate. Seth was of the opinion Aidyn should turn the humans now, before the damn curse took them all.

He backtracked to the last location he'd seen her. The place where they fought the demons. Darkness approached, and as much as he hated to do it, he selected a young, handsome male from which to feed. He much preferred to take his nourishment from a warm, curvy female but figured the men in the area would be more likely to know the pretty redhead he sought.

He sank his fangs deep and took several pulls of the coppery liquid, hoping this time he'd get lucky. Already, he'd tapped at least half a dozen men, seeking information. He was playing Russian roulette, waiting for the one that would send him over the edge into insanity. Unable to purge their memories because of the curse, he sometimes had to fight to keep his head above water. Many days, though, he drowned in the sea of voices.

What's this? An image drifted through his mind.

It was her.

The tall, beautiful redhead was walking into a building. The neon sign above flashed Fire & Ice, Seth recognized its location. Seth released the human and sent him on his way. He flashed to the outskirts of the city and stood across the street, watching the patrons enter the men's club called Fire & Ice. The woman he sought, her name was Kaitlyn and she owned this club. Images of her laid out flat on a dirty mattress, wrists bound, and a gag in her mouth flashed through his mind.

He shook them free.

The man he'd just sent on his merry way knew everything about this woman. Her name, where she lived. Where she shopped even. He was obsessed with Kaitlyn and had asked her out, but she'd rebuffed him. His ego was bruised so he was planning to kidnap her and keep her locked away as his little toy.

Seth rubbed his fists over his eyes. The images hurt his head, but they also caused his cock to harden. *You're a sick fuck!* Was he talking to himself or the man whose memories he stole? He could no longer discern where he began and they left off. He pulled at his hair, hoping pain would bring him back from the threshold.

He inhaled. *Strawberries.* He dropped his hands to his side and focused on the figure across the street. She turned to look his direction. His fangs descended, and he emitted a growl. His stride carried him across the pavement with visions of naked flesh dancing in his head.

LILETA GASPED when they stepped through the portal into the dragon's caverns. She blinked, almost blinded by the colorful display. Stalactites hung like enormous waterfalls from the cave ceiling. Traces of vibrant blue, purple, orange, and yellow coated the minerals and lit up the room like millions of tiny colored bulbs. She took a step forward and felt something warm on her face. She tipped her head back and looked up.

"Oh my gods!"

The cavern rose hundreds of feet into the air. Carved into the ancient mountain were hundreds—no thousands—of smaller caves. They dotted the walls as far up as she could see, several had dragons perched at the entrance looking down at them. It was then she noticed the opening at the very top, it explained where the sun was coming from that kissed her face. Dragons of all sizes and colors flew in and out of the gaping hole.

"Pretty amazing, isn't it?" Caleb asked.

"It's beyond words. I never imagined." Lileta pointed. "Are those their homes?"

Caleb chuckled. "No. Those are the dragons' lairs." He bent closer to her ear. "Where we keep our riches."

Her chin dropped. "Oh."

"We need to hurry. The ceremony will be performed in a private chamber. Only the leaders and their families will bear witness."

Caleb led the two girls down a smooth set of steps, through a maze of rock formations and into another chamber. This one much smaller than the last with torches hanging from the wall that cast an eerie glow on the room. At the far end, a fire burned in the large hearth that had been carved into the rock. The flames blazed with the same magical colors she'd seen coming into the cavern.

On either side stood a stone dragon. One white, the other black, their tails curled along the edge of the fireplace then across the top, forming a most unusual mantel. Diego stood in front of it, dressed in black slacks and a gray, button-up shirt. He gave her a wink, and she flashed him a smile. She owed her new brother-in-law a great deal. Not only had he rescued her while Caleb battled Odage, he'd rescued her mate more than once.

Her gaze slid from Diego to the three benches on either side of the room. Massive wooden structures with ornate dragons climbing up the sides. At her feet was a burgundy carpet that ran from the entrance to where Diego stood.

A commotion came from the door. Six oversized men and three beautiful women descended on the room. From what Lileta had been told, these were the other leaders and their mates. There were seven houses of the Draki now left with Odage gone. One day, Leria could reestablish her father's house when she mated.

The Draki leaders took a seat on the benches, and Caleb led her and Leria to where Diego stood. Caleb reached for a silver goblet adorned with diamonds and emeralds that sat on the mantel. Diego produced a silver dagger, the handle carved in the design of dragon scales. He made a slice across his right wrist, handed the dagger to Caleb and took the goblet. His blood trickled into the chalice then the wound healed over. Caleb repeated the process, allowing his blood to pour into the vessel. He then offered the goblet to Leria. She accepted, palming it in both hands, she brought it to her lips and sipped. Leria turned and handed the chalice to Lileta. She brought the cool metal to her lips and let the coppery liquid coat her tongue before allowing it to slide down her throat. Her eyes closed for a moment while she let the power of those few drops of blood course through her. Even though she and Caleb had mated, she now carried the blood of the Draki. These were her people. She hoped to make them proud.

"Qadira, goddess of fire. The house of *Vers* welcomes Lileta as the mate of Caleb." Diego pinned those sitting on the benches with his gaze. "Does anyone wish to object?"

Silence.

He gave a nod then looked to his brother.

"Qadira, goddess of fire. The house of *Vers* welcomes the daughter of Odage into its fold." Caleb reached for Leria's hand. "My mate and I wish to raise her as our own and call her daughter."

Energy engulfed the room and prickled Lileta's skin. The flames in the hearth flared and snapped at the air. A woman's silhouette formed in the center of the room. Blue flames danced around her feet.

"Your request is granted, Caleb, son of Andreas and Jonet." The goddess completed her transformation. Her crimson gown dragged the floor as she approached Leria. "You will follow the path your new family provides for you." She touched the girl's cheek. "One day, when the time comes, you will fulfill your prophecy."

"What if I choose not to?" Leria whispered.

Qadira smiled. "You will. Your heart will not allow you to do otherwise." She turned and took a step toward Lileta. "Welcome, daughter, I am pleased you and Caleb have finally joined." She stepped back.

A shift in power swirled through the room. Caleb growled, and Lileta's jaw dropped. A man clad in only black, leather pants, his raven hair tied back, revealing a strong jaw and smoldering eyes appeared.

Hades.

"I come with a gift." Hades moved forward.

"You left my mate to suffer at the hands of her father," Caleb growled through his clenched jaw.

"It made you stronger, didn't it, Lileta?" He ignored the dragon.

"I did terrible things, my lord." She fought back the tears. "Why are you here?"

Hades reached for her hand and placed it in Caleb's. "I am here to show you a glimpse of your future." He closed his eyes, still embracing their hands, and projected the image of a tiny babe into their minds. The little bundle was a boy with dark blond hair and golden eyes.

Lileta gasped. "Is he?" She held her breath, afraid to finish the question. Her hands trembled.

The god opened his eyes and leaned closer. "He is your son."

Lileta shook her head. "I don't understand. How is it possible?"

"You are the daughter of a demigod. Your power will protect you during the birth of your children." Hades stepped back beside the goddess. "A son of the goddess of fire and a daughter of Hell. Qadira, I could not have made a better match myself."

Caleb squeezed her hand, and Lileta realized tears were running down her cheeks. "Thank you." She could scarcely contain her joy and watched as the images of Qadira and Hades faded away.

"Welcome to the family." Diego pulled Leria into a bear hug, and she squeezed him back before breaking away to hug Caleb and Lileta.

Caleb kissed her forehead. "I am proud to call you daughter."

He pulled Lilcta closer. "Come, I must introduce you to the others before we proceed to the funeral." He leaned in. "We can practice making that baby later," he whispered in her ear.

CHAPTER TWENTY-EIGHT

CALEB LED the ladies back into the main hall and wondered if they should have saved the ceremony for after Odage's funeral. Lileta had insisted it was better this way. Leria would be in a black mood after coming to terms with her father's death and would want to be alone to process her feelings. He gazed at his mate through desire-filled eyes. Her raven hair had been piled on top of her head, leaving her long neck exposed. The black dress she wore was simple, but on her, it looked like a million bucks. Thin straps crisscrossed across her back, showing off soft skin and a slim backside. The dress continued past her hips and stopped a few inches above the knee. He wanted to lick every inch of her body.

She cast him a fiery look.

What?

This is not the time to think about sex, she chided.

Then you should have worn a sack.

She chuckled. *I somehow doubt that would have helped.*

You're probably right. He sighed.

Caleb, I don't feel right. She gave a weary glance around as they entered the cavern.

What's wrong, are you ill?

No. I just have a bad feeling. Furia is screeching to get out.

He flared out his senses and his dragon stirred. He didn't like hearing that Furia, Lileta's dark side, was restless. He sensed nothing out of the ordinary other than the guardians had arrived. He pulled Lileta close and brushed a kiss across her lips.

"Stay connected to me no matter what happens."

She nodded, worrying her bottom lip. They continued on to meet Aidyn on the other side of the expansive cavern. The vampire warrior stood tall, hands locked behind his back. Leria approached him, her chin up.

"Where is my father's body?" Her hands clenched at her side.

The vampire looked down at her, his eyes filled with sorrow. "He has been taken to his chambers."

She turned to Caleb. "I will go oversee the preparations."

Caleb nodded his approval and watched the girl leave before he turned back to Aidyn. "Are all your warriors here?"

"Yes. Lucan insisted we all come except for the children, of course. He said something about a nagging feeling crawling up his spine."

"Yes, I have felt it too." Lileta said, her voice shaky. "Caleb, what if my father is up to something?"

Caleb scratched his chin then waved Diego over. He wasn't taking any chances. "Tell the others to be on the lookout for trouble. Post a guard at every entrance to this mountain."

Diego tipped his head, turned on his heel and strode out of sight.

"We should head out; the ceremony will begin soon."

Minutes later, Caleb stood at the water's edge and helped his daughter light the fire that would consume her father's body. Several Draki pushed the small barge, with the shroud-covered form into the water and watched it float to the middle of the small lake that flowed through their cavern community. By the time it reached the center, it was fully engulfed. Caleb and Lileta stood on either side of Leria and held her close. The girl blinked back her tears.

"I'd like to visit Erebos and the others. With their family's permission, of course," Leria stated.

"I will arrange for it as soon as the ceremony is over." Caleb couldn't blame her for wanting to see her half-brothers, the only family she had left. He watched as she walked toward the water and placed a red rose at its edge.

An explosion rocked the mountain, shaking the ground under his feet. Screams rang out as rocks rained down upon them. Dragons shifted and took flight.

"Oh my gods, what's happening?" Lileta shouted.

"Flash out of here." Caleb grabbed her. "Go!"

"No! Where's Leria? I'm not leaving you guys."

More screams reverberated off the rock walls and pierced his ears. Demons. Hundreds of demons filtered in through cracks, flew down from the open sky above, and emerged from the water. They were everywhere.

Dragons dropped fire balls on the demons. Swords clanged together as hand-to-hand battles took place all around him. He could see Leria through the dust and smoke that wafted through the air.

"Leria?" Caleb shouted at the top of his lungs. Diego flashed beside him. "Status report."

"All the guards are dead. They looked to be taken out with a blade," Diego replied.

"Lowan's secret weapon," Lileta shot back.

"Fuck!" Caleb grabbed Diego by the shirt. "Have you seen Leria?"

He shook his head. "No."

"We need to evacuate, there are too many of them to fight in here." Caleb shoved Lileta toward Diego. "Get her out of here." The need to get his mate to safety overrode every instinct he had to save his people. He could think of nothing else until he knew she was out of harm's way. She was going to be sorely pissed at him, but right then, he didn't give a fuck.

AS SOON AS Caleb had shoved her into Diego's arms, Lileta flashed. Her need to find Leria outweighed everything else. Granted, Caleb was on the same mission, but he also had his hands full. She hiked up her dress and removed the dagger she'd strapped to her thigh earlier, the warm metal comforting in her palm. That nagging fear and Furia's scratching at the surface had warned her to be prepared. She threw off her heels then began her search along the water's edge, the last place Leria had been seen.

"Leria?"

A demon with thick, black skin and a small pair of wings stepped in her way. Furia snarled, and Lileta slashed at the beast, leaving cuts on its chest. The demon screamed and pushed its head forward only inches from her nose. She struck from the left and made a quick slicing motion to the right. The beasts head toppled to the ground.

"Teach you to stick your nose in my business." She continued her journey. Panic rose in her throat. What if the demons had gotten to Leria? *Stop, she's a Draki for Christ's sake.*

Damn it woman! You disobeyed me. Caleb's voice rung in her head.

"Shit." *I am not one of your warriors that you can bark commands at. I am your mate and I intend to find our daughter.*

Caleb growled, and for some reason, she found it sexy when he did that. She shook her head. Lileta needed to concentrate or be killed. Another demon attacked. She raised her hand and let the power rip from her fingertips, sending the beast sailing into a pile of rubble.

Gods damn it! I will find Leria. Just get out of here.

You need me. I can help. These are my people now too. It hadn't really dawned on her until she mentally said the words. These were her people now. She and Caleb were ambassadors, bringing the two species together. Would the gods see fit to mate more of their kind?

Damn it, woman. Just don't get hurt, and promise you'll let me know if you need help. I'll destroy everything that moves if something happens to you.

I love you too. She smiled.

"Lileta!"

She turned toward the voice calling to her and found Leria running toward her. She embraced the girl in a hug. "We need to get you out of here."

"I was so scared he was coming for me again." The girl was shaking in her arms.

Lileta sent a quick mental message to Caleb that they were all right and flashed them both outside. She'd taken them to the base of the mountain where several injured Draki were being treated by Marcus and Cassie.

"Can I be of any help?" Lileta asked Cassie, kneeling next to her on the rocky ground.

"We're fine. Most of the dragons can heal themselves. Marcus and I are taking care of the worst injuries." She glanced up from the wound she was tending, her brow furrowed in worry. "Any idea what happened?"

"No. They just suddenly poured in like ants taking over a hill." Lileta looked over her shoulder at the once majestic mountain. A gaping hole covered a large area of the upper slope. It explained the falling debris, but how had the demons gotten into Vandeldor? "I thought this realm was off limits to Hell's occupants?" Of course, Hades had made an appearance, but he was a god and could go anywhere he chose. Had he somehow opened a way for Lowan's minions?

"So did I and everyone else." Cassie stood, placed her palms at the small of her back, and stretched. The Draki she'd been working on jumped to his feet and flashed. Lileta assumed he was returning to the battle being waged inside.

Lileta worried her lip. Her mate was in that mountain, along with her brother-in-law. "I need to go back."

"No." Marcus stepped forward. "They found where the demons

are coming from. Somehow, they opened a fracture under the mountain."

Several dragons flew overhead, their massive bodies blocked out the sun momentarily. They were heading toward the beach. "What's going on?" She pulled Leria close to her side.

"We need to evacuate farther away." Marcus gave her a sympathetic look. "The only way to stop this realm from filling with the spawn of Hell is to bring that entire mountain down. Hopefully, the shift in the ground will close the opening."

"Why are you looking at me like that?" Lileta's nerves were already on edge, but a sudden feeling of dread crawled up her spine. It was as if someone had placed a concrete block on her chest. The weight of it constricting every breath she tried to suck in.

Diego appeared at her side. "Come on, we need to move." He flashed her against her will, his power engulfed her and kept her feet pinned in the sand. She hardly noticed the dragons who dropped fire onto the escaping demons or the stench of burning flesh. Her mind could only focus on one thing.

Caleb!

No response. She shot a menacing glare at Diego. "Tell me!" She fisted her hands and clenched her jaw, trying to contain the anger that boiled and threatened to spill over.

"Several men volunteered to stay in the bowels of the mountain where the demons are coming through." He inhaled. "Caleb was one of them."

Her jaw dropped, and her eyes widened with shock. "You're going to drop an entire mountain on top of him?" She ran quick calculations through her head. Not even an immortal was likely to survive. She flailed her arms at Diego, beating on his chest. "Release me. Now!" Furia screeched, even she wanted to go to her mate. Why the hell didn't her power work on the Draki? She was the daughter of a demigod. She should be much stronger.

"I gave my word," Diego replied.

Lileta slapped him across the face. "Screw your word. How can you let your brother die?" He winced, and she was sure her words stung him more than her slap did. Good. Right then, she'd do anything to break free and find her mate. *Caleb? Answer me, damn it!* He had put up his barriers, blocking her from his thoughts and emotions. She was about to lose it but fought to regain control. Leria watched her, the girl's eyes filled with tears about to spill at any moment. She had to remain strong for their daughter. She looked up at Diego who still had her arms pinned to keep from hitting him.

"Please don't let him do this," she whispered.

A look of sorrow came over his features. "I tried to stop him, but you know how stubborn he is." He cast his gaze back at the mountain. "He will not ask his people to put their life on the line if he is not willing to do so himself."

She slumped into his chest and wrapped her arms around him. He squeezed her. "We will leave. There is no reason for you to witness this."

"No." She raised her chin to look up at him. "I need to stay."

Diego closed his eyes and gave a quick nod.

"Aidyn is ready." Marcus slid in next to them. "We have to do this now before it's too late."

Lileta picked her head up off Diego's chest and pulled Leria in close so the three of them were huddled together. "How are you planning on bringing an entire mountain down?"

"Aidyn controls the elements, and his power is even stronger here at home. He will bring the mountain down." Marcus gave her a weak smile then walked away. She buried her face back into Diego's chest.

Caleb, if you can hear me, I love you. Warmth spread over her and embraced her then it was gone. It was his last communication with her. She felt as if someone had taken her emotions and tossed them into a basket then shook them around. She was angry he would sacrifice himself, yet proud he would do this to save others. Sad she might lose him forever, yet grateful for the time they had spent together. She clenched her fists in anger, pulling Diego's shirt between her fingers.

She fixed her gaze on Aidyn when he squatted to the ground, his palms touching the sand. The ground shook beneath their feet and thick, black clouds filled the sky, blocking out the midday sun. Lileta dug her nails into Diego's chest and held her breath, her gaze now riveted on the mountain. It exploded, spewing chunks of rock into the air, narrowly missing the few dragons who still patrolled the skies looking for stray demons. Her heart sank into the pit of her stomach and tears spilled down her cheeks. No one could survive an explosion of that magnitude, it would have ripped them to shreds.

She buried her face in Diego's chest and wept. Leria clung to both of them and cried.

"I am sorry." Aidyn had moved in beside them to express his sympathy.

Leria shot him a look that would kill most mortals. "It wasn't enough to kill my real father." She sniffed. "You had to break up my new family as well? I swear to the gods on this day, on our sacred soil, that one day I will kill you."

Aidyn cast his gaze to the ground and walked away. Lileta pulled the teen back to her side. "Shhh, I know it hurts, but one day you will understand he had no choice." She wondered if she really believed that herself.

CHAPTER TWENTY-NINE

SETH WATCHED Kaitlyn run through the glass doors when she spotted him coming toward her. Did she think she would get away so easily? Now that he'd finally located her, he was going to—what exactly was his plan anyway? He hadn't really thought out what he'd do once he found her. Procure the dagger, of course. That was the mission assigned him by his king, but he wanted more. *What do I want?*

He grabbed the cold, metal handle of the glass door and pulled it open. He found himself in a vestibule with a set of heavy, wooden doors on the other side. He flung them open and was greeted by a heavily muscled hulk that stood a good four inches over him. The man stepped in his path.

"You are not welcome here." The man crossed his bulky arms over his chest in an attempt to intimidate. Seth scoffed and bared his fangs, hissing at the steroid-induced piece of shit that stood between him and the fiery redhead. The guy's eyes widened then returned to normal. He shook his head. "We don't cater to weirdo's here."

Seth unclenched his jaw and stretched his neck, he needed to keep a lid on his emotions, and showing his fangs was already a huge fuck-up. Luckily, the giant thought him to be one of those vampire wannabe humans. Seth snickered to himself, if he only knew.

"What sort of establishment is this?"

The hulk threw his head back and laughed then leaned closer to Seth. "Like I said, not your kind. Now leave before I toss your skinny ass onto the sidewalk."

He quirked a brow. *Skinny ass?* He might be a bit shorter than the hulk here, but his six-foot-four frame was anything but skinny.

Seth grabbed the guy's shirt collar and pulled him closer. "Listen up, Brutus. You'll not only let me in, but you will escort me over to the bar, buy me a drink, and tell me everything I wish to know."

The guy blinked, his face expressionless. "Yes, of course. Right this way." He extended his arm toward the bar, and Seth strode past him, pleased with himself for having contained his temper. There were times when being a guardian had its rewards. Enthralling people was at the top of the list today.

Seth took a seat on a leather stool. Brutus sat to his right and motioned the bartender over. "Drinks on the house for Mr..." He gave Seth a questioning look.

"Ruiz. Seth Ruiz and I'll have whiskey on the rocks."

The man nodded. "Mr. Ruiz has an open tab."

"So, Mr. Ruiz, you're a whiskey drinker?"

Seth turned toward the velvet voice to his left. Kaitlyn had slid onto the stool next to him and was now wearing an emerald, satin dress that exposed more flesh than it hid. Her hair was swept up, showing off her long, delicate neck. He had to keep from licking his lips.

"Yes, I do enjoy a fine whiskey from time to time."

She looked past him to the man on the other side. "Gary, you are needed back at the door.",

Seth arched a brow. He thought Brutus was a more fitting name for the massive hulk, but whatever. He watched the man stand and scurry out of sight as if he was a puppy who'd just gotten caught chewing on his master's shoe. It would seem the beauty beside him was in charge here, and like a good owner, she had established her dominance.

"I hope you don't mind if I join you, Mr. Ruiz?"

He fixed his gaze on her brilliant blue eyes. Visions of her tied to the same dirty mattress as before consumed his mind. This time, she wore the slinky number she had on now. Her body writhed under its restraints, and her eyes begged for mercy. He felt his fangs lengthen.

"Mr. Ruiz?"

He shook the visions free and found her staring at him with a puzzled look on her face.

"Are you all right?" she asked. Was that concern she expressed?

"Yes, I'm fine." He grabbed the glass the bartender laid in front of him and took a big gulp, letting the liquid burn the back of his throat. Anything to kill the visions in his head. He was teetering on the edge of sanity. The clock was ticking, about to strike the bell for the last time before he was sucked completely into the darkness. Sweat trickled down the front of his chest, and he dug his nails into his thigh in one last attempt to keep himself in check.

He could almost feel the cold steel of his king's blade slicing across his neck.

"IS EVERYONE ALL RIGHT?" Caleb asked.

"Fine." Two voices shot back.

The barrier Aidyn had thrown over Caleb and his men had blocked out all communication to the outside. Both men had agreed not to mention the magical bubble placed around them when the explosion occurred. Neither were sure it would work, and Caleb had not wanted his family given any false hope. It would have been crueler than what he had already done to them. Lileta was sure to kill him once she realized he was alive.

"How the hell do we get out of here?"

Caleb turned his attention to his friend and fellow warrior, Jax. "I'm not sure."

Jax scratched at the scruff on his chin, his hazel gaze fixed on the rubble above their heads. "What a fine mess we're in." He sheathed his dagger on his right thigh. "Well, at least it seems we stopped the demons."

Darius approached. "Hopefully, they were able to take care of any that escaped." He shuddered. "I hate to think of what would have happened if we hadn't closed the breach."

Caleb looked from one warrior to the other and filled with pride. When Aidyn had told them the only way to close the fissure and stop the demons was to bring down their entire mountain...Jax and Darius didn't hesitate in volunteering to stay behind. They both understood their chance of death was about ninety percent. Shitty odds, but somehow, they had managed. Diego had pleaded with Caleb to let Diego take his place. Had said Caleb needed to stay alive for his mate and new daughter. He'd fought his inner turmoil, tempted by the soft, luscious curves of his mate. Almost broke too. Had nearly ran from the mountain to be by her side, but he was a warrior at heart. A Draki never ran from duty and never left his men behind. He only hoped she understood and would forgive him. He sat down on the cold floor.

"Aidyn promised he would find us." *Or what is left of us should we perish.* "It could take him awhile. I'm going to try and contact Lileta one more time."

Jax snorted. "She's going to kick your ass, and I'm going to enjoy watching."

Caleb arched a brow. "Should we get out of here, I'll give you ringside seats." He looked back up at the rubble suspended in mid-air above them. Even though the guardian king was powerful...powerful enough he had woven the elements around them and created a shield. Caleb grew uneasy. If that thing gave way, they would be crushed under tons of rock. As if to give merit to his jittery nerves, the rocks shifted and groaned above them. He sucked in a breath. It was now or never. He motioned for the other two Draki to come sit by him. It was time to test his theory.

"You two ever perform *Arcaniss*?" Caleb asked.

Darius and Jax looked at each other then back at him as if he had two heads. "No," Jax answered.

"Well, we're about to try." Caleb stood and assessed the space they had. It would be tight, but he was sure they could do it. Thankfully, while Darius was the same size as Caleb in human form, his dragon was built for speed and therefore much smaller.

"Are you out of your fucking mind?" Jax hissed. "You want us to shift in this tiny space?"

"I know it will be tight, but Darius is smaller than we are. We'll manage, if we do it one at a time," Caleb replied.

Jax thrust his fists on his hips and shook his head. "We'll be lucky to not bring the mountain down on our asses."

"If you two go first, I can make do with whatever space is left," Darius spoke up. "I'd rather try than sit here and wait. Gods know how long we could be here."

"Besides, it's the only way we can access our magic." Caleb knew he could order Jax but wanted to give his friend the opportunity to make the move.

"Fine. I'll go first." Jax began the shift. Bronze scales popped along his skin and bones shifted. Caleb looked up, the shield was holding. His turn.

He focused on his inner beast who had been itching to get out and back to his mate and let the magic transform him. Within seconds, it was complete, and the shield had withstood another blast of magic. Now for Darius.

In the blink of an eye, the small, green dragon appeared and wedged his way in between them. They were now all three nose-to-nose. Perfect.

I hope you know the incantation. Jax slipped into Caleb's mind.

Of course, I do. Caleb searched for the ancient words. A spell from long ago that would bring the magic of any dragon he touched to the chanter. Since he was currently touching Jax and Darius, he hoped to steal from both of them. Draki had no magic, and their dragons had only small amounts, but his hope was that, by taking from the other two, he would gain enough to boost his power and reach his mate.

He ran the chant through his head. His body began to tingle with electrical pulses, the other two men's images faded. They fought to hold their dragon form, but Darius shifted first. Caleb had taken all he could from Darius. Next Jax shifted, no longer able to hold his dragon. Caleb had all the magic he was going to get. *Qadira, don't let me fail.* He opened his mind, lifted the barrier and thought of his mate. Pictured her silky, raven hair cascading down her back. Her curvy hips he ached to latch onto.

Lileta.

LILETA GASPED and push off Diego's chest.

"What's wrong?"

"He's alive," she replied.

Her brother-in-law's brows knitted together. "You sure?"

"Yes, he just called to me." She threw her hands over her mouth and giggled.

"Caleb has made contact with you?" Aidyn appeared beside her. "I've been searching but have had no luck yet. The barrier I placed over them has blocked out everything."

"Barrier?" Leria asked, still clinging to Lileta's arm.

"Contrary to what you think, I did not leave them totally defenseless." Aidyn explained how he had woven a shield over the Draki to protect them but was not one hundred percent certain it would hold, and Caleb had sworn him to secrecy. He'd vowed to recover the men, dead or alive but had hoped for the latter. "If he has contacted you then he is alive, but now we have to locate them."

Lileta bent closer to Leria and cupped her cheeks. "I need you to stay here. Help Cassie in any way you can, and I will be back."

Leria nodded, and Lileta kissed the top of her head. She released the girl, grabbed both Aidyn's and Diego's hand, and flashed them back to the base of the mountain. Suddenly, she became overwhelmed when she looked at the sheer size of the rubble.

Her shoulders dropped. "I don't know where to begin."

Caleb? Where are you?

Under a shit load of rock.

She rolled her eyes. At least, he still had a sense of humor. "He has no idea where he is."

Aidyn looked out over the terrain. "I know where the breach was, but to find it in this." He waved his hand. "Nothing looks the same."

"Wait. Why don't they simply flash out?" Lileta looked at Aidyn and waited for an answer.

"With the magic I have in place, they have no idea where to go. They could end up materializing in the center of the rubble and end up in a worse fate." He gave her a sympathetic look. "I'm afraid my barrier not only protected them but also imprisoned them. I'm not even sure how he's communicating with you right now."

"I know. It's an old Draki trick. He's sucking the power from Jax and Darius." Diego scratched his head. "We need to find them in a hurry, before he loses his connection with you."

Lileta clenched her fists. "Oh." She tried to subdue her rising panic.

"I have an idea," Aidyn said. "Lileta, you need to shadow walk and find him."

Leaving her body again just as she had done in search of Lowan. She could go anywhere in that form, but there was only one problem. "I can't do it alone. Last time, Caleb was there helping me. I don't think he can do that now." Lileta chewed her lip. They were back at square one.

"I'll help."

She turned and eyed the dark warrior suspiciously. Lucan moved in next to her and grabbed her hand. "Come with me." He led her away from the others.

"What are you doing? I thought you said my darkness was too tempting."

"It is," he replied through clenched teeth. "However, I can't stand to hear her screeching any longer."

"What?"

He spun her and pulled her to his chest. Her backside rubbed against him, his arousal evident. "Furia has been screaming since your mate came up missing. I need her to shut the fuck up."

"You hear her?"

He gave a mocking laugh. "I can hear all the darkness, but she is the loudest." He brought his lips to her ear. "Another reason you should have been mine," he growled.

She swallowed hard. "Then, again, why are you helping me? You could let Caleb die."

"I still have my honor."

He slipped into her mind. A cold darkness spread across her, he was nothing like Caleb. He lacked warmth and light.

Find the link to your mate and follow it. I will be here to watch over you.

She hesitated, but only for a moment. As uncomfortable as the dark warrior made her, losing her mate was far worse. She found the light and grabbed hold. *Caleb, I'm coming. Pull me toward you.* She shifted through cracks and crevices. Making painstaking twists and turns, her soul determined to find the way. After what seemed like an eternity, she ended up in a small room. Her vision adjusted to the darkness and saw a dragon in front of her. She reached out and touched her mate. He nuzzled into her palm.

I'll relay your location to the others, Lucan said.

"They're coming to get you out."

Moments later, light filtered above her head as the rocks began to move. Finally, she gave a sigh of relief. Caleb was alive, and they were going home.

CALEB RAN his hands along smooth, silky skin. "He's lucky I didn't scorch his dark ass."

"He was only trying to help," his mate responded as she moaned under his touch.

"I know, but he was touching you," he growled.

Lileta opened a golden eye. "You should not have placed yourself in danger then."

He nipped at her thigh. "Will you forgive me?"

She sighed. "Perhaps I could be persuaded."

He delved his tongue into her folds and encircled her nub. He lifted his head to gaze at her beauty. "How's that for a start?"

"Mmm. Keep going and I'll consider it." Her breathing was heavy.

He smiled then dived back between her legs. He flicked his tongue and made circles around her clit. She wiggled her hips, but his right arm crossed over her abdomen and kept her pinned to the bed. He wanted utter control.

He inserted his left middle finger into her opening. She grabbed fistfuls of sheets. She was on the edge, ready to spill over. Her power engulfed the room and slid across his back. His demon was coming into her own, and he was damn proud of her. He pulled his finger out and thrust it back inside.

She screamed and clenched his head between her knees. The orgasm taking control of her entire body. When she finally relaxed, he crawled up and sucked a nipple into his mouth, his cock poised to strike. He couldn't wait any longer, he needed her. Craved her.

He thrust. Penetrating to the hilt. Her muscles clenched and pulled him in farther. He wanted to spend eternity there, buried in his mate. Forgetting the outside world and the hell that was being unleashed upon them all. War was imminent, and it would take them all—Draki, demons and guardians—to fight the battle. For now, though, he shut it all out and cherished the woman beneath him. A gift from the gods. His own true angel.

LOWAN SWEPT his arm across the desk, sending papers scattering and glass shattering. "Fuck!" His temper rose to heights that surprised even him.

"My lord?"

He turned his head and pinned his gaze on the Wendigo who dared speak to him. "What. Do. You. Want?"

"My lord, surely there is another way to prevail?" The demon clacked his teeth together.

Lowan straightened, brushed his hands across his silk shirt, and stretched his neck. His temper reined in to a more manageable level. He strode across the burgundy carpet, glass crunching under his boots as he made his way to the bar. He poured a glass of Merlot and swirled, watching the blood-red liquid coat the crystal. He imagined it was the blood of his enemies. The guardians, the dragons, and his daughter. Oh yes, his lovely daughter had even managed to free herself from his vise.

He sipped the wine and let it wash some of the bitterness in his mouth down his throat. He curled his lip in a snarl and let loose a chuckle. His grandfather, Hades, had underestimated him. His minions had been able to follow the god into the realm of Vandeldor. True, the fissure had been closed. However, he now had a way in, and soon, the realm would be his. He could almost taste the sweetness of victory. He looked back over at his demon.

"Yes, we will wait for the dust to settle and then move into Vandeldor." He raised the glass to his lips and sipped. "Soon, my friend, the humans will bow to their new god." He closed his eyes, tipped his head back, and took in a long breath. "I can feel my power growing. Patience, we must have patience."

"Of course, my lord." The Wendigo tipped its black, oversized head.

Lowan paced across the room then turned and made his way to the other side. His mind a whirl. "Let them think they have won, and they will become complacent. The guardians' curse will be our ally. Already, the one they call Seth is near the edge. Soon, he will be mine." The thought of wielding power over a guardian sent excitement through him. How would the all mighty Zarek feel about that? He would show them. Show them all one day what he was capable of. The gods would bow to him or die. Perhaps before he killed Zarek, he would force Zarek to watch what he did to the god's beautiful wife Qadira. The thought of parting the fire goddess's thighs and plunging his cock into her depths caused his shaft to thicken.

"What of your daughter, my lord?"

Lowan was snapped from his thoughts. "She will go on and live her happy little existence, but the day will come when I will take it all away. I will kill everyone she holds dear, and then she will be mine." His grip tightened around the crystal goblet until it shattered in his hand and blood dripped onto the carpet. He looked at his bleeding palm, smiled, and then fisted the shards farther into his skin. Pain sliced through him, bringing comfort. "Patience," he whispered. "My time will come."

ABOUT THE AUTHOR

Award winning and bestselling author Valerie Twombly grew up watching Dark Shadows over her mother's shoulder, and from there her love of the fanged creatures blossomed. Today, Valerie has decided to take her darker, sensual side and put it to paper. When she is not busy creating a world full of steamy, hot men and strong, seductive women, she juggles her time between a full-time job, hubby and her German shepherd dog, in Northern IL. Valerie is a member of Romance Writers of America and Fantasy, Futuristic and Paranormal Romance Writers.

 Sign up for Valerie's newsletter and be the first to hear about new releases, receive special excerpts and exclusive contests. http://valerietwombly.com/newsletter-sign/

Follow Valerie
www.valerietwombly.com

Taken By Storm Book 2

Jinn's Seductions Series

Spanish Nights

Sultry Nights

Beyond The Mist Series

Passion Awakened (Beyond The Mist)